A new luxury...	2
Mark...	7
Another day, another dinner...	13
Storms of all forms...	21
Another fine mess...	24
Lifelines...	28
The past starts peeking out...	33
Too much, too soon...	38
Shocked and shattered...	44
Facing it head on and on the head...	48
Stares and stairs...	54
The dinner party...	57
Social grace-less...	63
It begins...	69
Joan Howard...	72
Distractions...	76
Love let it happen...	80
Burn it down...	85
Adrift...	88
A new kind of pain...	90
Shedding Samcora...	93
Reminiscing, ruminating, reunions...	96
Sisters and surprises...	101
Tom...	110
It started with a sofa...	117
The beginning of the end...	120
The deception...	129

Opportunities...	137
Mission but no control...	139
A new normal...	142
Ground rules...	147
Coming home...	151
Ethics and opportunities...	156
Pay the price, penitent man...	165
Cash grab...	168
The vengeance...	173
Predators and their prey...	178
Back to life...	185
Fooled again...	190
Help for the helpless...	200
Monster in the making...	204
Evolution of an affair...	212
Payback...	215
Sins of Samcora...	221
Epilogue	223
Book Club Questions	225

The Sins of Samcora

Copyright © 2018 Sherry Derksen

All rights reserved.

ISBN: 978-1-9994747-1-3

All rights reserved. No part of this book may be used or reproduced in any manner whatsoever without prior written permission of the author/publisher; except in the case of brief quotations embodied interviews.

All characters in this book have no existence outside the imagination of the author and have no relation to anyone bearing the same name or names. Any resemblance to individuals known or unknown to the author are purely coincidental.

A new luxury...

Mark was sleeping spent from his lovemaking. Stretched out beside him, Madeline listened to the rhythmic drum of his breathing, the metronome of life. It had been three months since they married, and within the cocoon of their union she wondered if he would begin to show a softer, gentler side. Even before their marriage Mark did not demonstrate sensitivity to her sexual needs, addressing only his own carnal urges. The pace, the process, the possession, all set by him. She had no expectations that marriage would change either of them, though she felt somewhat different and it surprised her that she did. Perhaps that was exclusive to being female, to feel closer when bound by commitment.

Mark was a domineering and aggressive man but Madeline did not fear him or feel lessened by her submission to him. It was not her weakness but rather her strength that allowed her to yield without sacrificing her intrinsic identity. Madeline was always able to separate her emotions from her behaviour. Acting weak did not make her feel weak, and acting like she loved Mark did not make her love him. She knew why she was in this marriage, and it was not for love. Love was not a good enough reason to get married. It was dangerous to tie your fate to the whims of it. It was better to tie your fate to something tangible, like possessions and money. Those were the things you could count on, those were the things that you could control.

Madeline rolled onto her back trying to get comfortable. The day had been hot and humid and the sticky heat lingered on through the night. Cradled in the plush bed she began to

Sins of Samcora

feel claustrophobic as the creamy silk top-sheet pooled around her, clinging to her glistening skin. Careful not to wake Mark, she slipped out of bed and entered her walk in closet, quietly closing the door behind her. Standing inside wrapped in the darkness, she strained to hear if Mark stirred. Satisfied that he had not been roused she felt along the inner wall and switched on the lights.

After her eyes adjusted she began to admire all her new clothes. Most of them were bought after her wedding and were carefully hung on matching hangers. Pleasure coursed through her as she grazed her hand over rows of rich fine cotton, silks, and linens. In her eyes, the most beautiful fabrics ever created and crafted into magical garments which transformed her. She could do anything she wanted in these clothes. She could be anyone she wanted.

Mark never commented on how much she spent on her wardrobe. She was not sure if he noticed the rapidly accumulating balance on the credit card or if he just did not care. He certainly could afford her shopping habits. His comments on her looks encouraged her to dress and groom well and as his wife, she had a certain image to maintain.

Madeline was acutely aware of the importance of image. Image was instrumental in helping her escape her former life, helping her change who she was fated to be. How she looked, how she dressed, how she spoke all created the person she was now, this beautiful life that was not destined for her.

Her identity was purposefully evolved. A construction that she spent years refining. From gutter trash to socialite was a sacrificial transformation.

She did not often think of the past. Looking backward kept you stuck. Old memories normally held no reign over her yet tonight, unbidden, her ghosts began to rise. Perhaps it was her new luxury, the feeling that she had finally made it that triggered her mood? Her life should not have been filled with comfort but Madeline had tricked fate by taking charge of her destiny.

It had been hard growing up in Samcora, witnessing the destructive spiral of her mother's life who ended up becoming a casualty of her own deportment. The role model she provided seeded both Madeline's and her sister's life with low expectations. Her sister, Delta, accepted her mother's weakness, and like her,

Sherry Derksen

could not escape the chains of indulgence. Madeline fought back the complacency and ripped out the root of her heritage and rejected the example of her line.

Madeline's childhood had been coloured by fear. Fear not of those things that had hurt her and scarred her, but rather the fear of becoming like her mother and sister. Stuck and beat down. Over the years that fear transformed into an iron will of self determination to break away from the world her upbringing was conditioning her for.

She had been born into a place that had rules and cultural expectations that were prepared for her like a casket, waiting for her to lay down and get buried in the allotment of misery that was measured out for her. Delta had laid in it, perhaps unwittingly but still willingly. Madeline determined that she never would. She would fight for something better, fight for her justice.

Madeline did not miss her mother. Sometimes she did miss her sister. Not her real sister, but rather the idea of a sister connecting her to her born blood line. In truth, she could not stand the whimpering and whining of Delta. Madeline's sister was younger, and perhaps was not entirely to blame for her abdication of will. She obediently became what she was raised to be and either stupidity or youth made her vulnerable to the ease of acceptance.

Madeline felt gifted by her early sorrows as it gave her insight into the trajectory of her life and the implications of the limited options her financial and emotional poverty provided her. She was able to detach from and see how the unrelenting hardship, dysfunction, and addiction was trying to pull her down into its vortex. To escape its grasp she knew she had to leave and could never look back. The cost was the severance of all her relationships, even the one with Gran. Hard discipline, not desire, would determine her new destiny.

In the beginning the hardest part had been the guilt of abandoning Gran during her need, but the grief had long ago stopped hemorrhaging, and it no longer bothered her. Gran was long dead now. Ruminating on what she could have, should have done would not change any of it. Being there for the end would not have changed the end so what was the point of staying and watching and having another loss to bear? She did not want to watch her die.

Reconstructing herself had been more difficult than

Sins of Samcora

she expected, but in the end it was worth it to be where she was now. Mark would never have looked at her, and certainly would not have married her if he knew her true origins. If he knew who she really was underneath her facade. He would reject her if he could see her stains.

Madeline willed herself to clear her mind and think of something else. Despite the heat, it had been a lovely day and she did not want to continue to spoil it by allowing her thoughts to roam unrestrained. She had indulged enough and it was time to refocus. Madeline decided to go downstairs and make herself a cup of herbal tea.

Quietly leaving the bedroom she glanced over at her new husband and noticed that he was still asleep and undisturbed by her restlessness. He really was magnificent, sinewy and muscular. His masculine curves taut and ready to respond. Even in sleep he looked wound. He was all she wanted in a man. Strong, dangerous, detached. Rich.

She moved easily through the house as the darkness was lifted by threads of moonlight streaking in through the windows and stretching long shadows on the floors and walls. She savoured the tactile pleasures of the deep wool carpeting as the thick pile shifted beneath her footsteps. She loved everything about her new house, a magnificent mansion sitting in the most exclusive neighbourhood in the city of Summerton. The polished mahogany railing felt dense and smooth under her hand as she descended the curved staircase. The cool limestone floor extended from the foyer to the base of the stairs contrasting the warmth of the carpeting. It's stony coldness shocking and refreshing her feet. Reaching the kitchen, she snapped on the lights and admired the thick white marble countertops which anchored the ivory painted cupboards. The centre island was made of walnut and the deep rich colour provided contrast to the lightness of the polished limestone floors. There was nothing like real materials, the marble and wood had depth and glow. The limestone had texture and density that could not be achieved by cheap imitations.

Madeline thought how she herself used to be a cheap imitation but now that she was married to Mark she had gained the authenticity she craved. He was her passport to the good life and the stink of her low class had finally been washed off.

Sherry Derksen

Madeline waited for the kettle to come to a boil. Her hot water ready, she reached into the cupboard and retrieved the new teapot and one of the china cups she had purchased from Bennington's last week. Her smile was unrepressed as she recalled when she had bought them while shopping with Anne Layton and how pleased she felt when Anne was shocked at the price.

Anne's husband, Brian Layton, was a judge. Brian was one of the men that circled around Mark like sharks in chum water, waiting to consume the leftovers of the leader. Madeline considered him to be an unimpressive cowboy type. He had money by most people's standards but financially was no where near the league of wealth that Mark, and now Madeline enjoyed.

Madeline felt proud that she could spend whatever she wanted and Anne could not. There was a time that snobbish women like Anne would have laughed at her and dismissed her. Now she had to stand and watch Madeline buy what she could not. She had to stand there and suck it up because Mark was powerful and if she wanted her own husband to be in Mark's orbit then she had better kiss up. How deep the insult to her pride must have been, especially since Madeline was sure that Anne had noticed how Brian's seedy gaze lingered on her when his lust began to show.

Relaxed and soothed with her tea, control over her random thoughts returned easily as she released and dismissed her intrusive memories. The past had no power over her anymore and whenever her mind drifted to unpleasant thoughts, she just needed to look around her house and the pleasure of her possessions would make all the bad things go away. Finishing her tea, she left her cup on the counter for her housekeeper to deal with and then made her way back to bed to settle in for sleep.

Mark...

BUZZ...BUZZ...BUZZ... Madeline jolted awake at the insistent buzzing sound of the alarm clock. Her heart pounding from the adrenaline shooting through her, she jumped out of bed feeling that something was wrong, something out of place. She was in danger.

As her head cleared and her eyes focused in the bright morning light, she realized where she was and quickly settled down, glad that Mark did not see her. She often woke up in panics and in the past, there were times when there was good reason for it. Now, however, the old dangers that threatened to overtake her were gone. She was home and she was safe.

She could hear Mark in the shower. He showered twice a day. Once in the morning, and again after he got home and worked out in the home gym. Madeline liked that he was always clean. It seemed easy for him to be so immaculate. It enhanced his attractiveness to her.

Cleanliness was status, it signified luxury and money. She hated that there was never enough hot water or clean towels in Samcora. Poverty did not easily facilitate personal grooming. Even though she liked Mark's cleanliness, sometimes it gave her the uneasy feeling that she was not clean enough for him.

Madeline knew she was good looking and that Mark only married her because he was attracted to her physical beauty. She had the right image to fulfill his social and political needs for a wife. Her value to Mark was aesthetic and as such her relationship had a shelf life. She had no illusions that she would ever be more than a trophy wife.

Mark was always more mature than his years. He was raised to be stoic and strong. Even when his father beat him he was expected to show no reaction, weakness was a female failing and shedding tears an unforgivable crime.

Mark was born with survival instinct. He never cried in the presence of his father and never experienced the rebellious state normal for the teen years. He learned early on to control his emotions and reactions.

His face was a smooth white plane and curved in a delicate manner. It would have caused him to have a gentle appearance were it not for the intensity of his eyes. Almond shapes set deeply in his face. The pupils lost in the deep brown of the iris. His stare was hypnotic. His gaze penetrated through all facades that to talk to him one had to look away for fear of revealing the many secrets that lay beneath the surface of our faces. An imposing man, to be near him felt like a violation of personal space. With him in the room it felt like there was no territory left for others. His aura dominated and commanded respect. At six feet four inches, he stood ramrod straight never slouching, never yielding. An aggressive posture for an aggressive man.

Mark was weaned on violence, often witnessing the brutal beatings of his mother, Elizabeth, at the hands of his father, Elliot Jacobson. Those who did not guess the family dynamics would have said that Elliot adored Mark as a child, and it was true that Mark was often with him. Elliot loved Mark but only because Mark was never a person to him. Mark was considered an extension of Elliot himself, and the fact that father and son looked so much alike strengthened the core belief that Elliot saw his son as his own genetic marker in the world and not as an individual.

Mark grew up under the shadow of Elliot and learned his fathers business tactics early on. Elliot was a shrewd and clever man who ensured that his wishes were followed out with an iron fist. If his deal was not going well he was not hesitant to using intimidation or deception to sway the outcome. Victory and domination was his ultimate power. To guide Mark to this power was the responsibility of a good father, Elliot reasoned to himself. Any personality deficits that Elliot observed in Mark could be

Sins of Samcora

beaten out as they had been beaten out of him by his father, and the earlier you started the better.

Pain was an important part of growth and the sooner that lesson was learned, the more successful a man would be. Pain shaped and sharpened and the presence of it was a guide and motivator. Pain was a friend. This was known only by strong successful men. Weak men folded under the teachings of pain and as such, deserved to be stepped on, hard.

Mark exited the shower and wrapped a towel around himself. Bare-chested, he appraised his physique in the mirror. He knew he looked good. His body was chiseled with muscle honed by the cold steel in his personal gym. Lifting weights was also a good stress reliever for him. When he was physical, he was able to think more clearly.

The extreme exertion of his workouts helped him weed out unnecessary and redundant thoughts so he could focus more clearly on things that were important. Some of his best work had been thought out in the gym. It was there all alone that he felt the most comfortable. Able to be exactly what he was. He was able to work out his frustrations. He had to keep a handle on his frustrations.

He could not let what happened with his ex-girlfriend, Joan Howard repeat itself. He had gone too far and he knew it, but so had she. He watched his mother get beaten black and blue and he swore to himself that he would never do that to a woman. He never felt the urge to hit a woman until Joan provoked him. She tried to extort money from him by getting pregnant. It probably was not his kid anyway. There was no way he was paying for someone else's bastard. Mark recalled the aggravation he felt when Joan would not stop talking, trying to convince him. She would not shut her big mouth.

He barely remembered his fist driving into her face. He only noticed that silly gasping sound she made just before she fell backwards down the stairs of her condo from the force of the blow. Lying at the bottom of the stairs, she was still accusing him and threatening to call the police. Her mouth, going, going, going. Calling him an out of control monster. He was no such thing. He was in control. She was the one making a scene with her accusations and hysteria.

Sherry Derksen

He had to shut her mouth. He could not stand the noise coming from her. The raging in him ceased when she fell silent. Sure, he felt a little guilty afterwards about how far it went, but she had no right to threaten him.

It was not his fault that she miscarried the little bastard. It was not real anyway, a fetus only. Just cells. Life started at birth. What was the big deal, miscarriages happened all the time. Not everything was meant to live. Failure to thrive, end of story. Dying so easily, it would never have survived unprotected in the real world anyway. It was better off gone now.

Mark's first beating was in his mothers belly. She was not supposed to get pregnant when she did. His father liked to tell him the story how his mothers disobedience in getting pregnant without his approval ended up with a strong correction and how Mark was almost aborted in the beating but hung on and survived. That was the sign that Elliot knew Mark was to be his successor. From the moment that Mark survived in vivo Elliot was excited about the birth, knowing he had a strong seed planted.

Joan greatly miscalculated her value to him and she forgot her place, Mark thought to himself. He smiled as he remembered how Brian Layton helped her find her place. Nobody threatens Mark Jacobson and gets away with it. Nobody.

Mark began to feel the tight knots at the back of his neck returning as he finished dressing and walked into the bedroom. There was Madeline sprawled out on the bed in her satin negligee giving him instant desire to remove it from her silky skin. Just laying there she could make him hard. She was truly a beautiful woman.

Mark had never really thought he would marry. He toyed with the idea in the beginning of his relationship with Joan, but the first time he laid eyes on Madeline he knew that she was special. He felt an instant connection and knew that she was his.

It shocked him how strong his urge to possess her was, how after bedding her he still wanted more. She was perfect in every way. Beautiful, gentle, and cooperative. Obedient. Madeline appreciated the finer things in life, yet she never demanded anything of him. She had an innocence about her that appealed to him.

Mark recalled the first time he took her to Cimmarons for dinner. She seemed to soak in and enjoy the fine surroundings in

Sins of Samcora

a way that you rarely see in women who grow up in wealthy families like hers. Most women do not notice the opulence and the elegant touches like a fresh orchid on the table, they just take it all for granted. Like they try to take him for granted.

He knew that most women just wanted a money horse. Just like his mother who never appreciated the lifestyle she married into. His father had warned him not to get serious with women below his class.

"They drag you down, son," Elliot always said. "The rich ones are for marrying and the poor ones are for pleasure."

Madeline was unusual, vibrant and refreshing. He found his perfect wife. An only child, no annoying siblings to have to contend with, absent parents who have their own money and won't be looking at his, and better yet, live and work in Europe. The worst that could happen is that he would have to sign a Christmas card once a year to send to them. Madeline respected him and seemed to understand his possessiveness, she belonged to him. She was his precious treasure that he wanted to care for. Mark knew that he would never hit Madeline. She did not annoy him. She was almost perfect, and the few flaws that she did have, he knew that he could straighten those out in no time.

"Good morning beautiful," Mark sat down beside Madeline on the bed and ran his hand up her thigh.

"Good morning handsome. Are we going to have breakfast together?" Madeline already knew the answer would be no. He rarely ate before heading to the office, preferring his morning protein drink.

"No breakfast, I've got too much to do. If I was to linger it would not be for breakfast," Mark teased as he continued caressing her.

"Too bad," Madeline pretended to pout. She did not really care if they shared breakfast, it just seemed like the right thing to say. She rolled on her back and allowed her nightie to slip down further off her shoulder. She could see how she enticed him, excited him.

"I'll see you tonight." Mark casually ran his hand up her belly until it nestled between her breasts. He could feel her heart quicken and beat under his fingertips. Suddenly disengaging himself, Mark stood up. He really did have to go to the office and

Sherry Derksen

she was so distracting.

"Don't forget we are having Brian and Anne over for dinner. Also, Brian called. Anne wants to bring a friend who just came into town so now we are going to have one more guest. I want you to make sure everything is ready." Mark was enjoying having a wife to attend to his social obligations. It was closer to the vest than hiring personal assistants. Plus she was proving to be quite adept at pulling together successful dinner parties. She seemed to understand the proper environments that needed to be created for networking and business.

"Before I go, let me see your schedule so I know what you are up to."

Madeline bristled at his last comment, however she retained her composure and did not let Mark see how it made her feel. She noticed that since getting married, he liked to know where she was every moment of the day. He was almost as obsessed with her schedule as he was with his own.

"I don't have much happening today, just some grocery shopping for the dinner tonight and I was going to see if my hair stylist could squeeze me in today for a touchup." Madeline passed her scheduler to her husband. She did not understand why a high powered executive like Mark would care about her mundane appointments.

"Sounds fine darling, just make sure your cell phone is turned on. Now give me a kiss goodbye." Mark placed her scheduler on the night table. Madeline rose up and gave Mark a kiss goodbye, trying to act more upbeat than she was really feeling.

Another day, another dinner...

The day was turning out better than Madeline hoped for. Her mood always lifted when she went out shopping. Even grocery shopping was a pleasure for her because she no longer had to go to the huge super save chains. Every experience in her life was upgraded due to her marriage to Mark. Now she shopped in the upscale markets and the specialty organic shops. The stress of having to count her pennies to see how many packages of dried noodles she could afford was over. Now she could select the freshest and best cuts of meat and the ripest fruits and vegetables regardless of the season.

Madeline loved to pick out new foods that she had never tried before. She felt exotic and worldly when she selected unusual combinations. She felt smug confidence that her housekeeper Hazel would see she had gourmet gastronomical tastes. She was unaware of the strange looks that Hazel had on her face when she viewed the contents of the bags that were delivered to the house.

"That woman is at it again," Hazel would mutter to herself. "What am I supposed to do with all of this?" She felt better after venting about how uncomfortable the Jacobson household was getting, and how lucky they were that she did not throw down her apron and walk out. The thought of quitting ran through her mind more often in the last few months since Mark brought his new bride home. Even though she could not bring herself to like Madeline, she knew she was being paid well for her service. She could tolerate it a

Sherry Derksen

little longer.

Hazel had been working for Mark Jacobson for the last two years and for the most part, it went well. Hazel always felt that she had good instincts about people and she decided early on that Madeline was not 'good folk'. Madeline had rubbed her the wrong way from the first day she met her and she could not bring herself to like her.

"She's strange," Hazel would complain to her circle of friends as they gathered for Saturday Bingo at the Plaza. "I asked her once what her father does and she just glared at me and walked away. So rude. Normal people will tell you a little bit about themselves. You don't know anything about her and its impossible to make small talk with her." Hazel mimicked Madeline's blank stare and then she and her friends would begin laughing.

"Now, that Joan, she was a sweetheart. When she was over, you knew there was a lady in the house. She was always nice to me. Such a shame what happened to her. That horrible fall down those stairs. The way Mr. Jacobson dumped her after her injury for that woman he now has was awful. Its just not right. People just don't care about each other anymore." Hazel turned her attention back to her bingo game. She only needed two more numbers for the blackout. Her service in the Jacobson household was just a job and nothing more anyway. "You can't care about people who won't care about you," she reminded herself as she daubed her cards hoping it was her lucky night.

"That will be $357.93 please," droned out the cashier at the organic market with a bored look on his face. Madeline fished out her platinum credit card and gold pen from her purse. When she was given the sales slip to sign she scrawled out with an exaggerated flourish 'Mrs Mark Jacobson'. She loved signing her name that way. She knew it was antiquated. Nobody signed that way anymore but it gave her such pleasure to identify herself under the name of her husband. For that moment, when she was signing, she felt reinvented solely as Mrs Jacobson. She felt pride at the platinum status on her card. People paid attention when you had platinum.

"Thank you," Madeline smiled to the clerk as he returned her credit card. "Please deliver my items to 328 Royal

Sins of Samcora

Ridge Estates." Striding out of the store, she glanced at her watch and realized that she would be late if she did not start heading out to her next appointment with her hairstylist. It felt good to have places to go and to have the day filled with reasons to keep track of time. Madeline slid into the soft and supple leather seat of her Jaguar. She would have to take the Taylor freeway and connect to Lions Bridge if she was to get to her appointment on time.

Madeline disliked driving on the Taylor. Although the ring road was the fastest way to cross the city, she was not comfortable driving on the four-lane freeway. Traffic was too fast and with the new construction in the South leg, it felt dangerous. Although her powerful new model Jaguar was more than able to keep pace with the traffic, she was never comfortable driving fast. A performance vehicle was as new an experience to her as taking public transit would be to Mark, she thought to herself. Beyond that, Madeline was not a good driver, something that Mark often pointed out to her. Today she knew she did not have the luxury of taking the long way about if she was to get to the salon on time. She wanted to look good tonight.

Mark believed that regular entertaining was a business necessity and he expected her to coordinate a successful evening. As far as she was concerned, her looking good was part of that success. She felt validated every time Mark looked at her with pride and complimented her when an evening went well.

Mark was endlessly networking and Madeline loved it. She loved the steady stream of people to whom she could talk to without revealing anything about herself beyond the shallow layers she would invent. The superficial façade of intimacy at their dinner parties gave her the feeling of friends and connection even though she recognized that she had no real friends or connections. Madeline liked that Mark was just like her. They both knew and socialized with many people but no one really knew them or what they were about. Even though Mark and Brian had golfed together for the past twelve years, she could tell that Mark did not consider Brian a close friend. In fact, Mark really had no friends. Just a huge network of acquaintances and contacts, some of which like Brian, he has known for years. She could not recall a single time when Mark opened up on a personal or emotional basis to anyone, including herself. Madeline loved that he was that way.

Sherry Derksen

Madeline was worried when she first met Mark that he would eventually want to know too much about her private family life. Besides the basic questions, he did not care. Madeline had worked out a solid story about who her parents were, the business they worked in, where they lived and why they were never around. With Mark being an only child himself, he had no comments or questions when she lied and said she also was an only child. Lies about her education and the fantasy that she lived on a modest allowance from her parents were easily rolled off her tongue. She would only come into her wealth by inheritance. She smiled at what she felt was her coup de grace lie when she told him she would sign the prenuptial agreement only if it was changed to reflect that whatever was his would remain his and whatever was hers would be shared. He appeared shocked but pleased when she explained that it was her way of acknowledging his contribution to her upkeep in the marriage and it was her display of total trust and love for him. Madeline needed to convince him that she loved him, the man and not his money.

Mark would never know her real agenda, that her gesture was the perfect way to avoid messy investigations by lawyers into her non-existent assets. There was no better way to demonstrate to Mark that she loved only him and not his money. Sure, she was exposed if he ever divorced her, but she had zero plans to divorce her rich husband. She would do everything in her power to remain married for as long as possible. Besides, over the course of the next several years, she would squirrel away a lovely little nest egg for herself just in case the marriage went awry. That was always a possibility. In fact, it was likely that at some point the marriage would dissolve. Madeline had no illusions that her and Mark would grow close and old together. She anticipated that one day she would be traded in for a younger wife. Madeline would hang on as long as she could because when her marriage ended, she was not going to leave empty handed.

Mark had never questioned Madeline's authenticity. Madeline knew it was because she looked the part. She could thank Gran for teaching her to sew. Madeline could look at any garment in any magazine and duplicate it with fabric, needle and thread. As long as the fabric was a reasonably close match, the men never noticed her designer wardrobe was fake. The few high-end items

Sins of Samcora

she did buy like her Jimmy Choo shoes sometimes took her entire salary. In the end, the eviction notices from unpaid rent were worth it. The starvation from having no food made her look even more fantastic in her mock designer wardrobe. Yes, the sacrifices she made to project the right look paid off.

The only detail she worried about was if Mark wanted to meet any of her family or friends. That one was impossible to pull off. She had lost two other potential husbands before she met Mark because they kept pressuring her to introduce them to her family and friends. She did not have any friends and as far as she was concerned, she did not have any family. The day she left that hellhole of a city, Samcora, she divorced her family in her mind and soul. She would never go there again and she would never look back again. That door was closed. It relieved her that Mark never asked. In fact, he seemed pleased that she did not want to involve anyone else in their relationship. She was happy to be an extension of Mark and his credit card. Life was perfect.

At home from her errands, Madeline could not stop admiring herself in the mirror. Her new white cashmere Dolce & Gabbana cowl neck sweater hugged her curves and perfectly set off the Burberry Proscum skirt that she purchased to go with her new sweater. She knew she looked good. She felt good. She was finally able to stop dreaming of the life she wanted to live and was now living it. Life with money was easy and gracious. The only thing hard was deciding what you wanted next. Rich people knew nothing about living a desperate hard life. The kind of hard that tries to suck the life out of you. Mark no doubt would be proud of her look tonight. Done admiring herself, Madeline went downstairs into the kitchen to check up on Hazel who was preparing the dinner.

"So, how are the dinner preparations going, Hazel," Madeline inquired, enjoying the enticing smells in the kitchen.

"Everything is fine, Mrs. Jacobson, everything will be ready on time," replied Hazel with a dour look. It was feeling more difficult to paste a phoney smile on her face. She wished Madeline would get out of the kitchen and leave her to her work. Hazel did not like being watched when she worked, and Madeline had a way of making her feel like an indentured servant.

"Great," Madeline was not sure if Hazel was challenging her or if it was just her mannerisms. She was never obviously rude and Madeline could not say that Hazel ever did anything directly to show her disrespect, yet there was something about the way she set her artificial smile in her square face that annoyed Madeline.

"Just keep it up woman," thought Madeline "and I'll fire you so fast your head will spin." Madeline enjoyed the knowledge that she had the power to fire Hazel, to disrupt her simple life by taking her job away. She never followed through because although she found Hazel disagreeable, she had to admit that she was an excellent housekeeper and cook. The dinner tonight looked very inviting with barley and wild rice risotto, aged standing ribbed roast and broccoli and fresh mushrooms. A large basket of butter crust rolls were ready to serve as well as several trays of hors d'oeuvres. The wine was chilling and Hazel was preparing a beautiful molten chocolate cake. The first time Madeline tasted Hazel's dessert she almost swooned over the warm cake with the rich truffle ganache that flowed from the middle like decadent silken lava.

"I can fire her another day," thought Madeline, seduced into complacency by the thought of eating more of the confection. After surveying the dining room that was set up and ready for the party, she went into the living room. It was one of her favourite places in the house. Curling up on a plush chair, she sat to wait for Mark while she drank in all the beauty around her.

"Korak needs to be handled," bristled Mark to himself, thinking about the meeting he had with the head of Candlewood Corporation. Did he really think Mark was going to just roll over and accept the proposal the way it was? He was in for a big surprise if he thinks he can muscle in on the epigenetic program that Mark was developing at Jacobson Corp. Mark anticipated he was going to do battle with Candlewood at some point and it was giving him a headache just thinking about it. Mark felt enraged at how emboldened his business adversary behaved in the meeting. Korak has no idea who he was dealing with, Mark smiled to himself. How foolish and short sighted of him to not really know all the players before making demands.

Mark always smiled when he felt enraged, it was unconscious and automatic. Initially, he was taught to do it when he was a child. Whenever Elliot beat him, Mark was expected to smile

Sins of Samcora

and thank Elliot for teaching him good sense. To do anything other than smile would ensure a longer, crueler beating. As the years and the beatings wore on, the smile became ingrained. It was nothing more than a muscular reflex. As Mark turned into his driveway all he could think about was working off some stress in his gym, having a hot shower, followed by some smooth Lagavulin. He needed to fortify himself for his dinner guests tonight. His last nerve was strained and he was running out of patience to deal with the Judge tonight.

"Brian is also turning into a problem," he thought as his bad mood deepened. "He is at the limit of the money I'm going to give him for the Joan job, it is over. He is going to have to understand that." Striding into his house, Mark did not acknowledge the presence of Madeline.

"Hi honey, I'm glad you're home. How was your day..." Madeline was cut short by Mark.

"Not now, I need to catch a quick workout before our dinner guests get here."

Stunned by his abrupt manner Madeline surveyed her husband as he went past her. She was not offended by Mark's foul mood. She understood the need for space. She understood what it felt like to be on the edge of losing it and having minimal emotional reserves for small talk and social graces. Mark had been working out in his gym for about 15 minutes before he began to calm down.

"Madeline is a good wife," he thought to himself. "She knows when to back off." By the time Mark was showered and dressed, he felt renewed. He grabbed Madeline and gave her a passionate kiss.

"I guess I forgot to say hello properly." Mark pulled her close and Madeline pressed herself into his body and began slowly running her hands down his back. His muscles felt dense and warm and his kisses began to consume her. His caresses were confident and knowing, remembering her triggers. She knew what he was doing to her but she did not want him to ruin her styled hair and perfect new white designer clothes before the dinner party. Yet, as he entangled her, he weakened her resolve and she began to respond to his rhythms. Wanting more, she now wished there were no dinner guests arriving and that they had the night together uninterrupted.

Sherry Derksen

She knew if he wanted to have sex then it was going to happen. Her refusal of his advances would not change the outcome and would stimulate his aggressiveness. Intellectually she thought she should reject his behaviour, a normal person would have. She could admit to herself that it turned her on, his intense desire for her. She experienced his bellicosity on one of their early dates, some might have misinterpreted it as date rape. She was acting coy and playing with him, to hold out and not give him what he wanted, and if she was honest, what she also wanted. Her forced submission to him gave her permission to let go and allow herself to feel all the things he made her feel. She was not a victim. She used him to dispel her inhibitions and to place the guilt of the encounter on him, if there was any guilt to be felt. You can't rape the willing. Suddenly the doorbell rang, ripping through the passion, breaking the spell of desire. Mark broke off from his advances and hand in hand they walked to the front door to welcome Brian, Anne and Dr Gabe Brewel.

Storms of all forms...

It seemed to come out of nowhere. No warning was given, the violence unannounced, the intrusion unexpected. The storm cast a blanket of blackness over Samcora. Bathed in darkness, first came the lightning and then the rain. In angry torrents, it pounded down, obliterating any view. CRACK! Delta sensed the sound of the lightening strike with her body before the deafening assault on her ears. The power it contained seemed to vibrate through the entire house. The brightness of the display lasting only a moment until the power was spent and the fuses burnt in the backlash. The house darkened, fading into the night.

With the lights out, she could see nothing. Her eyes straining against the darkness, Delta felt small and insignificant. Howling and wailing, the gale conjured up surreal images of destruction as it battered the house and threatened to shatter the windows. The flashes of lightening illuminating jagged shadows in every corner.

Delta always hated storms, they made her feel powerless and insignificant. Cowering on the corner of her sofa, she called out to her husband, Tom. Over and over, she called his name, trying to drown out the howling of the wind. He did not answer and she knew he would not. Downstairs, passed out in a drunken stupor, he did not even realize there was a storm. Delta felt alone and abandoned, again.

He gave her no words and no love, Delta thought to herself. He did not care. Why couldn't he see that she just needed a little bit to hold on to? Just a scrap of affection from time to time to give her a reason to stay married to him. The pit of her belly ached and a cold void spread through her body as her terror of the storm morphed into a stifling depression over her marriage. Tom would never comfort her. She felt utterly alone. She could not breathe in her marriage. She could not breathe in this house. The darkness felt heavy, pressing down on her. She needed air. She needed to get out of her house, to feel something, anything other than what she was feeling now.

Mechanically Delta stood up from the sofa and felt her way along the living room to reach the front door. With each crack of lightning, the room lit up like a strobe light, blinding her even further when the light ended. She took slow deep breaths trying to expel her remaining fear as quietly as possible. Stealth now was her desire. She did not want Tom to come to her anymore. She did not want anyone anymore.

Urged by an overwhelming desire to escape, she needed to get out of the house. Groping her way along the wall, she found the front door and turned the knob. The door opened only a sliver when a gust of wind grabbed it out of her hand and almost ripped it off its hinges. Walking out onto the front lawn, the icy cold rain bit at her skin like hundreds of razor sharp teeth numbing her in its assault.

Shaking uncontrollably from the adrenaline surge and rapidly falling body temperature, Delta began to wonder if the storm was going to take her. Here she was, facing the power, boldly daring it to harm her. The sky was a ceiling of boiling black clouds. The sheets of rain continued to pound her body and the wind was pushing her back. She could feel the electricity in the air and the smell was magnificent. Earthy and wet and pure. The lightening was overhead, would it strike her? Better to be killed quickly in one night than continue living the silent suicide of her life, dying a little bit each day.

Delta pushed up against the wind and made her way to the lamppost in the front of her yard. She was growing weary of fighting the wind and wanted to stabilize her position. The grey metal was hard but she could barely feel it with her frozen fingers. She wrapped her arms around it embracing her anchor as she began to laugh.

"I am here," Delta screamed to the wind. She threw

Sins of Samcora

her head back and closed her eyes, wanting to etch the memory of this moment and the cold rain making her feel more alive than she could ever remember being.

Suddenly she felt a shift. The air electrified, the charge intensified and she could feel every hair on her body rise and tingle. She knew that the next lightening strike would hit the lamppost and take her with it and she did not care. Delta began to laugh hysterically.

"What do you think you are doing, you stupid woman?" Tom grabbed his wife by the waist and threw her away to the ground and then fell on top of her. At that moment, a bolt of lightening struck the huge poplar tree down the block splitting the main branch through the body of the tree. The flash, the noise, and the power of the blast was so intense that Tom felt like a bomb had gone off as he lay on top of his unconscious wife.

Another fine mess...

Holding her head in her hands, Delta could feel her temples pounding. The skin on her forehead felt tight and raw. This was going to be a headache to remember.

Delta had fainted at the same time that Tom pulled her away from the lamppost, her limp body landing headfirst on the ground. She knew she was fortunate that her head did not hit the concrete sidewalk, instead hitting the softer lawn. She supposed it was a blessing that Tom was too lazy and drunk to cut the grass the past week, it gave her more cushion. Except for some abrasions and her embarrassment she was unhurt.

Tom had called an ambulance and went with her to the hospital. It was uncommonly nice of him to go with her but instead of sitting by her and being supportive, he had to run around and spill his guts about what happened. Why couldn't he just make up a simple story for her like she had just tripped and fallen? Lying was always so easy for him, words slipping off his tongue without thought like leaves dropping from a tree in the fall, not caring where they landed. No, his need for drama was more important to him than protecting his wife's reputation.

"The idiot knows I work here. Why can't he just shut up," Delta thought to herself. Sitting on the stretcher in the emergency room, Delta felt mortified and exposed. She pulled the thin flannel blanket up higher. All she wanted was to be home and alone in her misery. It was humiliating being here where she worked.

Looking around she felt relieved that she did not

Sins of Samcora

recognize any of the nurses. It was unlikely any of them would be here from her unit but still it was unnerving. Delta worked as a nurse on the third floor geriatric unit. She loved her job when she first got it eight years ago because the money was good and she liked the old folks, but the daily grind of catering to old people's complaints began to take its toll. The beige walls and the mingled smells of sickness and antiseptic began to cave in on her.

Hating her job now, it gave her a desperate sense of entrapment. She grew so tired of caring for people. It made her too tired to care for herself. Delta had seen enough blood, shit, and urine to last a lifetime but the money was still good and paid the bills. She also liked the flexibility of her shift work. It was a real benefit especially when she had to deal with problems that Tom made for her. Problems that could occur anytime and anywhere.

"I don't know what to say," stammered Delta to Dr Brewel. She looked down, unable to hold his gaze. The floor looked so scuffed and yellow. So many feet shuffling around, unaware of creating all those scratches. She wondered how many people had sat on this same stretcher staring at this same patch of floor. It was uncomfortable with the doctor looking at her, assessing her. Judging her.

"Your husband says you were not acting like yourself tonight," began the doctor, easing gently into his assessment. Dr Gabe Brewel had spoken to Tom who relayed his version of the incident. Tom's obvious intoxication made him a poor historian, yet it was still clear to Gabe that Delta was in profound emotional distress.

"I'm embarrassed by what happened. I know what it looks like. Really, I'm fine. I hate being accused. Tom always exaggerates." It was difficult to answer the doctor's questions without sounding like a complete fool. How was she supposed to explain her actions to the doctor when she could not even explain them to herself? What kind of an idiot goes out into a full force storm hugging a pole like a lunatic?

"I know what my husband is saying but I wasn't trying to hurt myself. I was trying to feel more alive. I can't explain it." Delta did not know what else to say. There was nothing to say. She herself could not believe that she pulled such a stupid stunt. She had let her emotions overtake her and now here she was, stuck in

Sherry Derksen

another embarrassing mess. It was all so surreal. How did she let this happen?

"I know this feels uncomfortable for you," Dr Brewel was not going to tell her to not feel embarrassed, or that it was ok. She was entitled to feel whatever she was feeling and she obviously was not ok.

"You are not being accused of anything. I'm here to help you. I would like to listen to you and what you have to say if you would let me." Unlike Delta, Dr Gabe Brewel loved his job. Growing up in a medical family, it was no surprise that he would also enter the medical profession. He could not remember when he wanted to be anything else other than a psychiatrist. It was a standing joke in his family that between his father, mother, sister and himself, they could cure anything from head to toe. Last week, his six-year-old daughter announced to him that she wanted to operate on 'cats and ducks'. It amused him to think that the next generation would be able to add the claim of healing the animal world as well.

Gabe Brewel was an averagely handsome man, gentle in affect and mannerisms. He was one of the few who genuinely loved people and wanted to help them. Most of his patients could feel his sincerity and responded well to him.

"I don't know that I can stay overnight. I work here, and I know how people talk." Delta was having difficulty processing what was happening.

"It's in your best interest to be admitted for observation," reaffirmed Dr Brewel. "We need to make sure you are not going to hurt yourself."

Delta knew that if she did not voluntarily agree that she would be formed anyway. It was mortifying to be on suicide watch. Everyone would be looking at her. She began to heave and sob. Her aching red eyes squeezed out more salty tears down her puffy face. She could taste it in her mouth. She could feel the wetness on her face mingle with the snot that was collecting and dripping from her nose. Did the doctor really think she was that crazy that she needed observation? Delta willed herself to stop crying and to pull herself together but she could not. She felt ridiculous, but also powerless to stop the tide of emotions churning in her. She could not understand why she was having such trouble getting back in control, why it was so hard to settle down. She began to retch and watched as her stomach contents projected onto the floor, covering the scratches she had been so intently studying earlier on.

Lifelines...

Delta had been in the hospital for three days and was having mixed feelings about her discharge. She was looking forward to getting back to her home and her things, but at the same time she felt scared to untether from the support she had been getting from the hospital, from Dr Brewel. She never realized how stressed she had been, how bottled up she felt. She was exhausted by the last few days but it was worth going through. She felt different, more hopeful.

It felt good to talk to a man that really wanted to listen to her and to what she had to say. A man who was able to converse with her on her level. Not the stupid foolish babbling like her husband Tom did. He was always saying the same thing over and over again until she could scream.

Delta felt ambivalent with her diagnosis. She would not acknowledge that she was clinically depressed but she could at least admit now that she had been unhappy for a long time. She liked the way Dr Brewel made her feel important. He listened to her and cared about how she felt. She could say anything to Dr Brewel and she did not have to worry about recriminations or have to continually apologize for what she was feeling. Of course, she could not talk too much about Tom or her marriage, but there were plenty of other things to talk about. Her sessions with Dr Brewel at the hospital were intense, but Delta felt like she had a lifeline now. She had a plan to sort out how she felt about many things all the way from Tom, to her mother, to Maddy.

Sins of Samcora

"Like I said, that will be forty-eight bucks, lady. It's cheaper if you take a bus." The cabbie was pulled up in front of her house and the driver did not even bother to look at Delta as he rudely responded to her comment about how expensive everything was getting. "I take Visa and MasterCard if you don't have the cash." The ride only felt like five minutes long thought Delta to herself. Everybody was an extortionist these days and forty-eight dollars was too much to pay for a short ride that smelled like old wax and cheap pine cones. Delta had no choice, she had to pay her fare. Tom had stood her up again and did not pick her up at the hospital like he said he would.

After paying the fare, Delta slowly made her way up the walk and noticed that Tom did not bother to take in the newspapers and flyers that were strewn about on the front porch. The curtains in the front window were drawn, making it look like no one was home, but Delta knew that did not mean that Tom was not in the house. He never seemed to notice or care about anything. If the house was dark inside, he would never bother with opening the curtains to let in the sunlight, he would just switch a light on instead. It was a depressing habit he had. Why would he not want the natural light in?

Delta hated when her house was dark or looked untended, but today she was too absorbed thinking about the weekly appointments she had booked with Dr Brewel to dwell on it. That was the only thing that made looking at the mess Tom made tolerable, knowing that she would continue seeing her doctor.

"Dr Brewel is just wonderful," Delta announced to Tom. "He cares about me, unlike you." Delta placed her hands on her wide hips and stared at her husband. Deep down she did not really know what the doctor felt about her, but she felt more cared for by him than by her lazy husband. She felt hurt that Tom did not even look up when she walked in the door. She had made as much noise as she possibly could when she entered to get his attention but of course he did not respond. In turn, she tried to ignore him for as long as she could, but the more she tried to look nonchalant about his coldness, the more bitter she felt. She had to get that bitterness out before it ate even more of her away.

"After three days away, I don't even get a simple

Sherry Derksen

hello?" Delta knew that she should not expect anything better from Tom, yet it was always a shock each time she experienced how little he cared about her. It seemed that it was a lesson she would never learn. Why could he still affect her so deeply? The feelings of hurt began to grow and envelop her.

Tom was hunched over the small round kitchen table eating a can of cold spaghetti and knocking back another beer. He did not reply, he just raised his head up to look at her with a scowl on his face. Delta could see the traces of pasta that was stuck in the patchy beard he was trying to grow out. Although he was still lucid, his eyes were beginning to redden and Delta could tell by them that he was half drunk already.

"Did you hear me Tom Barr?" Delta went on against her better judgment, she felt compelled to let him know that he was hurting her.

"I said some people know how to show they care. They show they care with actions. Why didn't you come and pick me up at the hospital like you said you would? Do you have any idea how much the cab cost? Do you have any idea how sick I get of having to pay for everything around here? Do you really think I have extra money to waste on cabs? You act like you think I have a money tree growing in the back yard! What is the matter with you, why don't you care about anything?" Delta could see him glazing over as she spoke and felt her stomach starting to knot up. Although she was trying to keep calm, she knew she was starting to shriek.

Irritated, Tom stood up and threw the half eaten can of spaghetti at Delta. She ducked and it missed her but it did not miss hitting the white enamel stove that now bore the evidence of his attack in the form of a dent. Delta was not so lucky with the spoon, which hit her squarely in the forehead leaving a bright orange dribble of sauce to run down her face.

"If I didn't care, I would not have risked my life peeling you off of the lamppost," Tom spewed out. "I would have let you fry like a piece of bacon, you fat pig! You leave me without money for three days and think you can waltz back in here like nothing happened. You are as stupid as you look!" Tom saw Delta wince as she always did when he called her names. Now satisfied that she would stop nagging him, he took his beer and strode into the living room. He settled himself in for the night, surrounded by

Sins of Samcora

the things he did love like his flat screen TV and his universal remote control. From the corner of his eye, Tom could see Delta sobbing as she cleaned up the dripping, soggy pasta from the stove and floor.

"I am not nearly drunk enough to deal with her," he said to himself as he turned the TV up louder to drown her out.

Over the next two days, Tom continued to berate Delta every chance he got. Delta shrugged off his cruelty, knowing that he would calm down once her paycheque arrived and she gave him some money. He was so predictable. Tom would take her money and then he would disappear for a few days while he hit the bars. Delta had no more strength to fight with him. She only had the strength to survive his verbal attacks and black moods while she waited for her next counselling session with Dr Brewel.

Tom hated that Delta was seeing Dr Brewel but as the weeks wore on, he came to terms with it and never mentioned it anymore. As long as the money kept flowing, there was relative calm in the house.

Delta lived for her appointments with Dr Brewel. In small ways she noticed that she was starting to feel better about herself. Better than she had felt for a long, long time. Delta found herself thinking about the doctor a lot lately.

The image of his soft sandy brown hair and smooth skin found its way into her fantasies and helped her block out the image of Tom in her mind. She could not stomach Tom anymore. Just looking at him made her feel hopeless and depressed.

Tom had appealed to her when he was younger because of his full lips and big eyes. Time however, had not been kind to Tom. She no longer saw the soft sensuous curves in his mouth, instead only saw big fat flapping lips that were either belittling her or glued around the neck of a beer bottle. The only time Tom talked to her remotely sanely was when he was telling one of his has-been stories from the past. Then he would repeat the story over and over with such zeal, as if he were telling her the story for the first time. His repetition used to make her feel like she was stupid, that Tom had to repeat himself because he could see that she was too dull to understand the story the first fifty times. She now knew, however, that she was not the one with the problem. Dr

Sherry Derksen

Brewel had told her that advanced alcoholics repeat stories like that. They forget what they say. They forget their lives. They forget the ones they used to love.

As Delta sat across from Dr Brewel in his office, she was warmed by the bands of sunlight that streamed through the blinds in the window. She felt good today. She felt younger. Her life with Tom made her feel so old and tired. Over the past three months, the doctors office had become a safe and comfortable haven. Her therapy sessions gave her a sense of self worth that she had lost years ago. Talking with him made her feel relaxed, a sensation she used to think she would never feel again. Recently, she began to feel ready to talk about Tom, and had been slowly opening up.

"His chronic alcoholism has killed off so many brain cells that he now babbles like an idiot," Delta confided to Dr Brewel as she sat in his office. "Sometimes I wish I could meet some nicer people just so I could have normal conversations," she said dejectedly. Secretly, she yearned for that conversation to be exclusively with Dr Brewel. Even though she knew it was impossible, Delta had developed a crush on her doctor and wished the frequency of her appointments were more than once a week.

"That's good Delta." Dr Brewel finished his notation and lowered his clipboard. It was a sign of progress that Delta was opening up to meeting other people. She had been locked in her husband's destructive circle of enablers for a long time.

"It would be beneficial for you to expand your network of friends to include people that stimulate your intellect. So far, I understand that your only social network is people whom you meet through your husband?"

"Yes, That's right." Delta was feeling more comfortable revealing her secrets. "They are all drunks like him. I don't know anyone else. I could never bring anyone else to the house, Tom would just embarrass me. To tell you the truth, it is too hard to keep doing damage control. It's easier just to not have any friends. As much as I hate Tom's behaviour, I hate when other people judge me by him even more.

The past starts peeking out...

Dr Brewel looked over his list of attendees and marked them off in his binder as they arrived. He had two new patients joining the group tonight, one of which was Delta Barr who just walked in. She had agreed to join his group therapy sessions.

His individual sessions with her were progressing very well. Delta was a fighter even if she did not realize it. Life, circumstance, and poor choices had beaten her down but she was slowly emerging. She needed support to reduce her isolation by expanding her contact with other people. She was still unwilling to do so outside of the safety of the clinical setting. The group sessions would be a useful bridge for her to relearn how to interact with people unconnected to Tom's destructive world.

As Delta made her way in the room, Dr Brewel assessed her affect. He was pleased that she was starting to show positive signs that her depression was lifting. Dr Brewel noted that she was grooming herself better and standing up straighter. He continued scribbling notes in his files as each patient entered the room and took their seat.

He was relieved when he saw his second new participant arrive, a patient who had been referred to him a month prior. He was not sure she would show up. Assessing her, he was not as happy with her progress. A petite woman to begin with, she was emaciated and dirty, unaware and uncaring of how she was presenting in public. Unlike Delta, this woman did not want to survive. She was not a fighter and was not responding well to treatment. She often refused her drug therapy and was resistant to participating in her own recovery. Most of her behaviour was not her fault, she had suffered a devastating brain injury from a fall on some stairs which affected her impulse control and mood regulation. She was an inmate of the Samcora Women's Penitentiary currently out on supervised parole. Her incarceration had set her back even further, layering her injury with profound depression. Dr Brewel suspected she may have additional undiagnosed illness informing her behaviour but her resistance to therapy made conversation and diagnosis difficult to do. She had made it clear that she did not want to attend the group therapy sessions, however it was mandated by order of the court and was part of her parole agreement. Dr Brewel could only hope that she would take the opportunity she was being given to get help and connect with someone in the group who might be able to reach her.

"She is a difficult case," Dr Brewel reflected. "I will never give up on her. I will do everything in my power to help Joan Howard recover," he vowed to himself.

After pouring herself a complimentary coffee and sitting down, Delta observed the other people who attended. It felt strange to be in group therapy. What was expected from her? Was everyone going to be friendly? She felt uncomfortable but a little excited too.

Delta tried to decide if anyone was present that she could relate to. There were eight people in the room not including her. Three men and five women, all sitting quietly trying to hide their discomfort behind sticker name tags that announced them. None of the men interested her to talk to. She already had a dysfunctional man in her life and did not need to go searching for another one to listen to him drone on. Of the five women, only Irma and Beth seemed like possibilities. The other two women, Helen and Danielle looked too angry. Delta got enough angry at home and was in no mood to take on more here. The fifth woman, Joan looked like a zombie. Her hunched over bony body looked tiny yet there was something about her that frightened Delta.

"That is a woman who is ready to snap," Delta thought to herself as she casually got out of her chair and walked to the side table to pretend to refill her coffee. When she walked back to the group she sat down on another chair further away from Joan.

As the session unfolded, Delta decided that Irma was

Sins of Samcora

her favourite. Irma must have been well over three hundred pounds. Delta felt sorry for her that she was so fat but had to suppress her laughter when Irma talked about her problem and said that she was convinced that her overweight was caused by special depression hormones and not her food intake. She had admitted that she ate a dozen donuts most days. Honey-dip flavour in particular.

"No darling, it's the donuts," Delta smirked to herself. Later on, Delta found herself regretting her insensitive private thoughts as Irma talked about the abandonment of her family and her feelings of desperation with her own body. She felt for Irma and could see that she was trapped both in her body and in the nightmare of loving someone who would not love her back.

"A nightmare like mine," Delta thought to herself bitterly. "It's a wonder I am not six hundred pounds," she continued on to herself, feeling her misery increase with her memories of Gran and Maddy and her loveless marriage.

"I was abandoned by my family too." So engrossed in her own thoughts, Delta did not immediately realize that she had spoken the last part aloud.

"I'm sorry Delta," interjected Dr Brewel. "We did not quite hear you. Do you have something you would like to say to the group."

"Oh...sorry," Delta stammered, feeling stupid that she blurted out her thoughts the way she did. She was really starting to lose it. "I did not mean to interrupt Irma. Its just that..well..Irma's comments reminded me of something."

"No please, don't apologize Delta," sniffled Irma who began dabbing at the tears in her eyes with a tissue. Irma had been emoting for a while and needed a break. She was ready to pass the floor to Delta. "Tell us how you feel too." The group's attention turned from Irma to Delta, waiting for her to begin.

"When you said how your mother left the family, it reminded me of my sister, Maddy," Delta began, first speaking to Irma, and then to no one in particular. Delta could not believe she was dredging up her old history, but she could not seem to stop talking. She was tired of editing what she said. It did not matter if these people knew about her or her situation. What was the big secret anyway? She would not see these people in any other context of her life and that made her feel safe. It did not matter what they thought about her. Delta was noticing that when she talked about private things that hurt her, particularly with Dr Brewel, that those things began to lose their power over her. It seemed to hurt less when the secrets came out of the dark.

"I was raised with my sister by our mother and grandmother who we called Gran. Mom was an alcoholic. I know that she loved me and my sister in her own way, but she loved her whisky and boyfriends more. They always came first. She would go to a party and then not come home for days. You could never count on her. She always let you down and always had excuses why she let you down. She never took responsibility, to her it was never her fault. Mom always had someone to blame for the fact that she was never around for me and my sister. Most of the time it was just Gran, my sister Maddy, and I fending for ourselves. Gran was nice to us, and reliable, but she kept making excuses for mom. That used to bother me because it was like she was saying it was ok for mom to do what she did. Mom died from alcohol poisoning and then shortly after that, Gran got sick." Delta could still feel the pain, the rawness of it.

"Everything fell onto Maddy and me. I thought we were managing fine until Maddy decided she was sick of me and Gran so she just took off and left us. It was so unfair. Gran had been good to us, looking after us. It was so sad, the cancer was an ugly way to go. Maddy should have been there to help, to show her love, to show her loyalty. I was the younger sister and Maddy just left me alone with all of it. It was so hard. I loved my sister so much and she just left me without saying anything. There was no goodbye. Why wouldn't she at least tell me goodbye? To this day, I don't know where she is. I don't even know if she is dead or alive." Delta began to cry as the memory of her abandonment overcame her in a sudden wave of grief. She immediately regretted telling her story. What was the matter with her, revealing her family secrets to these strangers? Irma heaved her huge bulk up off the chair, walked over to Delta and put her arms around her.

"Oh you poor thing, I know exactly where you are coming from," Irma soothed as she patted Delta's back. "I know it hurts but keep on remembering that one day we will all be ok again." The words were generic and pithy but Delta could sense the sincerity of Irma and accepted her embrace. Delta considered

Sins of Samcora

herself a hugger too and Irma's fleshy arms felt warm and gentle. She smelled like a mix of the soft honey of her favourite honey dip donuts, and baby powder. The world needed more hugs.

As Delta regained control of herself, she glanced around the room to see who might be laughing at her outburst. She made note that Helen was nodding her head in understanding. Beth, who had anger and impulse problems took a break from her permanent scowl and was looking tentatively at Delta as if she had connected to what was said. The only women in the group who did not respond was Joan. Joan was like a ghost. Her body was present but her personality was absent. She was unmoving throughout the session, staring endlessly at the floor. The men, well, who cared what they thought. Feeling reassured by the reactions of the others, Delta was able to only feel a little bit foolish.

Too much, too soon...

Delta did not go straight home after the session. She wanted to drive her car around the downtown core to look at the skyscrapers and the lights of the city centre while she processed her experience in the group. She regretted telling her story. She also began to feel upset with Irma's hug. Delta realized she did not like her boundaries crossed the way it had been and decided that the world did not need more hugs. It needed more people to mind their own business. Then there was Tom to worry about. Delta knew that Tom would be roaring drunk again by the time she got home. She felt exposed and fragile.

Delta did not want to face Tom or deal with his hostility. Or worse yet, deal with his indifference. It was always one or the other, but in the past few years, it was more indifference. She knew within a year after marrying him she had made a terrible mistake but she had taken her vows. She was determined to make the marriage work.

"You don't just walk away because there are some difficult times," Delta would tell herself. "Life is full of tough times, and good times too." In the first few years of her marriage there were some good times but they seemed so rare and long ago that she questioned if they really happened. How long had she been making excuses for Tom. For herself?

After a couple of hours of mindless driving and thinking, Delta pulled into her lane and saw that Tom was not home because his Toyota was still gone. He should have been home by now, but she did not care. A wave of weariness spread over her as

Sins of Samcora

she realized how drained she was. The group therapy session took a lot out of her. She had not thought about Maddy, her mom, or Gran for a long time and was surprised she still felt so raw about it. Delta thought that she had come to terms with her past, but she had not. It was all too much. Her past. Tom.

Looking at her watch, Delta noticed that it was after midnight. It was clear that Tom was not coming home again tonight. Usually that upset her, but tonight she felt a wave of relief that she could just be alone.

Delta lay in her bed with her eyes closed. The morning sun was cutting through the crack in the curtains She had been awake for an hour but could not move. The inertia she felt was palpable and she thought she might just lie in bed all day. Delta did not want to think. She listened to the noises around her, the clanking hum of her old refrigerator when it began its defrost cycle and the groans of the wood in her walls as they stretched and shrunk with the change in temperature outside. She could not hear Tom. His favourite place to sleep was the well-worn sofa in the living room, but if he were home, Delta would be able to hear his snoring. She was not even curious where he had been all night. He often crashed at one of his drinking buddies places. Most likely it was Murray's but it did not matter to her. All she wanted was to be alone with her private thoughts. She had no room in her head to think about Tom because she could not stop thinking about Maddy. It was taking all her energy. The group therapy session the other night impacted her more than she realized. She got up and made some breakfast hoping she could shake off her lethargy.

"I can't do this. I can't deal with all of this," she groaned to herself. "I want to shut everything out." Although Delta hated lying, she could not face going to work and decided to call in sick. She needed a mental health day. As Delta began walking toward the phone it started to ring.

"Hello?" Delta tried to sound alert.

"Hey there, Delta," Tom sounded unsteady and slurred. "The boys and I are taking off for Vegas for a couple days."

"I don't understand, I thought you were at Murray's last night." Delta braced herself, knowing she was going to hear what she did not want to hear.

Sherry Derksen

"Well, I was but the boys and I went over to the King Eddy instead. It wasn't going well but then just before closing I hit and got three bars. I won three grand. I tell you Delta, I'm on a hot streak." Tom began to speak faster and more animated. It was getting harder to understand what he was saying.

"I'm taking a couple of days off work to run it out. Simon will be over today or tomorrow to borrow my golf clubs, so let him in to get them." Tom had a habit of being generous with his things with everyone except Delta.

"We could really use some of that money to pay some bills. Cable just sent a second notice." Delta knew he would not care but had to try.

"Stop being a nag and do what I tell you," snapped Tom before he slammed the phone down. Delta was not as upset at Tom's behaviour on the phone as she was at the reminder of their escalating debt load. Tom was always rude.

Delta felt enormous pressure when the bills were unpaid. Tom's credit card was his problem as far as she was concerned, but when the utility bills could not be paid, she began to worry. The last few months had been tough for her because she was still trying to pay off the roof repair on the house. Her entire paycheque went towards supporting the household. Utilities, taxes, food, maintenance, everything always fell on her shoulders. Tom contributed nothing, spending everything he made on his drinking and gambling habits.

Delta felt relief that she did not foolishly call in sick at work today. She had to protect her job, her income stream. Delta put the kettle on to make a cup of tea so she could wash down the toast she had eaten for breakfast. She had lounged too long in bed thinking about calling in sick and now she was running late. Looking out the window she saw on her driveway that her lovely blue Buick was missing and instead Toms ugly rusted beige Toyota was parked in her spot.

"Oh no." The toast was churning in her stomach." Where is my car?" Delta found the keys to Tom's Toyota on the hallway table. He did this to her all the time, he would switch cars. He must have come home last night after all. Searching through her purse, she discovered that her keys were gone and so was the forty dollars that was in her wallet.

Sins of Samcora

Delta had no time to worry about the Buick or she would be late for her shift. After throwing her uniform on, Delta pulled her hair back into a quick ponytail. She barely had time to grab the package of cigarettes in the freezer before she fled out the door.

"Thank goodness for small mercies," Delta said to herself as the Toyota fired up. Tom never maintained his vehicle and she was never sure it would start. "Please just let me get through this day!" Delta maneuvered out of her driveway, and lit up a cigarette. She did not often smoke, saving the habit for times when she was extra stressed or did not have time to eat.

"Damn!" Delta slammed on the brakes. She almost hit the neighbour dog, a barking factory which kept shitting on her lawn. She hated that dog. The jostling of the car made her drop her cigarette and it rolled under the seat. Frustrated, Delta tried to retrieve the burning ember before it set the mangled papers, flyers and wrappers on the floor of Tom's car aflame. Still unable to reach it she jammed on the emergency brake and leaped out of the car, kneeling on the pavement to search under the car seat. She grabbed handfuls of papers and threw them on the passenger seat, finally locating the burning cigarette. Delta threw it on the pavement and mashed it out viciously with her foot before she climbed back into the car and continued on to work, trying hard not to start crying. Hours later Delta was back at home in her bed, too exhausted to even think.

"Maddy, don't leave...Maddy...Maddy," Delta woke up at four in the morning to the sound of her own voice. She had another nightmare about Maddy. It had been years since she last dreamed about her.

Delta got out of bed and sat in her living room trying not to think. She did not want to remember. It was just all too much. Delta knew she would not be able to sleep until she processed her dream. She got up and reached for the old shoebox hidden behind a silk plant on the top of her bookcase. She needed to hide the box from Tom. He liked to throw things that were important to her when he was in his rages. He had destroyed most of her favourite objects over the years. It seemed that anything meaningful to her was a target for him. She was not going to let him get to her memory box.

Sherry Derksen

Delta gently thumbed through her private mementos until she found her favourite photograph. It was a small colour snapshot of herself, Maddy, Gran, and Mom.

Delta remembered the hot sun that shone down on them that day as they all sat on the blanket in the park, laughing and talking. It was a rare day when mom was sober and Maddy was happy. Tom was there too but they were not married yet. Maddy's boyfriend Jason had a brand new camera and was taking pictures. Everyone including Tom squeezed close together and they began to laugh. It was such a great day. When the picture came back, it was a perfect shot of everyone with the exception of Tom who ended up being cut off in the frame. The only thing you could see of Tom was a corner of his red shirt.

"Well, that was prophetic," Delta cynically noted to herself, "that is all I still see of Tom, just his laundry." Delta put her memento box back up behind the silk plant, except for the photo which she kept to continue studying.

Delta slept in late the next morning and when she awoke, she was feeling better. A good solid seven hours sleep was just what she needed. Her appointment with Dr Brewel was later in the afternoon and she was looking forward to it. Her private sessions with the doctor left her feeling hopeful and energized, unlike the group session that she felt set her back emotionally. Delta was going to talk to Dr Brewel about dropping out of the group, and perhaps having a second private weekly session with him instead.

She still did not know what got into her, dredging up the past like that, dredging up Maddy. Her sister did not want her, she needed to forget about it and move on. Delta thought she had already come to terms with it. Delta decided to leave for her appointment early. She wanted to walk through the mall for a while to relax, to break up her routine a bit and maybe buy herself a small treat. Walking in the mall usually took her mind off of things because she could distract herself easily there. She needed a little retail therapy. As she grabbed her purse from her bedroom, she noticed that her photo was on the bedside table and tucked it into her purse, intending to put it back into her memory box later. Delta walked out of her house towards the Toyota and began to worry where her Buick was.

"If Tom borrowed it out to someone again, I swear I

Sins of Samcora

will sell it," vowed Delta. The Toyota was a constant irritation to her. It was Tom's ugly car and he should be the one driving it, not her. He never looked after it like she did her car and it was a piece of junk, always breaking down. She expected the motor to seize up any day.

Lowering herself onto the drivers seat, she was about to fling her purse on the passengers' side seat. Annoyed, she looked at the stack of crumpled, dirty papers that she had dug out from under the drivers seat yesterday when she was trying to find her cigarette. She was not going to put her purse on that filthy mess. Delta grabbed the whole stack of papers and made her way out to the trash bin by the side of the house.

Demand for Payment. Delta glanced down at the papers and saw the ominous words on the page. She blinked her eyes thinking she had read it wrong. Her legs feeling weak, she sat down on her porch and mechanically rifled through the papers, not believing what she was seeing, not wanting to know, but having to know. Before she finished reading through them, she ran to the Toyota and searched for every tiny scrap of paper she could find. Gathering it all, she quietly went back into her house and spread everything out on the kitchen table.

Shocked and shattered...

It was all there. Tom had been lying to her and hiding the mail. He was in big trouble. She was in big trouble. The only credit card that Tom told Delta he owned had a two thousand dollar credit limit that was at its limit. Now Delta knew the truth and the truth was not two thousand dollars. Tom had more than one credit card and had fifty-seven thousand dollars in credit card debt. He had not made any payments for the past eight months. The collection company had begun suing Tom and were now advising Tom that unless he paid immediately, they would begin to foreclose on the house. Tom also had a nine thousand dollar loan that was secured by her Buick. That company stated that unless Tom paid immediately, they would repossess the car. Delta barely made it to the bathroom before she became sick.

"Don't think about it now, Delta." Delta still felt physically sick and had to talk herself through the motions of getting to Dr Brewel's office.

"That's it girl, watch your speed. Your turnoff is coming up," she coached herself. She felt detached from her body, watching and instructing herself as if she was an actor in a movie. A horror movie starring Tom.

"SIXTY-SIX THOUSAND DOLLARS!" Delta screamed aloud in the car as she pounded the steering wheel. She felt her body heave with dry sobs and started to feel nauseous.

"NOT NOW," she ordered herself. "Don't think about it now."

Delta could feel herself losing control, losing her

Sins of Samcora

mind. She started to take huge gulping breaths. The adrenaline was running like ice through her veins and she was trembling. This could not be happening. How could this be happening to her? How could her life continue to fall apart like this?

"Good Afternoon," Dr Brewel began as he noticed Delta entering his office with his peripheral vision. He was opening her case file and did not see her initially but he sensed her mood and quickly turned his head upward to look directly at her. He cut off his generic pleasantries when he saw her ghost white face and panicked eyes. He could see that she was in a highly agitated state and wondered what had happened. She had been doing so good and he hoped she was not experiencing a setback. He was aware that she shared more than she felt comfortable with at group therapy last week but he could not see why it should be causing her this level of distress at this point in time. Something else must have happened to her.

"Come, sit down here." Dr Brewel reached out for Delta to help her navigate to a chair. He could see how unsteady she was. She reached for his outstretched hand. Her shakiness destabilized her and she tripped, landing face first on the scratchy jute rug, she felt stunned and stupid, knowing she looked pathetic.

"Come, let me help pick you up," offered Dr Brewel. His tone was so genuinely kind. Delta began to cry again. Not the heaving sobs of frustration that she released at the house and in the car, but rather, a silent and steady wash of tears streaming down her cheeks.

"No, no...I am fine. Just fine." Delta raised herself to her knees and started to retrieve the strewn contents of her purse.

"It's my house. My house! Gran left it to me." Delta's tears flowed uninterrupted, years of tears stored that were no longer bound by her stoic sense of propriety. She surprised herself how long and how intensely she was crying. It was a cleansing wash of emotion, releasing anger and regret. She was glad Dr Brewel had the wisdom to leave her be and just let her express. When her body was too exhausted from her weeping to continue, she felt herself shutting down. Delta could not and did not want to speak. She looked at Dr Brewel, ambivalently waiting for his reaction. He looked back at her, his eyes revealing his concern and his care for her. His body language saying I see you. I am here for you. He

Sherry Derksen

knew just what she needed. All she wanted today was a witness to her pain, she did not want to be pushed to talk, to explain. He seemed to understand that the best thing to say to her right now was nothing.

"Are you going to be able to drive, would you like me to call you a cab?" The session was over and Dr Brewel wanted to make sure that Delta was back in control of herself and would not make any rash driving decisions.

"No, I will be fine, thanks," Delta, was finally able to compose some words for practical matters at least. Dr Brewel knew that Delta would be fine and also that she still needed to talk this out.

"I think it would be a good idea to see you back here tomorrow morning, all right? I can get you scheduled in and will have my secretary call with the appointment time later this afternoon." Delta nodded her head up and down and mumbled an inaudible thanks as she left the office.

After she had left, Dr Brewel was considering what had just transpired in the session. It always disturbed him when his patients were in such anguish, but despite his concerns over her distress, he was pleased that she was experiencing her emotions on a deeper level. As long as she stayed safe, she would survive this upset, whatever precipitated it. He believed that Delta's ability to stop feeling emotion had kept her stuck in an abusive cycle. The recovery process had great pain, but it could also end with even greater freedoms.

As Dr Brewel got up from his desk to get another case file, he noticed something on the floor. Retrieving it, he saw it was a photograph of Delta and three other women.

"It must have fell out of her purse when she stumbled," Dr Brewel surmised. "I will give it back to her tomorrow," Dr Brewel studied the photograph and saw Delta, who was much younger than she is now. The one woman looked like she could be Delta's mother and the other was perhaps the grandmother? The older girl must be her missing sister that she had talked about. Maddy was it? Dr Brewel lingered on her image for a few moments, struck by her stark beauty and wondered to himself what happened that she disappeared out of her family's lives without a trace.

The next day when Delta arrived for her appointment

Sins of Samcora

with Dr Brewel, she felt much more in control. Although she did not tell the doctor exactly what happened she did touch on her anger with Tom and his deceptions. She could not bear to tell the doctor that Tom had put her in financial jeopardy. That she might lose Gran's house, her house. She needed time to process what was happening before she discussed it with anyone. She needed to understand what was happening. Dr Brewel knew she was beginning to retreat into denial and avoidance again. He could plainly see that she was not ready to talk to him about it yet, however, he wanted to establish that he was present for her and available to her when she was ready.

Their session had no depth but that was not the purpose. The purpose was to reinforce the process of dialogue so that when she was ready she would know that she could rely on it. He did not push her and simply counselled her to face her fears head on. To solve her problems using actions instead of silence. He asked her to take positive steps forward and create new outcomes for herself. Delta listened to Dr Brewel and did her best to absorb it, but she was feeling weary and was slipping back into her inertia. It felt good to just listen to his voice though. She would talk to him, just not today.

After the appointment ended and Delta had left, Dr Brewel suddenly remembered the photograph. He pulled it out and studied the faces of the women again, and made a note in his file to ask Delta why she was carrying this particular photograph around.

"Doctor..." Dr Brewel's receptionist stuck her head in the door. "Your next appointment is here." He was going to be tight with scheduling today because he had added his emergency session with Delta to his appointment roster after it was already full.

"Thank you, please send the patient in." Dr Brewel put the photo in his jacket pocket intending to find a safe place to store it until his next session with Delta.

Facing it head on and on the head...

The initial shock of discovering the debt and the threat to the house was beginning to wear off for Delta. Even though Tom was an idiot, she refused to believe that he could be that foolish, putting the house at risk. How was it even possible? There must be a mistake. This was her house. Gran left it to her as an inheritance and it was hers before she married Tom.

"It is not possible that he could have used it as security without my signature," Delta reassured herself. If any of the creditors tried to take her house, she would sue them. They had no right. She never agreed to anything and never signed anything. How could they do anything to her or her stuff? It was Tom's debt and Tom's problem. They could throw him in debtors jail for all she cared. In fact, that would be a nice solution.

"I will get to the bottom of this when Tom gets home," Delta affirmed to herself, feeling more confident the more she thought it through. As she ran her approach through her mind, she decided a calm non-judgmental position would get the best results from Tom. Even if she had to choke out some garbage about understanding his pressures, she would say whatever was needed to find out the truth. Having her game plan in her mind, now all she had to do was wait until he came home, whenever that might be. As it turned out, Tom came home shortly after lunchtime.

"It's Thursday today, so his three day trip took him a week to do," Delta thought angrily as she saw him walking up the sidewalk to the house. He was looking greasy and dirty. It was obvious that he had been on a major bender and was still inebriated.

Sins of Samcora

She hoped that none of the neighbours could see him. Delta was tempted to fling the door open and demand he get in the house and give her an explanation, but she knew the coward would probably tuck tail and run. Tom sauntered into the house and when he saw Delta, he gave her a brief nod.

"Top of the morning, Delta," Tom said with an easy grin, looking happy and acting oblivious to the fact that he had been missing for a week.

'Idiot,' thought Delta to herself, 'it's the afternoon.'

"Well, top of the morning to you too, Tom," Delta tried to sound as neutral and friendly as possible. "Would you like me to pour you a cup of coffee?"

"No thanks, Delta. I need some shuteye. I'm going to bed," Tom rubbed his bloodshot eyes.

'That's what you think, Tom Bar,' Delta stewed to herself, 'we got business to discuss today. Big business.'

"Actually, Tom," Delta forced herself to stop fidgeting. "There is something I need to talk to you about."

"What? Did Simon come for the golf clubs?" Tom started swaying as he walked into the kitchen and sat down at the table.

Simon? Delta felt the pressure in her jaw from clenching her teeth and took a big breath trying to relax. "Yeah, Simon took the clubs." Why wouldn't he, thought Delta to herself? He's a big mooch.

"No Tom, it is not about Simon. I want to talk to you about the sixty-six thousand dollar debt that you have. I need to know what that is about and we need to figure out what to do about it." There. It was all out.

"What are you accusing me of?" Tom slammed his hand on the table, the reverberations knocking over her favourite penguin salt shaker. He was surprised she did not flinch. She usually did when he approached her with anger.

"I found the papers in the Toyota," Delta continued, glancing at the penguin salt shaker. Idly she hoped it was not chipped, she liked that penguin. "What is going on Tom?" Taken off guard by Delta's calm manner and feeling unbalanced that he could not get a rise out of her, he decided to tell her the truth.

"I had a run of bad luck with poker and the VLT's.

Sherry Derksen

The credit card companies kept sending me letters to apply so I did. All I needed was one good hit to get back on top but lady luck has left me."

Relieved that Tom was willing to talk about it, Delta pressed on. She had to know everything.

"How were you able to use the house as collateral, Tom? Is it true? Have you not paid your bills? Are they going to foreclose on the house?" Delta was afraid of what the answer might be.

"Well," Tom answered, looking down at his hands, feeling the unsteadiness that Delta could clearly see. "That was a bit of a surprise. I didn't sign anything that I can remember. I called lawyer referral and they told me that they could do that. They said you did not even have to know about it. This is my house too, by the way. I also pay the bills around here," Tom added defensively. He was beginning to feel uncomfortable. He hated to admit that the credit hounds and the lawyers frightened him. He did not want to think about it and certainly did not want to get into it with Delta. He had seen a lawyer who said they could take the house if he did not deal with his debt. The lawyer had some suggestions but it sounded like so much work. It was all too confusing. If his creditors did not want to give him money, then they should not have given him those damn offer letters asking him if he wanted credit. It was their fault. They could all go hang.

"You have never paid the bills around here." Delta began to raise her voice. Tom always knew how to hit her hot spots.

"You spend your entire paycheque on yourself and on your drinking and gambling. Now you have the nerve to sit here and pretend that you contribute?" Hyperventilating, Delta began to feel light headed. This was ridiculous. She was not going to take it anymore.

Tom knew that he had no answers that would please Delta. There was nothing he could do. She just did not understand his pressures as a hardworking man. He was entitled to a little recreation from time to time. Delta had a way of making him feel small. She never understood him, she just expected too much.

"Listen Delta, I am not happy about it either but there is nothing that can be done. They got me by the short hairs. Your nagging only adds to the problem. If you want to help, then get off

Sins of Samcora

your lazy backside and get another job and help pay for things around here." How dare she question me, Tom thought to himself. I am the man of the house. My bloody house too. Suddenly feeling like he was back in control of Delta again, Tom continued,"Now, I don't want to hear another word about it."

"Where is my car?" Enraged, Delta could hear the shrieking in her own voice. She did not care about being productive anymore, she just wanted answers.

"Where do you think it is?" sneered Tom sarcastically, "I sold it to Murray for three grand. I was not about to let the bank have it when my good buddy needed a car."

"Three thousand," Delta wailed, "you said you won three thousand at the VLT. Was that a lie? Did you go to Las Vegas on the money you got from selling my car?"

"Well, it looks like the great detective figured it out. Of course that was where the three thousand came from. Sometimes you are so stupid, I can't believe I married you," spat out Tom. "Now I'm going to bed for some well needed rest, not that you care. I'm warning you Delta, this conversation is over. If you want to pick a fight, just keep right on yapping." Tom stood up and turned his back to Delta and started to walk out of the kitchen.

She could not believe that he would just turn his back on her about something like this. This was her home. Her home! How dare he be so callous. Even she had her limits. That was when she snapped. She decided to take Dr Brewel's advice literally.

WHAM! Delta took her Teflon frying pan out of the kitchen sink and hit Tom on the back of the head as hard as she could. I am facing my fears...

WHAM!... I am solving my problems with actions instead of silence...

WHAM!... I am creating a new outcome for myself....
Delta's attack was interrupted as Tom recovered from his surprise and shock and whirled around. The pan was thin and cheap and was almost folded in half from the impact. Though a little bit stunned, Tom knew he did more damage to the pan with his head than the pan did to him, his thick baseball cap absorbing much of the force. Delta's arm was raised with her culinary weapon ready for another strike and as her arm swung around, Tom reached forward with both of his fists to knock it from her hands. As Tom leaned ahead to

Sherry Derksen

block the blow, he lost his balance and ended up lunging forward, his right clenched fist striking Delta in the eye and knocking her backward. After she fell down, he rushed to her side and looked at her in horror.

"Delta, Delta, honey, are you all right? I am so sorry. I did not mean to hit you. I just wanted to get the pan away from you. Are you all right?" Tom looked so distraught that Delta almost did not recognize him and he seemed to instantly sober up. Stunned that he actually used an endearment with her, Delta let him ramble on instead of pushing him away in anger.

"I am so sorry. You are right about everything. I screwed up. I promise you we will fix it. I have a problem with the booze and the gambling. I know it. I will quit and I will fix this. We will not lose the house. Please tell me you forgive me. Please Delta." Tom's voice broke as he cradled Delta in his arms and tried to think of the right words to say. What would she want to hear to make this situation better? He did not know what to do, he felt completely out of his element. His head spun and started to hurt and he was not sure if it was the pan or his hangover that was affecting him. He just needed to get away from this stress and sleep for a week. He could not believe that he had hit Delta. How could that happen? Only the lowest of the low would hit a woman. Even a nag like Delta. That was the only thing that he was truly proud of was the way he was good to women. His father taught him that you were no man if you hit a woman.

Tom was so ashamed of himself. His father would have been ashamed of him. Damn Delta. She just pushed and pushed. This was her fault. She did everything she could to strip him of his manhood and now she took the only thing any man truly has left, his pride. He hated her.

Delta could not believe she was hearing the words that she was hearing. It was so odd to have him care for her because it had been so many years of indifference. "Maybe this is what he needed to shake him up and make him come to his senses," Delta wondered.

Tom put his arm around Delta and helped guide her to the bedroom and helped her lay on the bed. He brought her a bag of frozen peas from the kitchen and held it against her face while he lay beside her. Tom continued with his apologies and promises until

Sins of Samcora

they both fell asleep and the bag of peas fell to the wayside.

Stares and stairs...

Getting out of bed, Delta went to the bathroom to survey the damage to her eye. "Wow, that looks really bad," she thought to herself. She could see the bruising begin to develop and her eye was swollen. She tried on her sunglasses, but it did not hide anything. It just made it look more obvious. Like she was trying to hide her injury which would make people think it was not an accident.

"Well, I'm beaten up on the inside, I might as well look beaten up on the outside," Delta groaned to herself. She hated what Tom had done. She was not angry with him about the black eye. She knew it was an accident. That was the one and only thing about Tom that she could count on, that he would never hit her. Sure, he would throw things in a tantrum, but he never raised his hand to her. He had felt so bad about it. She was almost glad for the black eye because it opened things up for her and Tom.

Maybe their relationship could be revived? His horror at hitting her surely proved that he still loved her? Perhaps deep down inside there were still the same feelings that led them to the altar in the first place. Does love ever die, or does it just get forgotten? Could those feelings come back again? Delta could hear Tom's loud snoring in the bedroom and wondered to herself if it was possible that there was hope for their marriage. There was so much to overcome. But she knew she wanted to try. You don't just walk away because there are some difficult times.

Despite it all, Delta still loved him. You don't spend all those years with someone, even if they are bad to you and not

Sins of Samcora

have some kind of feelings for them. Sure, it was not the kind of love that she used to dream that she could have but did that kind of love really exist? That kind of love was only in movies. Real life was different. It was messy and complicated.

Tom was now willing to talk about the house and their financial problems. They would sort this out together like the team that they used to be when they first got married. Delta did not forget that they had problems in the beginning too, Tom had left her for another woman. That had been painful. Then Gran had died and left the house to her. She was so sad after Gran was gone, the house was so empty and lonely. Her grief almost swallowed her up, and then Tom came back and moved in with her in the house. He had been good to her back then. Everyone else had left her but he wanted to marry her, and he helped her over her grief. At the very least she would always love him for that.

Despite the emotional upheaval of the day, Delta decided to go to her group therapy session that was later in the evening. She did not want to wait another week to see Dr Brewel. Even if she did not talk to him, just being in his presence made her feel more sane than she usually felt. She did not feel like talking tonight, but she wanted the presence of the others and to hear what they had to say. She was not even sure why she felt that way. Her therapy routine had become important to her, and she found some measure of comfort in the continuation of the stories of her fellow group members. She felt better when she could see them become stronger and healthier and that made her feel stronger herself.

Everyone in the group craned their necks to see Delta's black eye when she walked in. Dr Brewel took her to the side and asked her what happened. With the exception of Joan, Delta was beginning to like these people and knew they were genuinely concerned for her so she decided to make a group announcement and tell her version of what happened.

"Well, it is kind of silly actually, I tripped and fell down the stairs of my front porch and hit my face on my garden gnome. There was a loose board and I caught my foot on it. Dr Brewel can testify to the fact that I have been tripping over my own two feet lately. It really is quite silly and I hate looking like I was in a boxing fight," Delta forced an upbeat tone, trying to lighten and inject humour into the situation. She could not think of anything

Sherry Derksen

else to say, besides who would question or argue about a garden gnome? It was ridiculous enough to be believed. She surveyed the room to see if the group bought her little white lie. Delta knew they did because they all started chattering and murmuring at the same time. Their collective sentiments of sympathy pepperd the air.

Suddenly, the chattering stopped and the group went dead silent. Even Dr Brewel looked surprised as Joan Howard moved off her chair and walked over to Delta. Joan had never engaged in the group before, constantly sitting in silence and never looking at anyone. Now she was purposely making her way over. Delta was afraid of Joan and she was not comfortable with her in such close proximity. Her tiny bony body lurching toward her made Delta physically recoil both from her look and the smell emanating from her. Undeterred, Joan forced herself deeper into Delta's personal space, leaned over and an inch away from Delta's ear whispered, "I know what happened to you. I fell down my stairs too."

The dinner party...

"Well, good evening all," drawled out Judge Brian Layton. Brian enjoyed the slow measured speech of what he liked to call the western style. So many confused the cowboy style with the western style, the difference really being a matter of money. The ethics were largely the same: freedom, simplicity, honor. It was just that cowboys still walked around with shit on their boots. Westerners could afford to buy new boots.

Brian had been to dinner many times at the Jacobson house over the years and felt he had an established casual relationship with Mark. Still, he never felt entirely comfortable just walking into the house, preferring instead to wait in the expansive foyer where he, his wife Anne, and Dr Brewel were admitted several minutes ago by the housekeeper.

"Brian, welcome. Anne, good to see you again... and you must be Gabe?" Mark only acknowledged designations when he respected the man he was talking to and so far there was nothing impressive or compelling about Gabe Brewel that would inspire Mark to call him doctor.

"Let's make our way to the bar and get some drinks," Mark began to walk to the entertainment room where he did most of his socializing and the group dutifully followed behind. Mark realized that he was cutting short polite introductions but did not really care. He also noticed that Brian's gaze lingered too long on Madeline when they walked up. It was disrespectful to stare at Mark's property in that way and in his presence. He was noticing that Brian was beginning to make a habit of looking at Madeline.

Sherry Derksen

Mark carefully studied his wife to make sure she was not encouraging Brian's behaviour.

"Madeline, I love your outfit," gushed Anne after they made their way to the entertaining room. They lightly embraced and gave each other air kisses. Both women had put great effort into perfecting their makeup and took no offence in the lack of contact on greeting, mutually understanding that their makeup must be preserved as long as possible. Disengaging, Anne stepped back and pivoted to grab the arm of Gabe Brewel. Pulling him up beside her, Anne presented him to her hosts.

"Madeline, Brian," Anne positioned herself in front of her hosts and steered Gabe towards them by his arm. "I would like you to meet a dear friend of mine. This is Dr Gabe Brewel." Madeline and Mark turned their attention to Gabe.

"Welcome to our home Gabe." Mark was uninterested in the tag-a-long guest but skillfully disguised his distain.

"You really have a beautiful home." Gabe knew that general compliments were largely insincere and helped get conversation started, however, he was truly astonished at the opulence of the house. Clearly it took a shocking amount of money to create a space like they had. It was massive and looked staged for a magazine shoot. It was almost too perfect. Gabe could not envision children living in such a home. Or rather he should say, house, as homes were filled with personal intimate touches that speak to the personalities of the people living there. The space was beautiful but did not appear to have any personal touches like photos or trinkets and mementos from vacations. Nothing was out of place and all the decor seemed impersonal and intentional.

The creamy limestone floor stretching out from the foyer connected to gleaming Brazilian hardwood floors which then lead the way to two fifteen foot high white columns flanking the entrance to the room. The majesty of the space was enhanced by the prodigious chandeliers and the thirty-foot span of windows which lined the back of the room. It highlighted the immaculate gardens outside and made it feel as if the outdoors were part of the space. As Gabe gazed out the uncovered wall of windows, his eyes stretched past the Ridgeland Lake and ended on the horizon. Briefly Gabe fantasized about what it would be like to own a house like Mark and Madeline's. Despite the impressive views and opulence, he knew the

Sins of Samcora

only place he wanted to be was his Colonial back in Samcora which was decorated with the love and personality of his wife and little girl. He smiled to himself as he thought about how the artwork that hung in his home was not the expensively framed production of modern artists, but the creativity of his precious little daughter affixed to the wall with scotch tape.

"Well, thank you Gabe." Madeline decided that Dr Brewel had good taste and perhaps would be an interesting dinner companion. The entertaining room had been carefully designed to project the level of money and power possessed by Mark and had been the backdrop of many private business meetings.

"Rum and coke for you Brian," Mark knew the answer would be yes. Mark had been drinking with Brian for years and the judge was habitual. Mark only asked him what he wanted out of formality. He did not need an answer because the answer was always the same.

"That would go down pretty good about now." Brian was looking forward to the relaxing effects of his drink.

"Sounds good here too," interjected Gabe, not really caring what was served.

Brian drifted to the bar where Mark was fixing the drinks, needing to relax himself before assessing the general mood of Mark. Mark's mood was always difficult to read. Brian's gaze stretched out to the same view that Gabe was admiring. This was a beautiful property, he thought to himself. Except for the fact that it was in the city.

"Ladies, your usual." Mark handed the cocktails to Anne and Madeline. They also were habitual in what they liked to drink.

The group sat down on the deep leather sofas and began the interchange of conversation with the usual small talk. The ritual was always the same. Brian and Mark would start with their customary banter about their latest golf game, while at the same time, Madeline and Anne would discuss their latest shopping excursions. After fifteen minutes or so, and several sips of their drinks later, the conversation would bloom into something more interesting. Gabe Brewel understood the unwritten rules of social interaction and for the most part sat back out of the picture until the remainder of the group had completed their social customs.

Sherry Derksen

Gabe was glad he had a few minutes to blend into the background. It gave him an opportunity to distance himself and observe his hosts. Now he could sit back and study them in more detail. Gabe loved to people watch. As a trained psychiatrist, he learned that body language and mannerisms often revealed the true nature of people more than words and conversation did. Careful observation often exposed the hidden secrets that made a person interesting and it was a challenge for him to figure out the mysteries. Mark, Gabe decided, was an open book. He was obviously a controlling individual. Gabe surmised that he did not make attachments easily and his intense focus probably helped him to acquire wealth, power, women, and more than likely the occasional lawsuit if he was not careful. It was likely he was the product of domestic violence.

His wife did not demonstrate any fear or hesitation around him, so perhaps he was not perpetuating that dynamic into the next generation as so many do. Madeline, on the other hand was interesting. A definite air of mystery surrounded her and Gabe sensed a duality about her that he could not put his finger on. Plus she looked so familiar to him, but he could not place her. Where had he seen her before? Madeline was very beautiful, easily looking like she could be a movie star or a celebrity.

"That must be why she is so familiar," Gabe thought. "Perhaps I've seen her at a conference or function?" Gabe knew it was unlikely he met her at any of his normal social circles. He would have remembered her if he did. It was her appearance that was familiar, not her personality. Although financially comfortable himself, he was not even close to the league of money that Mark and Madeline enjoyed which put him in a different social circle. Then it struck him, she looked like the woman in the picture that he had in his pocket, the picture that Delta Barr had dropped in his office.

"So, what is your branch of practice," Mark turned his attention to Dr Brewel.

"Psychiatry," responded Gabe, "I have a rotation at a hospital as well as my own private practice. It keeps me pretty busy. I find the work very fulfilling."

"Gabe is one of the top doctors in his field", bragged Anne. "In fact, he is in Summerton for a couple of days because he

Sins of Samcora

is the key note speaker at the National Psychiatric Convention. Gabe also does a significant amount of charity work. That is how we met, actually. He was one of the original organizers of what is now the Annual National Psychiatric Convention. It would have been about four years ago and I was involved with the committee representing the Summerton Youth Rehab Outreach. It was supposed to be a one time symposium, but it was so popular that it became an annual event. Gabe and I just hit it off. I was so impressed by his dedication to the program."

"You do sound very dedicated...and accomplished," Madeline was about to ask where Dr Brewel hailed from but at that moment, Hazel entered the room and announced that dinner was ready.

"Shall we eat?" Although Mark posed the question, it was more of an instruction. Already he was bored with his guests. His bad mood from earlier still lingered and he wanted the night to be over. He did not care about Gabe or any charity he was involved in. He could see no use for Dr Brewel. Mark had enough doctors in his pocket. He did not need any more, particularly a shrink. He stood up, making his way to the dining room with Madeline while his guests followed behind. In spite of his surly mood, Mark still preferred to be viewed as a gracious host and put at least a small effort in to hide his attitude.

"Madeline, this is a beautiful table," Anne admired the delicate china and huge vases of fresh flowers gracing the table. Anne Layton loved beautiful things and felt jealous that Madeline did not appear to have to answer for her spending like she had to with Brian.

'If only Brian would not spend so much on his horses we could have some nicer things too,' Anne thought to herself.

Madeline was pleased that Anne mentioned the table. She had gone to enough trouble to make sure Hazel made it perfect.

"Oh, thank you, Anne. It was nothing. I personally love the mix of Pearl of Heemstede and Hillcrest Albino. Of course, I did not want to be too serious with the arrangement so I had my florist toss in some blanket flower as well for a fun twist," bragged Madeline, feeling very cosmopolitan after her floral speech.

Hazel was in the dining room serving the dinner as Madeline was going on about the flowers.

Sherry Derksen

"Unbelievable," thought Hazel as she imagined what Anne Layton would think if she knew Hazel had done the arrangements and had to repeat the names of the flowers multiple times before Madeline could remember the names of them that were in the bouquets.

"Such a phoney braggart," Hazel had to hide her feelings. She could not believe that hussy was taking credit for her flower arrangements. "I could have replaced the blanket flower with stinkweed and that woman would not even know the difference." Hazel slipped a quick smug glance towards Madeline. Madeline noticed and her suspicions that Hazel did not respect her position in the household was reignited.

As dinner progressed and the food, wine, and conversation flowed, Madeline began to feel less hostile towards Hazel.

"She is a brilliant cook," Madeline thought to herself as Hazel served her a generous portion of the wonderful molten chocolate cake that she had baked earlier in the day. Madeline was only partially listening to the table conversation now. She wanted to focus more of her attention to the silky texture and deep complex taste of her favourite dessert. As she slowly ran the tangs of her fork through the cake to get another bite, she was only barely aware of Mark's voice as he asked Gabe Brewel where he was from.

"Samcora," replied Gabe.

Samcora! The vile sound of that name sliced through Madeline's consciousness, instantly arousing her full attention. Samcora was a name Madeline never wanted to hear again.

Social grace-less...

"You know, Madeline," Gabe, turning his attention towards her, "I think you have a doppelgänger in Samcora." Gabe reached into his dinner jacket pocket and retrieved the photo that belonged to Delta. He began to pass the photo towards her. Even before she focused on the details of the picture, Madeline recognized it. She had seen this photo many times before. What the hell was he doing with it? What the hell was going on? Cold shock began to run up her spine.

Normally tightly controlled, her reaction was visceral as she gasped and jerked her hand, grabbing the photo and knocking over her tall stem wine glass in the process. It seemed like slow motion as she watched the body of the glass landing on the table and the bright red liquid continuing its trajectory, ending its flight in a large grotesque puddle on her white linen tablecloth and the bodice of Anne Layton's yellow silk dress. It looked like the blood trail of a murder scene.

"Shit!" Guttural and raw, Madeline erupted with the only word that seemed to capture the moment. Her utterance jarred her out of her startle as she regained her internal sense of control. She knew the damage was already done. The authenticity of her emotion was on full display and she knew she made an error. This was a side of her that Mark had never seen.

Mark gave her a sharp look. Was he angry? Shocked? Could he now smell the stink of Samcora on her? Could he see her secret? She knew he detested vulgarity, equating swearing with low class uneducated behaviour. She had always been so careful to

Sherry Derksen

present ladylike in front of him, in front of his colleagues and friends. Her docility had been so carefully planned and presented. Now here she was acting like common street. Did she lose his respect? Was he embarrassed by her outburst? Was he going to ask to see the damning photo? He looked stoic. Madeline could not read him. His mystery normally was exciting for her, but now it just made her feel unbalanced. Anne and Brian Layton were looking at her with surprise and Hazel was unsuccessfully trying to hide an annoying smirk of bemusement on her face. It could not be any worse.

"Anne, I'm so sorry. I'm such a klutz," stammered Madeline as she tried to recover and spin her outburst into something more benign while she crumpled the photo in her hand hoping to take the attention off of it.

Gabe looked at Madeline wondering what was going on, feeling upset that she had crumpled the photograph. He did not want to return a damaged photo to Delta.

"I'll just take that off your hands," Gabe interjected as he reached towards Madeline for the photo. He could feel her reluctance as she handed the photo back. He noticed she gave it another subtle crush with her hand. Annoyed at her rudeness he quickly tucked the photo back in his pocket regretful that he had been so careless with it in showing it to his hostess. Madeline avoided his gaze.

"Hazel, come quick and help Anne." Madeline knew she looked flustered. She had to work to get the anger off her face and replace it with something softer looking. She felt grateful that Gabe had stuffed that vile photo back in his pocket without offering it to anyone else and that no one else seemed interested, instead more concerned about Anne's expensive dress and the huge mess on the table. Hazel moved towards Anne and assessed the stain.

"Mrs. Layton," Hazel instructed, " Come with me to the kitchen and let me put some club soda on that stain before it sets." Anne let Hazel take charge and followed her into the kitchen, concerned that her new silk dress might be permanently ruined. She surrendered herself and her dress to the domain of the domestic.

"What a circus." Mark was furious with Madeline but kept his feelings under control, recognizing that he was disproportionality angry because he was already in a bad mood

Sins of Samcora

from the earlier part of the day. This was just one more thing in an unpleasant day but it was his wife's job to make the home serene for him and he was not feeling particularly serene right now. He hated the disarray and mess of the table.

"Madeline is lucky that our guests are not important people or she would be answering to me for this." Suddenly Mark wished he were in his gym. This was the first time since he married Madeline that she annoyed him. She was really asking for it. Mark knew that he had to get Madeline out of his sight. He needed a bit of space to calm down.

"Madeline," Mark kept his tone even which belied his internal raging, "Why don't you show our guests to the sitting room. Perhaps they would like some coffee or an after dinner drink? Brian, come with me to the wine cellar to help me pick a good bottle of cognac." Looking directly at Madeline he added, "we will join you shortly." Mark stood up , leaving the table. He could not stand looking at the mess that Madeline made. He did not have much tolerance for disorder. The other guests followed Madeline to the sitting room, abandoning the remainder of their desserts and feeling confused and dismissed.

Brian leaned back against the wall of the wine cellar and watched as Mark perused the bottles to find his cognac. He knew better than to make small talk. It was better to just step back and be quiet while Mark cooled off. He was well aware that Mark knew exactly where the bottle he wanted was, but needed space to ease his temper. Brian could feel the tension in Mark as soon as he arrived at the house and was aware that Mark was barely tolerating his dinner guests.

Mark was too much like his father, Elliot. They always had problems with the temper. Brian had been getting Mark's father out of hot water for years and now the apple was not falling too far from the tree. He looked so much like his father and the telltale signs of escalating rage were the same, angry eyes and smiling mouth.

Brian was not having a very good evening either. He had pushed Anne into orchestrating this dinner so that he could get Mark in a good mood and talk to him privately when Mark was relaxed. It annoyed him that all his plans got ruined when that damn doctor came into town and Anne dragged him along like a third wheel. If it was just him and Anne then he probably could have been able to uplift Mark's mood.

Brian had been waiting for an opening to get Mark alone to talk to him, but now that he had him alone, he could see that the timing was bad. Mark was in a foul mood. He had known Mark long enough to see the real emotions behind his behaviour. Years of dealing with Elliot and Mark taught him to recognize their nuances. Brian knew he would get nowhere with Mark tonight.

Brian was feeling pressured, he was running out of time and desperately needed to talk about FastBlast. The horse was making him hemorrhage money. Still, buying FastBlast was a good decision, regardless of what his accountant thought. Sure, the yearling cost him $750,000 but FastBlast was by a sire that had produced a total of 30 stakes winners. He was half brother to one of the nations most promising young stallions. Once he was ready, he would be an astonishing racer.

Brian fantasized how he would be standing in the winner's circle at Kentucky, Del Mar, or Belmont. There were a few problems that had to be managed first. The wins and the success would come, he was sure of it. First, however, he needed to get past the problems. The failure of the tie-forward procedure set his plans back badly and he had already invested so much. The only thing he could do now was wait for the horse to mature and improve its fitness with a better trainer. The expenses were piling up with his trainers, assistant trainers, grooms, hot walkers and exercise riders for FastBlast and the rest of his stable. Brian knew what he was doing. The ultimate issue was not with the horse, but with timing. He just needed a little more cash flow. Getting his return on his investment was a sure bet.

If Elliot were still alive, he would have been the first in line to help him out. As much as Mark and Elliot were the same, they were completely opposite when it came to money. Elliot understood that sometimes an up front investment could spin a little out of control, but you went with it and you recovered. Tenacity always paid off. Mark was much tighter with his money, he opted to shut the investment down when there were problems. He was more of a cut and run type. Sure, Mark helped him out with some cash after he did the Joan Howard favour, but Brian did not expect the obstacles he was having with Fastblast, and now it was not enough.

Sins of Samcora

He needed more money and needed it quickly.

Brian did not lecture Mark when he had beaten the broad half to death. Brian did not panic and pull out when Joan miscarried Mark's baby in the incident and she had tried to get Mark arrested. No, Brian had stuck by him and solved the problem. Tenacity always got the job done.

All of Joan's antics backfired on her when Brian told Mark to sue her for stalking and harassment. It was a brilliant move. Brian made sure he was the presiding Judge over the case and let Joan Howard cool her heels and change her attitude with a six month prison term. After he paid her a little visit in jail and explained that he could give her a six year prison term if she did not stop talking, she did the smart thing and shut up.

After she got out of jail she just drifted away. The last he heard, she had a breakdown and was shipped to the psych ward at the Samcora brain injury facility. Brian had completely cleaned up the Joan mess for Mark.

If Mark really appreciated it, he would spot him with a little extra cash to help him clean up his problem with Fastblast. Surely, Mark should know that he was good for the money once he started to get some flowing back in. That was the problem with this day and age. You couldn't take a man for his word anymore. There used to be a time when a man said he would help you, he would. Even if it did drag on a tad longer than expected. Brian decided it would be smarter to talk to Mark on the golf course. If there was one thing he learned through dealing with Elliot and Mark, it was that timing was everything.

As Madeline and Gabe sat in the sitting room, Gabe pondered her bizarre behaviour. She was acting very odd. Was it possible this was Delta's missing sister. It seemed unlikely but her reaction to him and the photo was strange. Madeline started out warm and gracious at dinner, but now she barely looked at him and her body language was clearly sending the signal that she wished he would leave. He was not sure what was happening, and felt uncomfortable and suddenly unwelcome. There was certainly something more here than embarrassment from some spilled wine.

Gabe was tired from the day, tired from the dinner party and just wanted to go home to his wife and kids. He did not want to think to much about it, he was anxious for Anne to join

Sherry Derksen

them from the kitchen to buffer the awkwardness and to advance the evening to its close. Perhaps he was misinterpreting her hostility.

"So, Madeline," Gabe attempted to restore some conversation and civility, "Have you ever visited Samcora? Do you have any family there?"

"No, and no." Madeline's constricted tone made it clear she was not interested in resolving the awkwardness. She was aware of her rudeness and did not care that she was impolite. She could not even look at him. He stunk of Samcora and she was not going to let the odour settle on her. "I've never been to Samcora and have no plans to go."

Madeline wanted to know how he got one of her family photos but did not want to pursue the query. So far everyone was forgetting the photo and she wanted to keep it that way. He seemed uncertain that it was her in the picture, thinking it was some look-a-like. She did not dare question further, scared that she would be opening a pandoras box. She wished she could take it from his pocket and burn it. Madeline sat on her sofa and looked out her window at the garden wishing this night were over.

Gabe understood the message in her tone very well and stopped trying to make conversation. Anne returned from the kitchen with Hazel, happy that the stain was lifted from her dress. Brian, and Mark also rejoined them in the room. The mood had been irreparably altered. After a short span of forced congenial conversation the evening ended, mercifully much earlier than expected.

Riding in the car back to Stone Pine Ranch with Brian and Anne, Gabe kept thinking about how strange the evening was. He could not understand where the undercurrents of hostility came from, but he knew he was glad he was getting back on the plane to Samcora in the morning, back to his practice and normal people.

It begins...

Madeline was glad that Mark had gone back into his gym. She did not know where he was getting the energy to work out again, but she was glad to have some time alone. Her dinner guests had been gone for a couple of hours already, but she still felt unnerved by Dr Brewel and she wanted to regain her centre before she talked to Mark. She surmised that she would be getting a lecture about the disaster at dinner and how uncomfortable the evening was. Mark seemed colder towards her after the guests left, but she did not think he was particularly angry. After all, he was smiling at her when he said that he was going to his gym and would discuss the evening with her later. Hopefully he would not make too big a deal out of it.

While waiting for Mark, she turned her thoughts to Gabe Brewel and kept racking her brain wondering where she might have seen him, or where he had seen her. In Samcora, she did not travel in good circles, so it was unlikely that they met in any normal social setting. He would not have been a doctor that treated her because he was a shrink. She never needed a shrink, she was perfectly able to sort out her own feeling without some overpaid fraud telling her how to be.

Madeline decided to call Anne the next day to apologize again for her dress and offer once more to pay for another one if the stain was not fully removed. She was tempted to ask a few questions to see if she could get any more clues on who this doctor was. Madeline knew she had to be careful. It was unknown what kind of relationship Anne had with the doctor and she did not

Sherry Derksen

want to stir up any questions or curiosity. Perhaps it was best to let the whole thing go. The world was too small. Why could she not shake off Samcora? It kept following her and haunting her. How far did she need to run to escape it?

Madeline's train of thought was broken when Mark called her into the bedroom and had her stand in front of him. Time felt suspended as they stood in the middle of the room watching each other and listening to each other breathe. Madeline was unsure of what was happening.

Should she should start speaking or wait for Mark to begin? She decided it was best to let him take the lead and stayed silent, waiting for him to steer the conversation. She really did not know where to start anyway. Although Mark's eyes looked angry, he started to smile to her. Madeline felt herself beginning to relax, thinking perhaps it would be ok after all.

Crack! It was so sudden and swift that Madeline did not even feel it. She only registered that Mark had hit her because she felt her face being knocked to the side. She felt stunned and suddenly detached from her body. She knew the feeling was from the adrenaline rush shooting through her veins. She willed herself not to react. She continued to stand in front of Mark. What else was there to do? Run? Cry? Fight? She supposed she must have known it, but did not want to acknowledge it. Now it was plain to her. She married a beater.

"Don't you ever embarrass me like that again," Mark said through clenched teeth. "Where did you learn to speak like that, in the gutter?" Madeline knew that Mark was not really asking her a question. She also knew that Mark was ramping up and she had better do her best at damage control. His voice was so cold. He seemed transformed into another person that she did not know. Though she did not recognize her husband she did recognize his type.

"Mark, I'm sorry. I was so shocked that I spilled the wine on Anne that I just blurted it out. I don't even know where it came from. Please forgive me. It will never happen again." Madeline tried her best to sound cooperative and steady. He was not focusing on the photo. He also missed the relevance of it. She subtly positioned her body and gaze to look as tractable and contrite as possible. Inside, however, she was furious that Mark hit her, but she

Sins of Samcora

knew that if she showed her anger it would be like pouring gas on a fire.

Mark felt his anger beginning to subside. Madeline looked properly repentant and after all, it was only Brian, Anne, and some forgettable boring doctor.

"You are forgiven sweetheart, just don't do it again," said Mark as he audibly exhaled. Crack! This one Madeline did feel. The side of her face felt hot and was stinging from the second blow.

"I thought you forgave me," quivered Madeline as her eyes began to fill with tears. She was not angry anymore. She was scared. She knew his kind. He was the most dangerous version of woman beater. His violence could not be abated from external cues. He had to switch it off in his head and no one could do that except him. Madeline knew that she had no influence on how far he would go. Some men just wanted to see the fear, some wanted to see the blood.

Without saying anything, he hit her three more times and then wordlessly turned on his heel and strode out of the bedroom. Madeline kept standing there not moving, trying to process what just happened. At least for now he only hit her with his open hand. Quietly she undressed and put on her nightgown. She would wait for him in the bed for when he was ready to reconcile.

Joan Howard...

After Joan Howard whispered in Delta's ear, she turned around and went back to her chair, oblivious to the stares that she had generated. Once seated, she arranged herself in her usual posture with her arms crossed in front of her chest and her head turned away from the group. She was not interested in looking at anyone. Fixing her gaze into open space, she began her familiar rocking, finding comfort in the rhythm of the movement. It gave her focus, making it easier to drive everything else out. She felt like she lived underwater, encased by atmosphere too thick to breathe, to hear, to move. Occasionally fragments of conversation would break through the buffer, but those moments were becoming less. Delta's voice, her story, had pierced through. Lies always pierced through, words like shards of glass cutting transparent slivers that bled her out, bled her trust.

That story about falling down the stairs was a lie. Joan was sure Delta was forced to say it. Joan had been forced to say it. Stairs and lies and pain and death. Deep injustice like the murder of her precious baby was the worst kind of death. Grief so deep it would keep her locked in its grip the remainder of her life. Innocence and justice buried with her because of those cruel and powerful men. Twisted, evil men unrestrained in their hostility.

Joan had no power against them, she had tried and failed. She spent everything she had, everything she was, fighting them. Now there was nothing left. Any residue of her resistance was stamped out during her incarceration. Brian warned her he had friends in jail who would visit her. As he promised, they visited her

Sins of Samcora

with all their rage until she was utterly stripped of hers.

Joan was surprised by her brief moment, when she had spoken to Delta, that she felt the urge to connect. To let Delta know that she knew the truth. Now, utterly exhausted from her effort she was unable to continue. Her will, her fight, a vapour vanished. It was too hard to think, to feel, to speak. She needed to retreat back to her place of rest, that place she found to protect herself, that place where she was hollow.

"Joan," Dr Brewel turned towards Joan, surprised that she had made a comment. "Thank you for participating today. Can you share your thoughts with the group?" This was the first time she had shown any engagement in the group. He wanted to reach her and to capitalize on this opportunity to help her before she retreated. He wondered what had triggered her unusual animation and what she had whispered into Delta's ear. He had been aware of the progression of her mental illness. Each time he saw her she was evolving further into her incapacity.

Joan did not bother looking at Dr Brewel. He did not exist for her. If he was a good man or a bad man she did not care. He was a man and that alone made her suspicious of his motives. No, she was not going to be fooled again.

"Not today," was all Joan could muster barely above a whisper. No, she knew better than to talk.

As the moment passed, Dr Brewel was aware of the rising din of the remainder of the group as their impatient murmurings called out for redirection. Self absorbed in their needs, they were oblivious to the significance of Joans sudden awakening and the tragedy of her complete retreat as she slipped further away from herself.

At the end of group, Delta got up to leave and as she passed by Dr Brewel, he called out to her.

"Delta, before you leave, I have that picture of your family that you showed me a few days ago. It had fallen out of your purse when you stumbled in my office." Dr Brewel was holding the crumpled photo in his hand for Delta to take. He felt embarrassed, knowing that his bad judgement in showing it was the cause of the damage.

"I'm sorry it's bent. I was showing it to a woman at a dinner party and in the course of that exchange the photo became damaged. It was inappropriate of me to show the photo in the first place. I can assure you that I gave no identifying information about you."

Gabe recollected the night of the dinner party, it was such a strange night and he had no excuse for himself apart from curiosity as to why he decided to show the photo. He hated having to apologize and explain himself like he was a rookie, but he had done it to himself and his honor and ethics demanded his disclosure to Delta.

"Ooh no, what happened?" Delta felt distressed by the damaged photo but was oblivious to the breached confidentiality.

"I was at a dinner and one of the hosts looked remarkably like your sister. She was so similar they could have been twins. I had put the picture in my pocket because I was going to return it to you. I took it out to show her and she crumpled it in her hand."

"Crumpled it?"

"Yes, there was an incident at the table. Some wine was knocked over. She crushed the photo in her hand. I'm very sorry. I can get the photo repaired or if you still have the original negatives, I can certainly get a new photo made." Gabe could see that Delta was upset about the photo and felt relieved that she was being reasonable about it. He had anticipated a much stronger reaction.

"Yes, I still have the negatives," began Delta, "who was this woman that looked like my sister?" Delta was more than a little curious. Could Dr Brewel have happened on Maddy? They say everyone has a twin somewhere. It was almost too coincidental to believe.

"Her name is Madeline Jacobson. She's very similar in appearance but not the same person. She was very clear that she did not know anyone in the photo. She said she had never been to Samcora." Dr Brewel felt relieved that Delta was not too upset about the photo. He got off this one easy. He swore to himself that he would never do anything like this again. He handed the photo over to Delta.

"Did you want me to send this out for repair or do you want to do it yourself and send me the bill instead?" Dr Brewel asked.

Sins of Samcora

"I'll just get another one made and let you know how much it is." Delta did not feel too worried about the photo. She had the original negatives at home, she would just get another print made. She was way more interested in who the woman was that reminded Dr Brewel of her sister. He said her name was Madeline Jacobson. Was it a coincidence. Or could it actually be Maddy?

'They think they will all remain unpunished.' Joan thought to herself as she laid on her bed. It was enough. Too much had been done to too many people. Enough women had been hurt. Delta got her black eye from a man, Joan was sure on that point. Delta was somehow connected to Mark's wife. They always thought she was not listening, but she heard it all. She heard Dr Brewels conversation with Delta. She heard the name Jacobson. It all tied together somehow. It was a pattern. It was continuing. Joan would not be the only one. He would keep hurting and destroying. He had to be stopped and there was no one to do it but her. She was the chosen one. It was time for Mark Jacobson to die and she was going to be the one to kill him. There was no other way to stop him. She had to gather her strength and make a plan. She had to find a way to get back to Summerton. She had to find a way to get away from Dr Brewel and her probation officer. First she needed just a little more rest.

Distractions...

It felt good to relax in the back yard. The prickly green grass poked at her bare feet and she enjoyed the shade that the trees cast over the patio. Off work for the day and her housework caught up, it was nice to have time to do nothing but enjoy the outdoors. A lazy day to lounge on her lawn chair and search the shopping websites on her tablet. It was fun to look for deals and imagine what she would buy if she had more money. As the sun warmed her legs, she thought she should get up and put on some sunscreen to prevent skin cancer.

That was one of the troubles with being a nurse, you could never just fully relax without thinking about how the world could make you sick. Delta recalled reading in her bible that knowledge increased sorrow. That quote always resonated with her because it was true. The more you knew about something the sadder life became. Knowing about skin cancer ruined the carefree enjoyment of the sun for her, knowing about Tom's debt destroyed her feeling of security, and dredging up memories of her sister Maddy made her depressed.

Delta gained a lot of personal knowledge during therapy and it had been good in the beginning. It helped her better understand her motivations and behaviours. Her awareness compelled her to master her impulsivity which was proving hard to do. It was difficult for her to behave the way she knew she should. She hated having to confront her personal failures. It was exhausting feeling aware of her compulsions, feeling restricted and deprived, feeling guilty for wanting what she should not want.

Sins of Samcora

Delta decided to stop going. It was time to move on. Her sessions used to make her feel better, but now it just created upheaval in her life. There was no point in dredging up old memories and pain. Ultimately what was it for? Just to relive it all over again? She had enough to deal with at present without layering on the past. The past was best forgotten. As for the present, Delta did not feel like talking about Tom or her newly acquired problems with money. It was nobody's business. She had spent too many years not talking to anyone and it was hard to change her ways. All these years she had been downplaying the problems in her life, trying to show that everything was normal at least on the surface. It was too much to ask to suddenly switch off her nature and let it all out.

"I need a break from this," Delta told herself. She had given it her best effort and the benefits she had gotten from her sessions were appreciated, but the sessions had outlived their usefulness. Counselling had opened up many raw wounds and old memories. She felt like she was going backwards. She needed to forget about the past and focus on her future. She needed to stabilize her life.

Delta knew she would not be returning to therapy. Sometimes she missed Dr Brewel because he was a nice man, but without him she was beginning to feel lighter. She did not care if it was delusion or denial. If solving or facing your problems meant continual pain then it was not for her. It was good to be able to take a break from thinking and analyzing. Therapy had made her too introspective. Besides, she was not as messed up as the other people in group. Compared to them she was downright sane.

Delta no longer needed Dr Brewel to help her label her feelings, she was capable of doing that herself. Putting labels on what she felt helped her sort out how she felt. Delta thought things were sorting themselves out fine on their own. She felt more confident with Tom than she had in a long time.

Delta was satisfied with how Tom was dealing with the debt. He got a lawyer and worked out a payback arrangement. The money was coming directly out of Tom's paycheque which made her feel more secure. Delta knew if Tom had to pay himself that he would not do it. He was irresponsible and would spend his money as he always did, on booze and the VLTs.

Sherry Derksen

Delta also knew the added financial pressure on her would not last forever. The garnishee on his paycheque left little for his gambling and drinking and he was pressuring her to shore up the deficit. His indulgences had to be fed to maintain a reasonable peace in the home. Tom would always be Tom, but she could see small changes that he was trying. Small progress was still progress.

Delta could not remember the last time Tom had taken responsibility for any of his problems. If he ever had. He was not much nicer than he used to be. Grumpy and disagreeable was his usual disposition. At least he was including her in the conversation about the money problem. He was unusually open when he explained how the lawyers were handling the orderly pay down. His mood did not matter to her anymore. He was what he was, and she felt ready to accept that fact. It was easy enough for her to pick up an extra shift at the hospital to help make ends meet. She lived with it this long, she could live with it longer. Her house was now safe, that was what mattered most to her. She felt a new appreciation for her home. Feeling like she was going to lose it strengthened her desire to protect it.

Yes, things were finally working out for her. Taking another sip of her iced tea she listened to the soft rustling of the leaves and felt the small shivers of coolness when the sun temporarily tucked once more behind a cloud. Contented she turned her attention to her tablet. Apart from surfing her favourite shopping websites she was spending a lot of time searching for information about Madeline Jacobson.

Delta found her thoughts drifting to Madeline Jacobson. Was it possible that she was her missing sister? How many people look like Maddy and have the same name? If this was her sister, what had happened that she did not contact her family? What kind of a person would cut off all contact with their family unless they were physically unable? It was just too cruel to be possible. Could Maddy be clever enough to land a big fish like Mark Jacobson? It seemed too fantastic to believe. Delta knew a bit about Mark Jacobson. The internet was a powerful tool and in her research she discovered that he was a very wealthy and influential man.

"If this is Maddy," Delta mused to herself, "she is rolling in the dough." Delta tried to find a current picture of

Sins of Samcora

Madeline Jacobson but was not having much luck. She had no social media presence, which Delta thought odd for a socialite. She discovered that Mark and Madeline had been married less than a year. Maddy has been gone for years. She just seemed to disappear off the face of the planet. How could it be this simple? This obviously was a case of mistaken identity by Dr Brewel. There are lots of people who look like other people. Still, marrying rich would be something that Maddy would aspire to. She was a user, always had been. Even so, it was unlikely that someone like Mark Jacobson would marry someone like Maddy. His kind did not socialize with her kind. As much as it would make a good story that type of thing did not happen in real life.

If she could get her hands on a good picture of Madeline Jacobson, then she would know for sure. The few images she found on the internet on the Summerton society gossip blogs of Mark Jacobson and his wife were not conclusive. His wife had dark hair. Maddy did not, but that was easy enough to change. In the photos, the woman kept turning her head away so it was difficult to see her face. Was it coincidence that her face was always shielded from the cameras, or was she deliberately trying to avoid being photographed? She would know in an instant if this was Maddy if she could see a full unobstructed frontal view. Sure people could look similar and it had been a long time since she saw her sister, but she would know Maddy from a mile away. The body of the woman could have been Maddy, but it was hard to tell. She was much thinner than Maddy used to be, but she did seem to stand in a similar manner. Delta could not decide if the woman in the photographs were her sister or not but the one thing that she was certain of was that it was possible.

Love let it happen...

It was an unremarkable Monday morning and Delta was finished working her five day stretch of day shifts. She should have felt happy and relaxed that she did not have to work for a couple of days but she woke up feeling restless. Nervous.

One of the benefits of living in an older subdivision was that she still got mail service right to her door. Of course that was going to change soon, the clowns at city hall decided that it was more efficient to put community mailboxes at the end of the block. So inconvenient and an eyesore to boot. It was outrageous how each year she was paying more in taxes and getting less service. The world was going crazy but today at least, the mail service would be coming directly to her door. She swirled some cream in her coffee and sat looking out the window. Sipping on it, not really paying attention to the taste she felt the tension building in her shoulders. Where was he? He usually delivered the mail by nine or sometimes a quarter after if he was delayed. As she glanced impatiently at her watch she saw the mailman strolling up the sidewalk. He finally stopped in front of her house and rifled through a handful of letters and then continued on to her neighbour. No mail. Again.

Delta began reviewing the things that Tom told her about what the lawyer said. She was relieved that the house was no longer at risk and she had been patient waiting for the documents to arrive that confirmed it. It was disconcerting when the postman walked by her house again. Delta had been confident that today was the day that her letter would be delivered. Tom told her that everything was settled and that the paperwork should have been in

Sins of Samcora

last week stating that the creditors were no longer proceeding with foreclosure on the house. So why did she have that nagging feeling that Tom was lying to her? Mail does get delayed especially from a lawyers office. That should not be happening. If they were delayed at all, then they would have let Tom know why. There was no denying it, her paperwork should have been in a week ago and there was no good reason why it should not have arrived. She was making excuses. Unease settled around her.

Delta knew there was no point in phoning the lawyer's office. She had tried before to get information but they refused to tell her anything, explaining that they would be breaching client confidentiality by answering her questions. After all it was Tom who was their client not her. How dare they say that to her. How insensitive and stupid could they be. She was the one who had been breached by her fool of a husband who racked up gambling debt and then put her house at risk. It felt pretty damn intrusive to be told that a creditor was going to foreclose when the debt was not even yours. Delta still had trouble coming to terms with how she could be responsible for financial decisions Tom made without her consent or knowledge. It made no sense to her.

Suddenly she had to talk to him and get some reassurance. Better yet she had to see him. Delta decided to meet Tom for lunch. She would buy him a greasy burger to make him happy and then she would personally escort him down to the lawyer's office to get a copy of the documents stating that the creditor had no further interest in her house. She would not be able to relax until she had it in her hand. If they were having trouble mailing it to her, then she would just go and get it. Besides, it would be a nice surprise for Tom to see her at lunch. She never came to his workplace, this would be a new thing. New things can improve marriages.

Delta stood in front of Tom's boss while he was explaining why Tom was not at work. It was difficult to process what she was hearing. She hated the side glances that she was getting from Tom's coworkers as she pushed her way to look around for him. How could he not be at work? She could not understand what was going on.

"Mr Barr has not worked here for five weeks, he was

let go," informed the site manager, droning out the fact of it with no emotion, no sensitivity to her shock. Delta store at him, stunned how Tom's boss was so unaffected by her sudden calamity. Tom hid his unemployment from her. She knew exactly where the bastard was. Once again, she was right. Here he was, a stinking liar, sitting in the Town & Country bar getting drunk and gambling what little money she had left on the video lottery terminals. He didn't even have the decency to look surprised when he saw Delta.

"What the hell are you doing," Delta tried to keep her voice down so everyone in the room could not hear her anger and disgust. "What happened to your job? When did you get fired? Why didn't you tell me?" Delta felt like she could barely breathe. Her body felt cold. What was the label for what she was feeling? Fear, betrayal, rage? All of them? None of them? The torture just never ended with Tom. Delta could feel the spasms in her jaw from the pressure of her clenched teeth.

"Well, that was a fine way to greet me," Tom slurred in Delta's direction. "I don't think I like your attitude at all."

"You answer me right now Tom Barr. You explain to me how you are paying off your credit card when you don't have a job. You explain to me how you are fixing your mess by sitting in a stinking filthy bar." Delta found it hard to restrain herself, she wanted to throttle him.

Tom took a long sip of his drink and put the glass down on the counter. Turning toward her, she could see he was having trouble focusing because he was so drunk. She hated him. The betrayals did not end. The nightmare did not end, she was a fool to believe him. All this time he had lied to her and she believed him. She felt sick to her stomach.

Still wobbly, Tom managed to stand up by holding onto the edge of the bar.

"Who do you think you are, grilling me like this? Nothing I ever do is good enough for you. I do everything and I pay for everything and all you do is complain. The last couple of weeks have been total hell on me, having to deal with all your nagging about that overpriced lawyer. As for work, that is none of your business. I'll go back when I feel damn good and ready. As for you, you'd better learn to shut your mouth and stop nagging me. So get your ass out of here before I show you the door." Spittle was

Sins of Samcora

beginning to fly out of Tom's mouth. Delta could feel the wet drops landing on her face. It repulsed her. Tom repulsed her.

"I want my letter you dirty bastard," Delta hissed out. "We are going to the lawyer right now to get my letter. You promised me the house was safe and now I don't believe you. I want to see it in writing. I want to hold it in my hand."

The only place that Tom felt important was in the bar with his friends. Everyone else made him feel judged. It takes a lot to live up to people's expectations of him but here it seemed easier. A man needed to have a place where he could relax and feel accepted. The Town & Country was his bar. The people here were his people. They respected him for who he was and understood the stresses that he had to face. Now Delta was in his face yelling at him and embarrassing him. She was treating him like he was a common drunk. Who the hell does she think she is trying to drag him out and scold him like an irresponsible child? Could she not see that his friends were watching?

"I'm going to explain something to you and you better listen carefully. Unless you get off my back the only lawyer that we are going to see will be the divorce lawyer." Tom saw a flash of fear passing over Delta's eyes. He knew he had her. Feeling empowered he raised his voice so that his friends could hear what he was saying. He was not going to lose face in front of them and he was going to put Delta in her place. He would make sure everyone could see that he was a man and not a whipped dog.

"There is no document you stupid woman. I just said that to shut you up. It is your debt too. If you weren't so selfish and paid your share I would not have had to rack up my credit card. So what if we have to sell the damn house. It is not like I spend any time there anyway. You were so interested in seeing my lawyer. Well, he will see you. I want a divorce and you can bet your ass that I'm going to get my full share of what I deserve because we are going to sell the house and I am going to get my half."

Delta had to faint. Or vomit. Or both, she was not sure. She turned and ran out of the bar to the Toyota trying to suppress the dry heaves that she felt building up. She just knew her house was already gone. That bastard had done nothing. Nothing. He let it all slip away in his drunken stupor and she let it happen. Belief in marriage let it happen. Faith in him let it happen. Hope in

Sherry Derksen

fairness let it happen. Love let it happen.

Burn it down...

Divorce. The sense of loss, even for a bad marriage, was staggering. Sure, her life with Tom was horrible, but this was her life, her world and even though she was deeply unhappy, it was what she knew. Change terrified her. Delta did not know how to be alone. She did not know how to live without irritation. Provocation was the motivation for most of her activities. What was the point of doing anything anymore? Delta had given so much to her marriage. Tom never acknowledged that anything good that occurred in his life happened because of her. The ease of his life, which she provided, was not even appreciated. She bought his clothes. She washed the damn things. She bought the food and cooked it for him. All she was, all she had to offer, her entire identity as a wife was being thrown in the garbage by him without tears or remorse. All those years of sacrifice and compromise and effort, all for nothing. A tragic waste of years. Delta had no clue who she was outside of the context of Tom Barr.

Despite this, Delta was still not sure she wanted a divorce. Tom clearly did because he saw the divorce as a solution to his financial problems. She as his wife did not even factor into the decision. Knowing this, and seeing her neediness contrasted against his distain made Delta feel even more pathetic. Why could she just not resent him and feel happy about divorcing him? Where was her dignity? She had no dignity. Some days it felt like she had no will.

Delta decided she would leave the decisions about the dissolution of her marriage in his hands. She had finally become aware that her fate was always in his hands, right from the first day

Sherry Derksen

she married him. She had long ago abdicated her will to him, not realizing until now just how complete his control was. The entire pacing of her life had been dictated by his needs and his alcoholism. Now, after all those years of cruelty and emotional neglect, he was going to just throw her away without a care. She had always thought that she was the strong one in the relationship.

Delta realized Tom was always much stronger than her. He could walk away happily, and not spend one more second of his life in regret for what he did to her, wasting none of his life in remorse or consideration of his behaviour. She would be the one to bear the permanent scars of his desolation. She would let him do it. The notion of winning or not winning in the divorce was not even a concern to her. She was already a shell of a woman so nothing else that could happen would matter to her. Let him burn it all down. She had no fight left. Perhaps she needed to see just how far he would go? In the end, would there be some thread of love left that would survive and knit them back together, or had their love truly been severed on some unremembered day in the past? Briefly she pondered, which was worse? Being alone and unhappy, or just being unhappy?

Delta did not know how to define herself outside of her relationship with Tom and it was a pathetic thought to her. Fine. Let it be done, get a divorce. Delta knew that the divorce did not just mean being apart from Tom, it also meant being apart from her home. The only true home she ever knew. Delta had to remind herself that her home was gone anyway, the creditors would see to that. What did it matter anymore? Where was she going to live? It was not easy to pick up and begin again.

There were only two years of her life when her mother had dragged her and Maddy to live at a couple of boyfriends places. With the exception of those two disastrous episodes, the place where she lived all her life was Gran's house, her house. It was the only thing that was ever stable in her life. The only thing. Now, it was feeling unstable, the foundations suddenly on shifting sand.

Delta considered going back to see Dr Brewel to get some support, some perspective. Some new labels to help her cope. She decided it would not help, her experiences had taught her there was no real safety net. She would simply be trading needing Tom

Sins of Samcora

for needing a therapist. She was better off alone. Dr Brewel was nothing more than a diversion, a distraction. Perhaps if she had not spent so much time with him and that damn group therapy, she would have noticed what was happening right under her nose. Delta could now see that Tom never had any intention of making a payment. It was one thing if he just failed at it, but this was not failure. This was refusal. How could she have been so blinded to that? How could she let herself get fooled again?

Delta was shocked how fast you could get an uncontested divorce. It could be accomplished in two weeks, but that was not what she wanted. When it came down to it, she could not deal with losing everything all at once, and surprisingly, Tom complied with her. They would divorce, for sure, but slower. Tom agreed to starting with a legal separation because he could still get the money he wanted from her house. The spoils of her life were counted and divided up and the creditors and Tom made sure they both got their full measure. Delta even got stuck with the lawyers fees for the separation and Tom made sure he got the Toyota. He had also tried to get alimony, but thankfully the judge did not agree. The house would be put on the market immediately. Once sold, they would go their separate ways. After two years being legally separated, all she or Tom had to do was file a paper with the court and they would become legally divorced. As long as they did not reconcile in those two years. Tom vehemently assured all who would listen that there would be no reconciliation.

Adrift...

The new owners had been in her home for the past three months yet Delta could not stop feeling unsettled and adrift. She knew it was unreasonable to hate the new owners, to feel jealous that they now got to enjoy the house that had been her home for most of her life. She often drove by her old place, watching with resentment as the new owners made changes to the landscaping, as if there was something wrong with how she had done it.

Out of her portion of the proceeds and after setting herself up in an apartment, there was precious little money left. She felt nothing but loss and diminishment and Delta knew she would never be able to afford another house. She bought new but meagre furnishings for her apartment. She could not deal with taking her old furnishings and possessions with her. If she was going to start a new life at this stage of the game, then she wanted nothing of her old life. She needed a fresh start.

Delta sold whatever she could and got rid of the rest in the garbage. She felt discarded and it made her feel better when she discarded all the trappings of her old life too. If she could not have everything that was hers then she wanted nothing. Delta threw it all away. She thought briefly that she should give her things to charity, it would be the Christian thing to do but her bitterness would not allow it. Other peoples needs were not her concern. She only had enough emotional reserve to deal with herself and she was entitled to discard whatever she wanted without caring about strangers needs. She had bought everything with no help from anyone else and she would do damn well what she pleased with it.

Sins of Samcora

No one was going to tell her what to do anymore. She owed nobody. Too much had been taken from her already. She would rather see everything burn than one more person, whether worthy or not, benefit from the back of her labor.

Her entire household was thrown away one garbage bag at a time. She did not have much time to sift and sort her belongings. The new owners had requested a thirty day possession date and she had agreed. Every day she packed up bags and bags of her household and drove it to the dump. Tom said that she could rent the Toyota from him until the money came in from the sale of the house. She did not even respond to that insult, she just gave him the three hundred dollars he wanted for the use of it. Tom did not need it anyway. He was already moved out.

Of all the years they spent together, Delta was astonished that there was nothing that he wanted except for a few of his clothes. He took nothing else, no pictures, no mementos, nothing that might remind him of the life that they had together in the house. To Delta, it seemed so cold to not want anything, to have never attached himself to anything that was shared with her. He had come into the marriage with nothing and after all their years together, he was leaving with nothing. Except her money.

She should have fought it harder, but she did not have the emotional strength or the financial resources. He did not pay one cent for the house, the upkeep, the taxes, the utilities. He paid nothing for all the years he lived with her in Gran's house, and yet he was still walking away with more than she got. Her lawyer told her that she would spend more money fighting for a larger share than she would receive. Women had come a long way with equalizations, his debts were now her debts too. The lawyer said it was unfortunate, but it was the law that he was entitled to half the assets. The lawyer looked sympathetically at Delta when he was explaining it to her, but Delta could see that what he really thought was that it was her fault for marrying so stupidly.

A new kind of pain...

Delta had been in her new apartment for four months. Laying on her bed smelling the mingled odours from the apartment hallway she felt her body sink heavily into the mattress. She felt tired from life and work. Too tired to cook supper and add her own smells to the emanations of apartment life. She picked up extra work shifts and the fatigue was catching up with her. She needed more money to upgrade her living arrangements. It was proving difficult to save only working her normal rotation.Her bank account seemed like a sieve, money slipping through it as fast as she put it in. Delta was shocked how expensive living was when you did not have a home that was paid for. How did people survive when they had rent and new car payments?

Apartment living was a difficult adjustment for her. The walls separating the units were thin and her tolerance for other people's noise, particularly from their music and blaring televisions were low. She hated her apartment and tried to spend as much time as possible away from it. Feeling the scratchy sheets she had bought rub her skin, Delta thought about the butter soft 1000 thread count sheets that she had thrown away when she disposed of her old household. They were so soft and comfortable. How could she look at the sheets she used to sleep on in her old house? Or look at the sofa that bastard Tom used to sleep on? Or the table where she made him supper? She had no choice but to throw everything away the way she did. The old stuff had too many memories attached. Her new beginning had to be started with everything new. She wanted a clear line between the life she used to have and her new life now but

Sins of Samcora

in her despair and haste she had grossly miscalculated how expensive it would be to buy everything all over again. She also miscalculated how barren all the newness would make her feel. Each sensation was so different, all the way down to the sheets. There was no comfort, no place to retreat and escape the newness. Her life was automated drudgery. Go to work, pretend you are happy, go home and descend into depression. This was all she had. That was all Tom left her. Damn him.

Sill, she could not bring herself to completely hate him. She saw him every so often. Tom had sold his Toyota and would call her and ask her to pick him up in her new car and take him here or there and sometimes she would do it. Not out of a desire to be with him again. More out of curiosity as to how he was managing. Delta pitied him. He saddened her because he was unable to see how pathetic he was. He felt he was living the life now. Tom did seem much happier.

He was living in a small camper that he had bought with the proceeds of the sale of her house. It was parked in an inner city mobile home park that had been in the newspaper a few months back because of the crime in that area. The park had over two hundred stalls which were mostly filled with camper sized trailers that had been there for decades. The poorly built porches and extensions gave the area a shanty town feel. The park was close to several bars, pawn shops and pizza parlours. The city was planning to close the park next summer as part of a revitalization project, but according to Tom, none of the residents were worried. The city had threatened to clean up the area many times in the past and nothing had ever happened. Tom was unconcerned and happy to be living there.

He invited his friend Bob to stay with him and all they did was sit in the trailer and drink. Sometimes if the day was nice enough they would grab a couple of lawn chairs and sit outside and talk about their glory days. Drunks, at least her drunk, never seemed to talk about the future, never had plans or aspirations. Stuck in his perpetual past, retelling the same few stories over and over. Delta used to hate to hear it but now their stagnancy reminded her how much better emptiness was than the anguish she used to feel with Tom.

Her life now was a new kind of pain, but somehow

better. A steady lonely pain she could settle into and manage more quietly. What she felt was reliant on her alone now, not on whether Tom came home or not or what new problem he created for her. She did not realize how tied her emotions were to Tom's behaviour until she was apart from him. When did she lose her boundaries? When did she lose her sense of self? How did she allow her life to get so entangled with someone so toxic for her?

Shedding Samcora...

It was hard to move to a new city, but now that it was done Delta knew she had made the right decision. She was enjoying lying in the sun, feeling it warm her as she lounged on the balcony of her new apartment in Summerton. Her new space was on the third floor and the building was surrounded by huge pine trees and tall poplars. One poplar tree reached up as high as her balcony and the canopy spread out, its full heavy branches fluttering with leaves in the slight breeze. The sound transported Delta into a relaxed state and she felt the stress in her shoulders fading as she slumped further into her lounge chair. It had been a good day at work and she felt more contented than she could remember feeling in a long while.

Delta reached over and took a sip of her iced tea and felt grateful that fate had motivated her to make the change to where she was now. She recalled the desperation she felt in Samcora. She had started scanning the job posting board and discovered there were several nursing positions opening up in Summerton. She was particularly interested in day surgery and sent her resume in, feeling that this could be an opportunity to get off of the geriatric ward and her night shifts. Delta had been working night shifts for months and was growing tired of them. She had asked to be assigned to the night shift shortly after her separation and thought it would be a good for her but it did not take long for her to realize she made a mistake.

She had been embarrassed by the nervous breakdown she had earlier, and with her marital failures adding to her shame, she could no longer face her regular coworkers. What if they asked her about Tom and how he was doing? She had not told anyone she was separated. She pretended that everything was the same as normal and all her lies saying everything was ok was taking its toll on her. She wanted to be anonymous and thought she could disappear on the night shift. The money she made with shift differential helped her out financially, but even the extra cash was not worth feeling so out of step with the world. She never realized how crucial the sunlight was for her moods.

Delta had two interviews with the Summerton Hospital recruiter and not heard anything back for a month. She thought that she did not get the job. She was a good nurse, but certainly not a superstar. She had to admit that she never focused on her career as she should have, Tom was the one she gave all her attention to. Delta did not blame the hospital for not hiring her. She had been out of touch for a long time and they likely saw that in her. Then suddenly, she was called and offered the position. Feeling off balance she hastily accepted the position without really thinking about all the implications of a move to a new city or of being sure that she really wanted to move to Summerton. Now that it was done, she was happier. She liked her new apartment and felt more comfortable than she did in the Samcora apartment.

Delta knew she could not keep going on as she had in Samcora. Everywhere she went she saw something that reminded her of Tom and the life that she used to have with him. There were too many memories, and most of them were bad ones. Ultimately she had a choice, live her life unhappy, or try to move on. When Delta finally decided to move forward she began to notice that the constant reminders of him were like an anchor, keeping her stuck. She would avoid going to places where Tom had made a scene. She did not like to leave her apartment because she did not want to run into people that knew her or Tom. One of the things that Dr Brewel had taught her was that she had to make peace with her past and put it in its place. She understood now what he was saying. She alone had the power to create a new future for herself, and she needed to do that in an environment that was healthier for her. One that gave her hope for success. She wanted to be somewhere where she was not known and defined by her relationship with Tom.

In shedding Samcora and the past she once again abandoned all of her possessions like she had with her house. All

Sins of Samcora

those items were also too painful to keep. Those belongings were a reminder of her sadness and unwanted transitions. The furniture for the old apartment had been sold. Everything else had been left behind, either given away or thrown away. She had taken only a few of her clothes with her, mainly the newer ones that she did not associate with Tom. She realized that she felt better with less possessions. Lighter and more free. The sparseness made her feel less tied down. Yes, it was a good move coming to Summerton, Delta decided as she got off her lounger and went into her apartment for a refill of iced tea.

Reminiscing, ruminating, reunions...

Delta had been so busy with the move that she did not spend much time thinking about the changes in her life. It was nice to have her days full of activity. There was no time to ruminate. She spent her free time shopping for sales to furnish her new apartment and it was looking good to her. Life had a comfortable order to it again. Enjoying her day off and all her chores caught up, Delta began feeling nostalgic. Instead of taking her iced tea back out to the balcony, she placed it on her new table and walked to the hallway closet to pull out her memory box. She had a desire to look through the contents, to rifle and ponder through the trinkets of her past. Her memory box was the only thing that survived Samcora. All other memorabilia and sentimental items had long ago been discarded and Delta felt wonderfully unchained from it all. Yet as freeing as being unfettered was, she was still unable to let go of the memory box and did not understand why she dragged it around with her. Perhaps because it was the only tangible link to a past that she had not come to terms with yet. She thought that she should have gotten rid of it, that if she did get rid of it she would truly start with a clean slate in Summerton but she could not part with it. The items reminded her of her life before Tom. Plus, she had loved Gran, and it felt like a betrayal to leave behind the only physical items that connected her to when Gran was alive.

Delta took the box to the kitchen table and began to go through it. She was aware that her feelings of nostalgia were beginning to depress her yet she felt compelled to continue. She decided that she would look at everything once more and then put

Sins of Samcora

the box away, hiding it in the furthest corner of the closet. As she examined the remnants of that time, old photos, cards, and small pieces of wrapping paper and ribbon, Delta remembered the toughness of those days. She looked at her favourite photo, still crumpled. She never did get it reprinted, being too distracted with the general disaster of her life with Tom. It still was her favourite photo. She liked looking at her mother's smile and wished she had lived a life where there were more of them in it.

Having an alcoholic mother was hard.The broken promises and the unreliability were difficult to deal with. Many times when her mother disappeared on a bender she did not call for days to say if she was ok. The fear of not knowing was hard to cope with.

Delta had looked up to and loved her mother dearly. She was fun, lively and spontaneous and Delta loved being in her orbit. Delta was too young to understand or see the dysfunction. Problems came when her mother decided to orbit someone else, then Delta dropped off the radar. Abandonment was normalized. Her mother lived for her own pleasure and blamed the people around for saddling her with too much responsibility. Anything that interfered with her fun or addictions were targets of wrath. Lingering on thoughts of her mother, Delta realized that it was her mother's choice to marry and then divorce the man that had fathered Delta and Maddy. Delta had nothing to do with the unhappiness of her mother's marriage, despite being accused of being the reason her father had left. It was her mother's choice to run from man to man, only leaving them when even they protested about her irresponsibility.

In the later years before her mother died from alcohol poisoning, there were fewer men around and the ones that were there were as screwed up as her. The most painful memories Delta had were of watching her mother sitting in the living room with her glass of whisky. Delta remembered how hopeless she felt watching her drink herself into oblivion. It was frightening to to see such addiction and desperation. Delta gave up begging her mother to stop smoking, to stop drinking her whisky. Those two things which would eventually kill her. It was tragic and unnecessary, the way her mother died. Her real pain though, came from the guilt of giving up on her. If Delta had continued to encourage, and yes, even nag

Sherry Derksen

her mother, perhaps she would still be alive. Maybe she would have quit or gone to AA. Delta would never know. Delta could now see that it was her guilt that made her susceptible to Tom. Although she did not realize it at the time, he had been her project. If she could reform him with her love, then perhaps she could be forgiven for not being able to reform her mother.

Maddy was different. She seemed unaffected by it all, the raging fights, waking up and finding her mother passed out in the living room, or waking up and not seeing her at all, knowing she was on another bender. Delta was sure she felt it deeply too but she never showed it. Maddy was a dreamer, and it was as if she could willfully insulate herself to it all. Maddy was always trying to pretend she was something she was not. She pretended to be a loving sister, but she was not. She pretended to be a good daughter but she was not. It was always a source of friction between her and Delta. How could Delta love her mother so much and Maddy not really care? Where was her heart?

Maddy knew how to work their mother. She manipulated her mom so that she would keep buying her things. Delta had to admit that Mom was good like that, she would buy you what you wanted no matter what it was but there was a terrible price to pay. The more demands, the more her mother complained about her burdens and the further she descended into alcoholism. Why could Maddy not see that? Delta never asked for anything except essentials and only when it was really important. It deeply disturbed Delta to watch Maddy exploit her mother, particularly for frivolous wants. If Maddy was not so demanding then maybe her mother would have put the drink down? Why could Maddy not see how she kept the problems going? How could she just exploit her mother like she did with no remorse or care?

After their mother died, Maddy tried to exploit Gran and suck out every penny that she could from her too. Gran was more savvy though and would not put up with the games. Gran provided what was needed but no more. There was no favouritism with Gran, and Gran did not try to buy love with money or gifts. She just loved you plain and simple. That was not good enough for Maddy, she did not want your heart, she wanted clothes and makeup and money.

Delta placed all the items back into the memory box

Sins of Samcora

and carried it to her bedroom. She lifted the box to the top shelf of the spartan closet and pushed it as far back as she could. Delta's mood had soured and she was beginning to feel resentful and angry. She shut her closet door and went to the small galley kitchen and opened her freezer. Her mother liked to freeze her cigarettes saying they stayed fresher and it was true, they did. She removed two and went back out to her balcony. Lighting one up and inhaling deeply, she tried to think of something else. Delta was unable to change her mood and she kept going back to the day Maddy left.

No one saw it coming, Maddy did not say anything to anyone, she just left one day. Just like that. There was no fight or hard words beforehand. There were no announcements or complaints. Nothing. No warning, and no reason. She was just gone, leaving behind a simple note that read, 'I want a different life and I'm not coming back. Don't look for me...Maddy.' Delta could still feel the devastation. Even now, after all these years she could still feel the ache radiating from the pit of her stomach when she thought about it. Mom had just died, she was barely in the ground. Gran was in grief over her death too, yet she still took over the full responsibility of raising both of them. Cutting through the midst of that incapacitating haze was that solitary note, white and pristine. It was a shameful way to say goodbye. It seemed wrong that the note was not crumpled or stained. There should have been some evidence of emotion or of Maddy wrestling with her decision. The paper should have been held, folded, cried on, anything. There was nothing. The white crisp smoothness of the paper denied the emotion, guilt, or grapple that any proper sister would have had.

It seemed clear at the time that Maddy had no respect or love for anyone but herself. She had no consideration of the worry and anguish she caused Delta or her grandmother. Delta felt enraged remembering how Maddy made sure she did not leave empty handed. She had taken all her clothes and makeup, Delta's favourite CD, and half of the food in the pantry with her. It was a disrespectful way to leave. It was unsettled, there was no closure, only loss. Delta held anger over that incident for a long time, thinking it was Maddy she hated. She could now see that she did not really hate her sister. Looking back, Delta recognized that what she hated was the courage that Maddy had to move ahead and take charge of her own life. Delta was jealous that she did not have that kind of courage. Her resentment towards Maddy was not that she left, it was that she did not take Delta with her. Delta realized that she still had a thread of love for Maddy, a bond of sibling attachment that, although strained, was not broken.

Delta mashed out her second cigarette. She was tired and wanted to take a shower and wash her sadness away and go to bed. It was time to stop thinking about Maddy and why she left. The reasons did not matter anymore. What mattered was what was happening now and her new life. Her old home was gone, Tom was gone. The only family she had left was Maddy. Delta felt so distanced from her sister, but was there really any reason to be estranged anymore?

Delta knew that the person who Dr Brewel called Madeline Jacobson was in fact, Maddy. It shocked her to her core when she looked up the wedding announcement photo at the Summerton Post and saw her sister's face looking back at her in the picture. The realization that Maddy was alive felt surreal as Delta stood in the archives office trying to process her discovery. The woman behind the counter had asked if she was all right, if she needed some water. Delta could not speak, she just shook her head and shakily made her way to the door. She did not see the relief wash over the face of the clerk who was worried Delta would get sick and that she would have to deal with it. It took several days for Delta to process that she now knew where her sister was. Her desire to see her sister burned in her, tempered only by her intimidation. She felt paralyzed to act, uncertain of what she would say, how Maddy would react. Delta removed her clothes and stepped into the shower. The hard spray of hot water felt good and helped interrupt her stream of thought. The water washed away her tension and Delta decided there was only one way to find out how Maddy would react. She would go and see her. The past was over and it was time to try to establish a new relationship with her sister. Maddy was now her only family. It was worth a try.

Sisters and surprises...

  The outdoors always soothed Madeline. She loved the feel of the air when it was hot and biting into her skin. She was glad that Hazel was off today and Mark had said that he would be late coming home. Madeline needed some time alone. She stretched her body out on the padded chaise by the pool and silently winced as she rolled too far to the side and her hip came in contact with the cushion. She had another argument with Mark and he pushed her. She stumbled backwards into the corner of the dresser, creating a goose egg on her hip. She needed the time alone to heal. Madeline felt like she had been in a war.

  Her relationship with Mark had been changing real fast. Madeline was trying to please him however she could, but it seemed like nothing she did was good enough for him anymore. He had so many criticisms and it was becoming harder to predict his mood or what would set him off. His need to know where she was every second of the day was beginning to strangle her. Last night added to his disturbing trend of manhandling her.

  The first time he hit her was at the dinner with the Judge, Anne, and that awful doctor from Samcora. There had been many more episodes since that night. She still felt fortunate, however, that he did not hit her that hard. She knew it could be much worse and eventually would be. Mostly he slapped her and pushed her with the occasional fist in the stomach. Madeline did not know if it was intentional but he stayed away from her face, making her bruises easy to hide. The money was still worth the abuse. She had been hit for free by boyfriends in the past after she had left

Sherry Derksen

Samcora. At least now, she was getting paid for it by living a good life.

The only thing that bothered her was that it would not be easy to walk away from Mark because she was married to him. Her old boyfriends only had to lay a hand on her once and she was gone. She knew that the level of abuse would keep on escalating, and she hoped that she could siphon enough of Mark's money before it became intolerable. She could live with a little action, but drew the line at any real injuries.

Madeline found a comfortable spot and closed her eyes. She gently let her bad thoughts drift away and concentrated on the heady perfume of the flowers in full bloom in her back yard. She felt herself start to doze off when she heard the doorbell ring. As tempted as she was to ignore it, she decided to get up and see who was paying her a visit. It was unusual for anyone to call at this time so she speculated it was a delivery. Mark would be furious if she did not accept it. He hated when the delivery men left cards and he had to go to the outlet to get his parcels. Not only would he be angry, he would accuse her of not being home. She slipped her arms into her cover up and tied it at her waist. She was not too modest to answer the door in her bikini, she just wanted to hide the bruise on her hip. Swinging the door open she was ready to greet almost anyone who was there, except for the person who was there. Delta. Madeline froze.

"Hi Maddy," Delta began fidgeting, pulling at the hem of her sweater. "Or should I be calling you Madeline?" Delta immediately regretted her opening to Maddy. Even to her own ears it sounded critical. It felt awkward saying Madeline, that was not who she was. She had always been Maddy. Delta had rehearsed what she was going to say but when the door swung open and she saw Maddy, the gracious and clever greeting she had practiced disappeared from her mind.

Madeline could not believe what she was seeing. Delta! Here on her front porch. She stood rock steady facing her. Madeline had tightly controlled self composure which did not fall apart under stress.

"Delta? This is a surprise. Yes, I do prefer to be called Madeline. Why are you here?" Although she asked the question, Madeline did not care why Delta came. She just wanted her to go,

Sins of Samcora

and quick at that.

"You...You...are my sister," stammered Delta, stating the obvious and feeling foolish. This was not going the way she hoped it would. She fantasized about this moment, about how Maddy would react. Of all the scenarios that Delta had imagined, she did not even consider the greeting of cold disinterest that she was getting. Her embarrassment began to turn into anger but she did not know what to say so she stood there, stunned.

Madeline felt the discomfort too, but she did not want to encourage Delta to explain or to stay. She just stood there herself and looked at Delta, trying to contort her face into a placid mask. There would be no explaining this to Mark if he were to suddenly come home. Madeline felt her fear rise. She had to get rid of her. Delta could ruin everything.

"That was not the greeting I was expecting," huffed Delta. She could never stand uncomfortable silences. "I'm your sister, what is the matter with you?" This was going so bad. She was feeling rejected, but still, Delta did not want to have a bad first meeting. She was having trouble controlling her emotions. "I'm sorry, I would have phoned first but your number is unlisted. I could come back another time. I wanted to visit you and meet your husband. I was hoping we could catch up," rambled Delta. Disappointed tears began welling up, ready to launch. Her emotions were a rollercoaster. Was there any way to rescue this situation?

Delta was unaware of the cold fear shooting through Madeline. No, no, no, the absolute last thing she wanted was Delta meeting her husband. Madeline decided to change her tact. She needed to do some serious damage control. She had to get rid of Delta quickly. If Mark came home early to check up on her, the fallout would be irreparable.

"Delta," Madeline adjusted her approach, softening her voice. "I'm sorry. I'm in shock. You were the last person I expected to see at the door. I didn't mean to be rude, I just can't believe that you are here." Madeline reached forward and stiffly embraced her sister. Delta looked bewildered. Madeline was not sure if Delta was balanced, she looked like she was going burst into tears again. "We have to leave the house now, Delta. Step in and I am going to get changed and then we are going to go out for a coffee and a chat, ok?" Madeline tried to sound enthusiastic. She did not even wait for an answer from Delta. She just pulled Delta into the house by her arm and closed the door behind her.

"One sec... I will be right back," Madeline turned on her heel and raced at top speed towards the staircase. Bounding up the stairs two at a time she ran into her bedroom and threw on some clothes as fast as she could. She had to get Delta out of the house, immediately. Every second felt like an eternity and all she could think about was Mark walking in on this little scene.

Downstairs Delta just store as Madeline raced away from her. She did not even know what to think, there were too many emotions to process and she felt herself shutting down. Confused, she sat on the love seat in the foyer and waited for Maddy to return.

It had been three hours since Delta got home and still she could not stop crying, her eyes were puffy and sore. It was hard for her to calm down. Hard for her to decide what she felt. Was she sad? Was she angry? Her meeting with Maddy was bizarre. After Maddy had rushed her out of the house, she told Delta to follow her to a coffee shop, which ended up being halfway across town. During the drive it was hard not to be resentful.

The contrast was sharp, Delta driving her cheap midsize Chevy following Maddy who was driving a gorgeous Jaguar. Delta surmised that the car cost more than she made all year. The opulence of Maddy's house was astonishing, the foyer where she waited when Maddy went to change seemed larger than her entire apartment. It was abundantly clear that Maddy had it made. She hit the jackpot. Any happiness for Maddy's fortune was swallowed in Delta's raging jealousy. The contrast in their lifestyles exploded her resentment. Maddy had so much and Delta had nothing. The little bit that she used to have with the house in Samcora was taken away from her by Tom and his greed. She stayed and looked after things, looked after Gran when she got sick. It was Delta who held it all together, and there was comfort in owning Gran's house after she passed on. She always thought that wherever Maddy was, she would have been jealous to know she forfeited her share of Gran's inheritance by disappearing. It was only fair after all, she had walked away and Delta stayed. By all rights, she should have had less than Delta. Life was not fair. Maddy did not deserve her wealth.

Sins of Samcora

Delta continued to review her first meeting with Maddy. It was not even close to how she imagined it would go. She thought she might feel some sort of closure but she ended up feeling more conflicted than before.

"What was I hoping for anyway?" Delta thought. She wanted to hear a story about how Maddy could not take the situation with her drunken mother anymore, that the stress became unbearable and she decided to run off. That she got so immersed in trying to erase her pain that she just did not call. She wanted to, but did not. As the years passed it had felt too late. Delta wanted to hear that Maddy had hard times and regret too, but Maddy had no story and no regret. She made no excuses nor explanations for why she left. She did not even want to talk about it. It was only after Delta pushed her that she exasperatedly said that she wanted to leave and so she did. She said it was nothing personal. Nothing personal! It was very personal to Delta, and Maddy's refusal to talk about it felt like another rejection. They were sisters, the same blood, and yet Maddy was unable to grasp how her actions affected Delta.

Delta felt hurt after she explained what happened with Tom and the house in Samcora and Maddy just listened stoically, without asking any questions or offering any kind of support. Maddy did not seem to care so Delta dropped it and the conversation moved on.

Delta finally understood Maddy's strange behaviour as she began to explain how Mark did not know her background and did not know she had a sister. Maddy had invented a complete life of lies and Delta could understand why she would. There was nothing good to tell about her past and certainly nothing that a man like Mark would be interested in. Would Delta keep her secret? Of course she would. They were sisters after all. Sisters were supposed to help each other

Delta would keep the little secret to herself and stay away from Maddy's house. In return, perhaps Maddy would help her by giving her a little hand up financially. Just something to help her restart her life after Tom.

Summerton was more expensive to live in than Samcora. Delta was tired of being by herself and living hand to mouth and Maddy had so much. Certainly she could share a little of her good fortune. After all, she was surrounded with astonishing abundance. The pittance that Delta asked for must be like lunch money to Maddy. Even if her sister could not share her heart, she could share her bank account.

Blackmail?

Why would Maddy call it blackmail? Delta would not deliberately hurt Maddy by revealing her secret. It was Maddy who hurt everyone. It was Maddy who took from everyone. She took her CD player and all the food from the pantry when she left. She knew that Gran was poor. What did she think they would eat? It was Maddy who leaned on mom so hard with her wants that she just gave up and drank herself to death. No, it was Maddy who caused the pain with her secrets and her exclusivity. She always thought she was better than everyone. She owed Delta for picking up her slack after she left. She owed her for the years of worry and stress wondering if Maddy was alive or dead. While all along, here she was, living in the lap of luxury while she struggled. It was enough to make a person bitter. It was an honest trade as far as Delta was concerned. A secret for a helping hand. It was not blackmail. It was justice.

Wiping the blood off her mouth, Madeline thought this day could not get any worse. Mark was upset because she had looked at the waiter for a moment too long when they were out to dinner. She did not think that she did, it was only an unconscious glance, but Mark made up his mind that she was flirting with the waiter. She had no idea that he was mad at her until they got home, even in the car Mark provided no clue that he was upset with her.

Examining her lip in the mirror of her bathroom, she felt fortunate that the split was on the inside. Her tooth must have cut the soft tissues. The outside of her lip was not bruised and only slightly swollen so she would be able to disguise the injury easy enough. Madeline did not know why Mark was in such a foul mood but knew it was not her fault. He probably had a rough day at work and was taking it out on her. It was not unnoticed that when he had stressful days at work that he was more difficult at home.

Madeline was grateful that she had gotten back home from her nightmare meeting with Delta before Mark arrived home. She did not want to even think about how bad it would have been if

Sins of Samcora

she was caught going out when he told her to stay home. It was a huge risk leaving the house, but it would have been even worse if he had run into Delta. Today was a new beginning for both Mark and Delta, thought Madeline. They have both achieved new lows. Mark had hit her on the face for the first time and Delta had gotten into the blackmail business. Madeline was outraged at Delta's greed. Her sister had promised not to tell Mark about her background, but Madeline would have to deposit money into her bank account every month.

She had asked for a ridiculous amount but Madeline was able to convince her that she did not have access to those kind of resources without being noticed by Mark. Madeline was barely able to keep siphoning enough off for herself without feeding her treacherous sister. This situation was going to set her financial plans further back. No wonder she hated Samcora and everything and everyone connected with it. It was the same all her life, everyone was always leaning on her, her alcoholic mother, her needy grasping sister. Only Madeline had the backbone and strength to get away from all of that and make something of herself. Even if her life was an invention, it was a lot better than anything she could become if she had stayed where she began like Delta did.

Madeline had no sympathy for Delta or her situation. It was Delta who decided to marry that loser Tom Barr. That he turned out to be what he was, did not surprise her at all. Anyone could have seen that there was no real future with him. Except of course for Delta, who was now so shocked that her loser husband lost everything. She was unable to see her incredible gullibility and stupidity. All the road signs were there. Why would she not want to look at them? Now, here she was looking for Madeline to bail her out. Why could she just not live out her own life? Just because she was born her sister did not automatically make her someone she wanted to know. Madeline never liked Delta. Never liked her whining ways and her weakness. She was always leaning and now she was leaning again.

Delta seemed to think Madeline owed her. It was not a helping hand. It was blackmail, pure and simple. No matter how she tried to justify it, her threat was clear. If Delta was to keep silent about Madeline's past, then Madeline would have to keep forking over money. Between Mark and Delta, Madeline was feeling trapped.

There was no way to salvage the situation. She had limited choices. Run away again? That would be a poor choice because she was legally married. If she just disappeared how could she possibly marry her next benefactor? No, she would have to divorce Mark before finding another man. Second choice, get rid of Delta. How? All she wanted was money. If she would stay with the fixed amount they agreed on, then perhaps the situation could be workable. But, if she became greedy and wanted more, which Madeline suspected she would, then the situation would no longer be possible.

Madeline replayed in her mind how she tried to be honest with Delta. She tried to explain in a way that would not hurt her that she just wanted to be alone. Delta kept pressing for explanations of why she left. What could she say? She left because she wanted to live her own life independently. It was nothing personal against Delta. Madeline was a loner and did not want a relationship with anyone. She did not want to be friends back when they were younger, and she did not want to be friends now. She wanted to be left alone. Madeline was tempted to tell her the truth, that she is her own individual and she has a right to choose who is in her life. Just because they are sisters does not mean that she should be obligated to have a lifetime relationship with her. It was not Madeline's choice to be born into her family, but as an adult, it is her choice who to associate with. Madeline knew she could not say those things, that Delta would be unable to accept that truth. She just said she did not want to talk about it. So she didn't.

She especially did not want to talk about her mother. She both hated and loved her mother. It was complicated. She wanted her mother to rise above her addictions and be someone Madeline could be proud of, but she was unable. Her weakness and failures killed her and Madeline knew she had to be someone completely different so that she did not end up the same pathetic way. She could see her mother in Delta, they looked the same and their personalities were so much the same. They both wallowed in their neediness.

Madeline did not need other people the way her mother and Delta did. She did not need to be told who she was or have her ego stroked by others. She did not need to live through the

Sins of Samcora

approval of others. She knew who she was. It did not matter what anyone else thought. People like Delta were dead weight. They just dragged her down. Delta had no right to make any demands on Madeline. She was utterly unable to understand that a blood connection did not give her a free pass to intrude on Madeline's life. Madeline could see that there was no easy way out of this complication. All she could do was continue to siphon off as much as she could from Mark's bank account until his abuse and Delta's demands became intolerable. She needed some time to think. Blackmail would be fine in the short term, but Madeline knew that she would need to find a longer term solution.

Tom...

The ending of his marriage felt like a new beginning for Tom. For a long time he had felt trapped, strangled by the oppressive feeling of accountability that Delta demanded of him. She was always so busy reminding him of everything she did for him that she failed to realize that he did not want any of her help. Delta had a way of making him feel small and useless. Whenever she complained to him about his failings, he felt scolded. Her approach erased any feelings of guilt he might have mustered up, for he also knew that he was not entirely innocent of all her grievances. Not being around her removed the stress he felt from her reminders of his incompetencies. But as wonderful as his new freedom had been, he now had to admit that in the last few months, he had fallen on some hard times.

The money from his separation agreement was almost gone and Tom could not understand how it went so quickly. He had been on such a hot streak at the casino. When did the tide turn? He had felt golden, rejuvenated and happy and now, all too suddenly, his carefree lifestyle was threatening to be over. The same old problems of money that haunted him all his life were clinging to his back again, and yet try as he might, Tom could not figure out why. It was impossible that he had spent all of his money already. He clearly remembered winning more than he lost at the VLT's, yet his bank balance was hard evidence that he must not have.

Tom store blankly at the eviction notice taped to the door of his small trailer and briefly wondered if Delta would help him. His pride turned those thoughts aside. He did not need her. He

Sins of Samcora

never needed her and refused to give her the satisfaction of seeing him down on his luck. Besides, how could the trailer park just tell him to leave? He always made sure that he paid his rent like everyone else. He had a right to be here. Tom did not give a damn about their revitalization plans. He stayed in denial and waited until his was the last camper in the small trailer park.

It was late morning when the knock came on the door from the sheriff. He arrived along with two deputies to make sure that Tom did not interfere when the tractor came to tow away his tiny trailer to the impound yard. Tom felt too tired and hungover to make a fuss, so he just nodded his head in agreement and walked out of his camper and headed across the lot.

There was no grass, it had long ago been replaced by gravel, garbage and dirt. The trailer park was circled by an uneven chain link fence, grey and baggy looking, stretched out in areas from years of people leaning and climbing, and being pushed up against it. The too few trees were gnarled looking, yielding sparse leaves on their branches. The fence had always seemed ridiculous to Tom. There was nothing to keep out, and even less to keep in.

Tom just sat down in the hot stale dirt, propped up against the sagging fence as he watched them hitching up his home. Everything he owned was in that camper and he had left it all in there. There was no point in taking it. He had nowhere to go and no place to store any of his possessions even if he had wanted them. It did not matter anyway. Tom had set backs before and survived all of them. He still had everything he wanted, a brand new twenty-six of rye in his pocket and his friends. Tom hauled himself up off the ground and dusted off his clothes. He needed a drink and to pay a visit to some of his buddies. He was sure he could crash on one of their sofas tonight. As he walked away from the trailer park, Tom did not even bother to look back. It was over and there was no point in dwelling on it.

The slats on the park bench outside the Regent apartments were rough and Tom had to be careful how he sat on them to avoid a splinter. The faded and peeled paint exposed the dried out wood which was cracked and worn from the elements and neglect. There were twenty-two of the ugly Regent buildings cramped into four city blocks. The subsidized cross shaped

Sherry Derksen

complexes were built out of dirty red bricks and small windows giving them an institutional look. They were three stories high, had no elevators, and stunk of overcrowding, cooking odours, and squalor. The neighbourhood was referred to as the slums of Summerton, and rightfully so, but it had been home to Tom for the past couple of months. He was staying with his old buddy Murray which would have been ok except for Murray's wife and three brats. Or at least, he used to live with them.

"You're not pulling your weight here man," was all that Murray said before he showed him the door. Ingrate, thought Tom. Murray should have helped him more than he did. After all, Tom had sold Delta's Buick for three thousand lousy bucks to him. He could never buy a car like that for so cheap anywhere else and he did not even have the decency to be grateful. Murray was driving around in that car like he thought he was the king of the mountain, parading with his ugly wife and screaming kids. Forgetting what he owed Tom. To top it off, for Tom's generosity, what was he offered? Nothing, but a lousy job that did not even pay him a decent wage and left him stinking with paint smells every shift. He did not even have his own room in Murrays apartment, having to sleep on a lumpy sofa bed that he had to be out of in the morning because the wife did not want to see him in the living room when the kids got up. They did not care even a little bit how hard it was to get up in the morning everyday. Where was he supposed to go? He did not want to work everyday. He was sick of eating that wife's breakfast every morning, how much oatmeal could one man take? How hard would it be to make a decent bacon and eggs sometimes? Murray was the one not pulling his weight thought, Tom irritably.

Murray had landed a sweet job as a supervisor of a painting crew that got a contract to paint the new wing of the University in Summerton. So Murray packed up and left Samcora. When he heard that Tom's trailer had been taken he suggested Tom join the paint crew and move to Summerton with him. It seemed like a good idea at the time but then Murray got all big headed being the boss. All he did was walk around and tell everyone else what to do, and what they had done wrong. It seemed to Tom that Murray picked on him more than the others. He always had something to say about how he painted wrong, that he missed spots, that he painted sloppy. Nag, nag, nag. Nothing was good enough for

Sins of Samcora

Murray. Tom continued to adjust himself, trying to get comfortable on the hard bench.

What kind of friend was Murray to ask him to start paying rent? What was he supposed to live on? Pay rent for that lumpy sofa bed? There was no privacy, and the three kids were loud and obnoxious. Why should he pay for listening to those brats and eating the horrible food the wife cooked? They should pay him for putting up with it. Plus, Murray was not understanding that Tom hated painting and needed to step out for a couple of days every now and then for some relaxation and to get away from the chaos. Tom was sick of Murray whining that he could not keep covering for Tom at work. It started to feel like he was married to Delta again, Tom thought grimly. Just because he did not show up for work for a few days and still had not paid any room and board, Murray had the gall to fire him from his job and toss him out on his ear from the apartment. Well, good riddance to that unappreciative bastard, thought Tom. He did not need friends like that.

Tom decided that the best course of action was to take back the Buick. Murray had gotten enough out of him and now he was going to get back what was rightfully his. It was simple. Tom walked to the construction site at the University where he and Murray had worked. Supervisors and managers were allowed to park near the West wing and there it was, parked as pretty as could be in its usual spot. It did not take too long to find the car, even though it was hidden between a white half ton and a dirty green van. Murray had driven Tom to work many times and he usually parked in the same spot if the lot was open. Three thousand dollars, Tom snorted as he unlocked the door and slid into the drivers seat. He was glad he still had his keys with him.

Tom always kept his keys with him. Even when the lawyer wanted the house keys after the sale of the house in Samcora, Tom said he did not have any, even as he felt them in his pocket rubbing alongside the Buick key and others. He liked to jangle his keys in his pocket, a habit that he did when he felt nervous. There was something about holding onto keys that made him feel better. He enjoyed his secret, that he could open doors he knew he should not. It made him feel like he still owned those things.

Tom's brooding continued as the engine roared to life

Sherry Derksen

and he put the car in gear. Tom would have never sold the car to Murray if he had known what a lousy friend he would turn out to be. It was unreasonable. Tom had known Murray long enough to know his habits and he confidently reached under the seat and found a three quarters full bottle of whisky as he knew he would. Pulling out of the parking lot Tom reached over and looked in the cubby hole to see if Murray left any cigarettes in there. He did not, but there was a camera. Bonus, thought Tom as he grabbed the camera and stuffed it into the inner pocket of his jacket. He should get enough at the pawn shop to buy some good tailor made smokes to go with his whisky. It was turning out to be a good day after all.

Feeling excited and free again, Tom rolled the window down and enjoyed the breeze as he cruised down the road. He turned on the music and it pulsed through him. He was feeling good. He had forgotten how much he missed his own wheels. He missed the freedom of being able to go where he wanted when he wanted. He felt like his old self and even began to think about Delta and his old house in Samcora.

He did not miss either, but had to admit that his life did seem easier back then. Delta always had a steady job and although she was a pain, at least he could get a few bucks out of her. She was not as stingy as Murray, and grudgingly he had to give her credit for that. Briefly he toyed with the idea of driving to Samcora and trying to find her. He wondered if she would help him get back on his feet but he realized that he did not have enough gas in the Buick to make it there. It was something he would think about later, but right now all Tom wanted to do was to head to the South Side shopping mall so he could park the car and blend into the sea of metal. He wanted to sit back and have a couple of drinks from the bottle he found under the seat. Then he would find a pawn shop.

Even though Tom had been in Summerton awhile, he did not usually venture far from 114th, his favourite street. It was only two blocks from the Regent apartments where he used to live with Murray. Pablo Pizza was there and made great pepperoni pizza which he often enjoyed washing down with a cold beer on tap. He felt at home there and everything he needed was close by including a drop in shelter which now he would have to consider going to. There was a pawn shop with its bright neon sign offering instant cash and payday advances. A couple of doors down was Jim's

Sins of Samcora

Billiards. Tom always had luck finding pop bottles in Jim's garbage, and it was always his last stop before he went to the bottle depot. He was usually able to find enough cans and pop bottles in the trash bins up and down the street to trade in for a few dollars to buy some comfort at the liquor store. He realized he would have to head back to his street soon, before anyone else began to rifle through his garbage cans, thinking that he was not going to show up today. But first he needed to park awhile at the South Side mall so he could have a drink or two and maybe a little nap. There was no place private enough to park on his street without being noticed and the last thing he needed was some do-gooder calling the cops and telling them he was drinking in the car. Tom remembered how one of his buddies back in Samcora got a DUI from sitting and drinking in his parked car. Parked! It was ridiculous. Tom was not going to let it happen to him.

Tom barely had half a drink and then he saw her. What the hell was she doing in Summerton? Tom rubbed his eyes thinking distractedly that his eyes were playing tricks on him but he was still sober and it was no hallucination. It was her. Her hair was a little longer and Tom noticed that it was a little lighter as well. The bags under her eyes were a bit bigger and the slightly dour turndown of her mouth was even more pronounced. She looked unhappy, or perhaps it was only the stern look she got when she was preoccupied. Whatever it was, she was definitely Delta. Her clothes were new, at least Tom could not remember seeing them on her before, but he usually did not pay much attention to what she wore anyway. In her arms were a stack of shopping bags and she was making her way to what looked like a new car.

Tom lowered himself in the Buick. He did not want her to see him, did not want to talk to her just yet. She was obviously doing better than he had with money if she could afford whatever was in her shopping bags. She must have tricked him and hid some money from him in the separation. If he was broke by now, she should have been too. Tom began to feel jealous and angry at Delta. It was him all these years who contributed everything in the marriage. All she did was shop and spend money. Tom made the decision to follow her. He needed to know where she was going and what she was up to. She needed to explain where she got the extra money from and why he did not get a fair share. She needed to help him, she owed him that much. Delta finished putting her parcels in the trunk of her car and made her way to the drivers door. Tom kept his eyes riveted to her as he fired up the Buick and backed out of his lot. He had to be careful not to lose her.

It started with a sofa...

It had been awhile since Delta had gone to the mall and treated herself. The South Side mall was the largest in Summerton and she loved it. All her favourite stores were there and she loved the distraction of the displays. Shopping had always relaxed Delta and there were so many sales going on that she could not resist buying just a few things for herself. As she walked to her car, she felt somewhat guilty about her splurge, she should be more responsible. Summerton was more expensive to live in than Samcora. But she would manage fine once she got a little more on top of things. Although her new job at the Summerton Hospital was paying well, she was spending most of it trying to furnish her new apartment and buy some decent clothes.

Delta was pleased with her new apartment, even though it cost more than she wanted to pay. It was comfortable and quieter than the apartment in Samcora. She was beginning to see the benefits to community living. No yard work and basic maintenance only a phone call away. She was adjusting to the noises and smells that were part of apartment life and was starting not to notice them so much. Her balcony was south facing and the complex was on a high section of Summerton which gave her a wonderful view of the skyline. Delta liked to sit out on her balcony after the sun went down and stare at the city lights in the downtown core. The lights shining out from thousands of office windows in the skyscrapers were mesmerizing.

Delta made the decision that this was it. She was going to stay in Summerton and rebuild her life. She had to move

Sherry Derksen

on from Tom, from the sadness of all those wasted years. There was nothing she could do about the past, but she could do something about her future, and she did not want to spend the second half of her life mourning the disaster of the first half. She was tired of crying and being unhappy. It was good to have her sister again, that was all the family she needed.

Delta's mood darkened slightly when she thought about Maddy. Her sister was not as receptive to Delta when they first met as she had hoped for. But Maddy was still probably in shock. She would open up in time. Her whole life with her husband, Mark, was a lie and she was afraid of being found out. It was complicated but Delta had no desire to rock the boat. Delta could feel the distance between them, yet as distressing as it was, Delta knew that eventually they would be closer together. They were blood after all. That had to count for something. If Maddy was unloving, she certainly offset that with her generosity. She was never late with the money she gave her to keep her secret. The money was coming in very handy as she was trying to set up a better quality of life than she had in Samcora. But she was starting to feel guilty and deep down inside she had to admit to herself that it was wrong to take the money. She knew she should stop.

Pushing it out of her mind for a moment, Delta thought about the leather sofa she saw in the mall. It was just perfect for her and her apartment. The only problem was it cost four thousand dollars. But, it was marked down from six and it was very high quality leather. Unfortunately, she was a little short on cash for that type of expense and decided to go directly to Maddy's to ask her for a bit more.

Maddy had made it very clear that Delta was never to come to the house. Mark could never find out about her. Maddy and Mark had been going through a rough patch and she did not want to add anything more to the growing list they had to argue about. Delta could understand that one. She lost count of the times she avoided inviting company to her old home because of Tom. So she agreed that she would never go over to the house, that instead she would text Maddy's cell phone and they would meet somewhere else. She had texted but there was no response. She knew she should not go to the house, but this was urgent. It was rude to not respond to a text message in a timely manner. That sofa would not last long at the

Sins of Samcora

price it was and Maddy had so much money. Surely she would understand and find it in her heart to help out her only sister. It was early afternoon and Mark would be at work, so it should not be a problem. She would be very careful and only stay for a short moment to ask Maddy for help with the sofa purchase. In and out, and then back to the mall. It was not unreasonable and Maddy should have no complaints about it.

Delta also wanted to talk to Maddy and tell her thank you, that after the sofa, she would not accept any more money except of course if there was an emergency. Delta decided that she needed to make it on her own. She knew it was wrong to take the money and although it was nice to have she realized that if she was going to rebuild any kind of decent life she needed to do things herself. She allowed herself to be emotionally tied to Tom and she must not continue to become financially tied to Maddy. She needed to feel fully independent. Maddy gave her enough money already to appease how robbed she felt when Maddy left Samcora all those years ago. Delta never had intention to reveal Maddy's secret whether she paid or not. All she really wanted was her sister's love and friendship. She wanted to be real sisters again, the way they used to be when they were little. Payback for the past was over.

They never fought as small girls, and Delta did not know why they grew apart as they got older. Perhaps the stress of what went on with Mom and the situation at home was behind all the distance. It did not matter anymore anyway. The past was over and should remain in the past. Delta wanted Maddy to love her just because she was her sister, not because she was afraid she would unravel her life of lies. She wanted to tell Maddy that to her face, not over the telephone. Just one quick little stop at the house should not hurt, Delta reasoned. Maddy will understand.

Instead of taking the exit to go towards her apartment, she turned to go to Royal Ridge Estates, playing out in her mind as she drove exactly what she would say to Maddy. Delta never noticed her old Buick three cars behind her, nor Tom hunched over the wheel trying desperately not to lose her in the heavy traffic.

The beginning of the end...

Madeline felt cold. She knew what was coming and this was going to be a bad one. Mark never came home at this time and he never sent Hazel away on her work day unless he had a plan for Madeline. Undoubtedly Hazel had no clue as to what was going to happen between Mark and Madeline because he was gregarious and charming as he gave her the afternoon off. But Madeline had learned all to well what was underneath the smile. That was Mark's mask. He put it on to hide his perversions, the malignancy of evil inside of him.

"I am going to ask you once. Where is my money? Why have you been stealing from me and what are you doing with it?" Mark's voice was low and monotone. He looked emotionless and that was when Madeline knew the beating would be severe. He had distanced his feelings far from her so that he would be able to do horrible things without limits. She knew no matter what she told Mark, that even if he was satisfied with her answer, that she would still be punished.

Madeline could see that he wanted to hurt her, even if there was no real reason to. This was the end. At this moment she knew her marriage was over and her survival was in question. The only possible way out was to escape him and the destruction that he had planned for her. She had no explanation for her conduct, what could she say. That she took his money because she was afraid they would not last as a couple? That he would find out she was a fraud? He would not understand that she needed her own financial security. He would not understand that she was not from a good family, that

Sins of Samcora

she had to recreate herself just to feel worthy enough to marry a man of the calibre that she thought Mark was.

The danger felt tangible and electric, almost as if it were a third presence in the room with them, breathing and waiting to interact. Madeline could feel the hairs on her body rise up. The air in her lungs reached deeper and she was vaguely aware that her capacity to breathe was improved. She knew it was the adrenaline surge and she could feel it shoot through her legs making them responsive and trembly at the same time. Madeline did not dare let Mark see that she was ready to run until she was closer to the door. If he sensed her resistance in the smallest way he would be all over her and she would have no chance to escape.

"I...I've been saving it....it was for ...for....a surprise....." Madeline stammered, not even knowing what it was she was trying to say. She was off guard and rambling, hoping to delay his attack. The adrenaline was making her shake, making her voice quiver.

"I have it...it's in the kitchen... I'll get it...." Her voice faltered, and he could hear the fear in it. She began to take long strides towards the kitchen. Madeline hoped that her legs could propel her quickly towards the door and yet look as if she was relaxed. She willed herself to look calm so he could not see that she intended to bolt. But he could read her intent and plainly saw that she was trying to run from him. He was like an animal recoiled and ready to attack. Mark lunged towards her, enraged but still smiling, insanity in his eyes.

Madeline ran. She pushed every drop of power that she had into her legs. Determination for escape surged through her body, driving her heart and pounding the blood through her veins. Her thigh muscles fired with responsiveness as she hitched up her skirt higher allowing her legs a larger stride so she could cover more ground. She visualized reaching the exit door in the kitchen and felt that if she could reach it she would have a chance. If she was outside perhaps someone would see her and help her, or at least call the police. She could feel herself flying. Madeline had never moved so fast in her life. She made it into the kitchen and past the centre island. It was a huge barrier in the middle of the room, dark oak with rich carved moulding and topped with a thick slab of white marble. She reached for the edge of it and grabbed it, using it as a fulcrum to force her momentum around the corner to reach the exterior door. The door was so close, she was almost there and her eyes looked through the glass window in the upper half to orient herself as to where to go once she passed through to the outside. So close now, she reached out with her hand and her fingers closed around the knob ready to turn it. Every moment counted. Every second mattered. She could feel the possibility of escape now. It seemed as if time had slowed down and everything was moving in slow motion, the doorknob in her hand rotating and she could feel the bolt start to slide back. Within herself a sliver of hope rose but then quickly vanished as she felt his hand on her neck.

His palm was under her ear and his long fingers reached around the front of her throat. Before, when he still loved her, he used to pull her to him in the same manner when he approached her from behind, only gently, and she would spin around and kiss him. But there was no love or softness now. Instead of cupping her gently his fingers curled tighter and dug into her throat, holding her back. She was surprised how much it hurt and how it completely cut off her breath. She had let go of the doorknob and had both hands up to her throat trying to pry him off so she could breathe. She was aware she was starting to lose consciousness. She revived when the impact of his fist in her back spiked her adrenaline once more. He must have made sure his knuckles were forward because it was a sudden sharp pain. She had never heard the sound of a rib breaking before. The pain was excruciating and overtook her, but at least he let go of her throat and she could take some ragged painful breaths.

Madeline crumpled onto her knees and wondered how long her adrenaline rush would hold out. She hoped it would last much longer so that she would not feel the full force of his attack. He had stopped for just a moment, he also had to catch his breath from his exertions and excitement. Madeline began crawling on her hands and knees but she felt so disoriented. Where was the door? She did not immediately realize that she began to crawl back towards the kitchen until she saw with sinking devastation, the table and chairs. Absently she thought that she did not want to die in this house, she wanted to be outside in the sun. She pulled herself up by grabbing onto a chair back and tried to explain better to Mark. "Please... Stop.... Mark, let me explain...," her words, falling on deaf

Sins of Samcora

ears, were so hard to get out. Each breath inward felt like a knife stab. Madeline surmised that her broken rib must be pressing into her lung. She focused her eyes on Mark and realized that she did not need to use up her energy on words. There was no point. He was committed to hurt her bad and there was no stopping it. She recognized that all she could do was try to minimize the injuries and survive. She knew that there was no point in trying to plead and there was no point in expending herself trying to fight. His desires would only be satisfied with her terrible injuries. Madeline never felt so helpless in her life. Her legs gave out under her and she was back on the floor, looking up at the ceiling. She must have blacked out for a moment or so because she could not quite remember how or when Mark had straddled her on her chest. There was so much blood everywhere and it must have been hers. She tasted it and was swallowing it. It was in her eyes and blurred her vision of Mark above her as he rained his fists down on her face.

She was grateful that she did not hurt so much anymore though. It was just so hard to breathe, but now the pain was gone. The only sensations she felt were in her chest which was like hot fire and her face which felt wet from her blood. She knew her hands were to the side of her, but like her legs they were heavy and she did not have the strength to move them. Briefly she wondered if she could actually survive this beating. She felt herself begin to pass out once more. Her eyes rolled upward and then she saw...Delta? There was no time to think or process as her overwhelmed body overtook her and she spiralled into unconsciousness.

Whack! It was a direct hit on the forehead. Mark went down like a ton of bricks and did not move. Delta knew he was out cold. This was the second time she hit a man on the head with a frying pan. The only difference was when she hit Tom on the head, the frying pan bent because it was a cheap thin aluminum one. This one was cast iron. It did not bend.

The scene that she was witnessing was unbelievable.

Delta did not want to alert the housekeeper that she was visiting Maddy so she decided to enter the house without ringing the doorbell and to see if she could spot Maddy from the entryway. She tried the doorknob and the door opened. She had no intention of going any further than the foyer, deciding that if she did

Sherry Derksen

not see Maddy then she would announce herself. As soon as she stepped in, however, she heard some strange sounds. It sounded like someone was...working out?

The breathing was guttural and strange, but there was also a moaning noise, a noise that frightened Delta as she followed the sound into the kitchen. She was horrified at what she saw, Maddy was on her back stretched out on the floor with a man straddling her on her chest and punching her in the face over and over again. Delta did not take the time to think. She just reacted. What was there? Knives in the knife block? No. What was she going to do with a knife? What else was there? Pans were hanging from the pot rack over the kitchen island. She just grabbed one and walked up beside the man whom she now recognized from his photographs as Mark, and swung the pan like a bat. His head snapped backwards as his hands dropped and he crumpled to the side, his legs still on top of Maddy.

Delta hoped he was not dead. She grabbed his legs and pulled him off of Maddy and then bent over her sister to assess her injuries. Maddy was still breathing but unconscious. Delta got a cold cloth from the kitchen sink and began wiping the blood off of Maddy's face. She inspected her body and realized that Maddy had a broken nose and probably a broken jaw and ribs. Her battered face was appalling to look at as her nose was swayed and swollen and both eyes were swelling shut. Maddy was barely recognizable.

Delta gently rolled her sister on her side and Maddy began to regain consciousness. She began to vomit the blood that she had swallowed. The odour from the mix of congealed blood and bile was strong but Delta barely noticed. Her nursing instincts kicked in as she focused on stabilizing Maddy to help stop her from going into shock. She needed to call an ambulance. As she helped her sister she kept one eye on Mark. He was breathing and it sounded funny. He should have been coming to by now. It both worried and frightened Delta thinking about what she would do if he did regain consciousness before she got help. There was no movement from his body. He was out cold and she hoped he would stay that way for a little while longer. Delta kept the fry pan near her just in case he needed another tune up.

The traffic was heavy and Tom was worried that he

Sins of Samcora

would lose Delta. He was the fourth car behind her but he could still keep his eyes on at least one of her taillights. A few times when the cars drifted within the lanes he would lose sight of her for just a moment and he would feel panicked, gripping the steering wheel tighter as if his grip on the wheel would somehow keep him tethered to Delta. He had no idea where she was going and was surprised when she turned into Royal Ridge Estates. Although he was new to Summerton, he was still aware that Royal Ridge was the rich area of town.

"What is she doing going into here?" Tom slowed the car and drifted even further back because the cars between him and Delta turned off and there was nothing for him to hide behind. If she looked in her rear view mirror she would see him behind her. It made it even more difficult to follow without being detected. Fortunately she did not notice him. He watched as Delta pulled her car up into the driveway of an enormous house.

Tom did not approach where she had driven, deciding instead to park the car and walk the rest of the way. He felt dwarfed by the mansion as he walked toward it, thinking that it was more like a hotel than a house. Irritably he determined that there were probably more workers in the mansions than there were owners living there. It seemed so unfair, how some could have so much and he had so little.

He felt uncomfortable, like he was being watched. He imagined judgmental eyes peering around the tailored curtains and looking at him and finding him lacking. Tom bristled at the thought and felt out of place, like he should not be walking down the sidewalk alongside the perfectly groomed lawns and gardens. He reached the house where he had watched Delta drive up and saw her parked car. She was not in it.

The entrance to the house was imposing, with a large covered veranda giving shade to the thick carved double oak doors. Tom speculated that each single door was probably four times the size of the modest entryway door in his old house in Samcora. How did anyone even open the damn thing? Feeling intimidated, Tom realized that if he knocked on the door he would have nothing to say. This could not possibly be Delta's house. It was impossible to believe that she would have a friend who had such wealth, so what the hell was she doing here? She was likely a cook, or something

Sherry Derksen

similar. She could barely manage to keep his house back in Samcora clean, so it was unlikely she was a housekeeper. He had to admit that Delta was a very good cook when she got around to it. She was also good with plants. Maybe she was a gardener here, Tom speculated.

Feeling confused, Tom decided that it was better to go around the side and see if she was in the back yard or if there were any rear entry doors, maybe to a kitchen. The further Tom walked around the house, the more amazed he was. It just went on and on. The gardens and landscaping made him feel hidden and protected until he was at the back of the house. There, the thick old trees thinned out a little, allowing the sun to shine on him outside the cool canopy that their leaves provided. Tom could see that the house backed onto a lake. The lawn looked like velvet and further down was a swimming pool. Several small seating areas were created around pagodas and stunning garden-scapes that looked like they came out of a picture. He had never seen such opulence up close before.

Suddenly Tom felt exposed and knew that he should not be here. He turned around to retreat and head back to the car when suddenly he caught a glimpse of Delta in a window. He sidled up closer and pressed himself against the side of the house. After one more glance around to make sure no one was watching him he turned and peered deeper into the window. He was prepared to see anything except what he was seeing.

A man and a woman were both on the floor of what appeared to be the kitchen. The woman looked real bad, coated in blood. Delta had a blanket in her hand and was walking back to the woman and then crouched down beside her and covered her with it. There was something about the woman that seemed familiar but he could not place her. Maybe she was someone famous? Her face looked swollen and fresh blood seemed to be seeping out of the cuts that were on her lips and eyes. Tom felt nauseated at the sight. When he was angry at Delta he would throw things, but would never hit her. Men did not do that. Some of his buddies had beaten their wives and he could tell that was what had happened here. Except this was more brutal than anything he had ever seen. It seemed obvious that the man had done this, but what happened that he was now unconscious himself?

Sins of Samcora

Stunned to his core, Tom continued to watch through the window as the beaten woman tried to sit up. She was speaking to Delta and Tom could see tears streaming down her face, squeezing out of her swollen orbits and mixing in with the blood. Delta began stroking her hair and seemed to be saying something back to her. The woman began to vomit blood and Delta supported her and helped her through it. It hurt Tom to see a woman so injured. It was not right. He should go in and do something but he felt paralyzed and incapacitated by what he was witnessing. For a moment he felt a swelling of pride that Delta was a nurse. Tom could see her competency and knew that she could and would help this woman. What could he do but get in the way? Delta would handle it. The woman began puking again and his repulsion triggered his gag reflex. He strained to control himself and began to take deeper breaths to calm down. He blinked back the tears in his eyes, that sprung unwilled, another reflex from his dry heaving. He raked his hands through his hair and ran them down his chest, signalling himself that he was in order again, he was back in control. Tom renewed his scrutiny in the window and while his hands were still on his chest he distractedly felt the camera that was still in his inner jacket pocket. Without breaking his gaze at the scene in the kitchen, he pulled it out and held it in his hand without really thinking why. Should he just go? It was too horrible to watch, and too horrible to turn away and yet he could not tear himself away from what he was seeing in the window.

Then he saw something that made his blood cold. The man was beginning to stir and regain consciousness. He rolled away from the woman sitting on the floor and then stood up slowly and grabbed the edge of the kitchen island for support. He reached over with one of his blood stained hands and grabbed a large kitchen knife from the butcher block that was sitting on the countertop. Holy crap he was huge. Tom could see that he was a big man. His shirt did not hide the large muscles and the hardness of his frame. He looked dazed but still feral, lethal. Tom surmised that both women combined would be no match for him. Tom wondered if he should enter the kitchen from the door he had seen to the left and protect the women, but he felt too afraid himself and it paralyzed him. Even from the distance he was, Tom felt like a boy in stature to him.

Sherry Derksen

Tom felt like he had to do something but fear rooted him to his spot. There was nothing he could do. He was no match. This was not his fight. The woman on the floor began to cower and tried to crawl under the kitchen table. Switching his gaze to Delta he could see that she was speaking to the man and gesturing wildly with her hands. Delta looked scared and placed herself between the man and the woman on the floor. Both of her hands were out as if she were pleading and reasoning with him. He did not appear to be stopping and ominously began walking towards Delta and the other woman. The knife in his hand weaving in the air sending a clear message as to what was to come.

Do something, Tom willed himself but felt impotent to act.

He could only watch as the horror washed over him. Delta looked like she was speaking more animatedly. She was gesturing wildly, desperately, as she inched backwards. But the man just kept approaching and when he was close, Delta suddenly bent down and picked up something. What was it? A frying pan? She swung it and hit the man in the face with an unrestrained blow. He fell back on the floor again and did not move. Delta rushed towards him and leaned over him and hit him a couple more times. Why did she do that, he was already down?

Tom was on automatic pilot. Without thinking about it he just began snapping pictures of the scene in front of him with the camera that was still clutched in his hand. He did not even know why, or if the camera was on or the lens cap off. He just felt like he should start snapping pictures. This needed to be recorded. Something terrible has happened in front of him and Delta was mixed up in it. He needed pictures. Suddenly Tom felt he should hide himself better. He crouched down lower as he continued to peer through the window.

The deception...

"Is he...dead?" Madeline looked up at Delta and could barely speak above a whisper. Her mouth felt thick and swollen and she was still oozing blood out of the cuts on her lips. The taste of her blood was metallic and felt sticky in her mouth. She wondered how much blood she lost, she felt she was bathed in it. She was alarmed at the thought of Mark being dead but also relieved that he was not coming after her anymore. Breathing was hard and she hurt all over, but she felt a deep euphoria that she survived.

"I think so," replied Delta as she started to shake uncontrollably and sank down quickly on a kitchen chair before she collapsed. She began to take deeper, slower breaths to calm herself. Delta wished she were dreaming, that she could just wake up and walk away from this kitchen and the man she just killed. She felt sick. What had just happened here? Delta could not think, she needed help. Maddy needed an ambulance. Mark needed a coroner.

"I killed a man," Delta repeated the sentence over and over. She could not process what was happening, was she going mad?

"Delta...stop," Delta could hear Maddy's thin voice above her panic and focused on it, she needed to direct her attention onto anything other than what she had just done. She got off the chair and sat beside Maddy who was still on the floor by the table.

"Maddy, oh, Maddy. What have I done? I was so scared and I think I killed him," Delta's eyes bore into Maddy's, she was pleading, confessing, seeking absolution for what she had done.

"Calm down," Madeline forced herself to have a calm

Sherry Derksen

voice. She had to keep Delta from escalating her panic. Speaking made it even harder to breathe and she could barely see out of her swollen eyes, but Delta was becoming unglued and she had to stop it. Delta needed to get back in focus.

"Oh Lord, we need to call the police," Delta tried to make sense out of what happened. She just reacted instinctively. She told him, she pleaded with him, to put down the knife. She told him to stop over and over again. But he would not stop, he just kept coming. She had no choice but to hit him on the head with the fry pan again. Anyone else would have done the same thing. She did not mean to kill him, it was self defence. Delta kept trying to justify her actions. Justify why she hit him more than once when he was already down. Justify why she was calling him Tom when she was hitting him.

"We should call the police now?" It was more a question than a statement. Delta knew they needed help but at the same time was feeling less certain that calling the police was a good idea. Delta glanced over at Mark. She could not bear to look at his head where she hit him so she just looked at his lax and motionless legs, reaffirming that he was dead.

"No." Madeline could see the conflict in Delta. That was good, it would make it easier to sway her and convince her to let Madeline handle the situation her way.

"You need to go to the hospital." Delta knew that the doctors at the hospital would question the origins of Maddy's injuries and that they would call the authorities in. It was obvious that Maddy was brutally beaten. "Where is your phone, Maddy," Delta asked, resolved to do the right thing and call the authorities in "I'll call the police and an ambulance." Delta knew that Maddy needed medical attention. She probably had internal injuries. There was no way to avoid police involvement if Maddy was to go to hospital.

"No...Delta," Madeline could see the situation was a bomb. She had to handle it with great care. "No...police...no ambulance...will cause...problems for us."

"What do you mean?" Delta was confused. Why would she not want an ambulance? Maddy needed help, and probably a couple of units of blood. Delta could understand the hesitation about the police but still, it was the right thing to do.

Sins of Samcora

Madeline had to pace herself, she did not know how long she could talk before the pain and the fatigue would make her pass out. She spoke in short sentences, trying to conserve her breath.

"They will investigate...I've lied...about who I am..Mark never gave me money..I stole it..money traced to me...to you..Mark found out..police will say..murder for money...you went beyond defence..cameras in house record sound..Tom." Madeline was sure Delta would pay attention to the fact that she saw her hit Mark more than what was necessary. That she was yelling out Tom's name as she was hitting him after he was down. Self defence aside, that was a bit of transferred rage right there. Surely Delta could also figure out that the police would say she was extorting him because that was exactly what she was doing. She was not going to let Delta know she had also been skimming a significant amount of money for herself. It was better for Delta to feel uniquely implicated, it would make her more cooperative to do what Madeline wanted.

Delta began to whimper. "Oh no, no, no. That is not how it is. I didn't know that you were stealing. You should have told me you did not have your own money. I would have understood. Now the police will think that we did this on purpose. What are we going to do Maddy? What are we going to do?" Delta felt panicked and cornered. How could they avoid the police? Maddy had to get to the hospital. She needed intervention. Delta struggled for an alternate explanation.

"Your injuries will prove it, Maddy. We just tell the police the truth, that he was beating you for taking money and we were defending ourselves. It's the truth, they would believe us." Delta began to hyperventilate. The truth was always the best way. The police can see all the blood around. They have special investigators who would be able to tell that it was Mark who was the aggressor.

"Calm...down," Madeline began again. She was able to pull herself up a little. She discovered that if she held her ribs with her hands that she could breathe a little easier. "We have no credibility..Mark owns lawyers and judges..in this town. Owns some police..Think, Delta..Mark is connected..no justice for us..only jail." Madeline was exhausted. Speaking was too hard right

Sherry Derksen

now. She could only hope Delta would agree. Madeline did not know how much more energy she could waste trying to make her idiot sister understand.

Delta felt trapped. This was a nightmare. Maddy was right. They were both in way over their heads. Besides, he was the one waving around the knife. It was not right that they should go to jail when it was all his fault.

"I have...an idea..." It took a long time and a lot of energy for Madeline to explain. It was an elegant solution and would solve all their problems. They would wait until it was darker out and then put Mark into the Jaguar. The city was still in the middle of construction on Taylor Bridge and the side railing of one section had been removed and had a temporary guard rail on it. They would let the car go through, over the edge with Mark in it, and it would roll and crash down at the bottom of the ravine. The car crash would explain Mark's injuries. Everyone would think he died in the accident from blunt force trauma from the steering wheel or roof. Delta would help Maddy down the ravine and she would lay in the crashed car and then Delta would call an ambulance and report the crash. It would look like Maddy was injured in the crash and Maddy would get the help she needed. Delta would make sure everything in the house was cleaned up. It was a brilliant plan.

"I don't know Maddy," I think we should still call the police. Delta continued to waffle, unable to commit to a course of action.

Madeline pressed harder, upping the stakes. Using every ounce of her strength and energy to convince Delta.

"We did not kill him...you did. Your fingerprints on the pan.... not mine. Police see money going in your bank account...not mine." Speaking was getting unbearable for Madeline. "I want to protect you...protect us... You are my sister...I love you." Madeline hoped that throwing in the last part would be enough to sway Delta. She had been whining and begging for a relationship since they first met, and now Madeline was dangling it out to her like a carrot. Madeline certainly did not want any kind of relationship with Delta, the thought of it was repulsive. But Madeline could see that Delta was dangerous right now. Stupidity and fear always got people in trouble, and Delta was both afraid and stupid. It was better to keep Delta closer to her and under control

Sins of Samcora

until Madeline was back on her feet again. She did not know the extent of her injuries, but she knew they were severe and going to take a long time to heal. It was better to have her enemies close while she was weakened herself. At least until she was able to figure something out. Madeleine needed action now. She could not continue much longer.

"Ok, Maddy. We will do it your way." Maddy was right, thought Delta. They were sisters and they needed each other. Sure they had a rough start when they first met but that did not matter anymore. Terrible circumstances always brought out the truth in people and the truth was plain, Maddy did love and need Delta. Even if she could not admit it in the beginning, it was clear now. The bond of blood was unbreakable. They needed to stick together. Delta made a mental note to herself, to wipe down the frying pan.

Both women waited in silence until it was dark outside. Madeline felt too weak to continue to talk, and all Delta wanted to do was blank out and stare. She did not want to think about anything until she had to. Earlier, Madeline had told Delta where the sheets were and Delta ripped one up and bound Maddy's ribs. Impulsively, Delta also took a pillowcase and put it over Mark's head. She could not bear to look at him, look at his dead half closed eyes. She needed to get some mental distance from him and hiding his face helped. Madeline had tried to help drag Mark's body out through the back mudroom and into the garage but she could do little more than whisper words of encouragement. She could barely walk, let alone drag Mark. Madeline had to admit that Delta was pretty strong as she hefted Mark into the passenger's side of the car. Delta just pretended that he was Tom, drunk and passed out again, and that it was just another typical night as she hoisted first his torso and then his lower body into the front passengers seat.

Still in silence, Delta helped Madeline gently slide into the drivers seat.

"Do you think you can do this? Can you drive?" Delta did not know how Maddy was still conscious, let alone getting into a car to drive it to Taylor Bridge. Her face looked unrecognizable with the swelling and bruising. It was shocking to see.

"I'll be fine," Madeline did not admit that she was feeling light headed and was concerned that she would pass out

Sherry Derksen

while driving. It was a risk she had to take. There was no other way. If she felt herself blacking out she would just pull over as quickly as possible. Hopefully she could pull over in time. Delta would be following close behind in her car. Fortunately there was very little traffic on the road and the darkness kept her face and injuries hidden from other motorists who might look into her windows. All Madeline had to do was stay focused and strong. She glanced over at Mark strapped into the passengers seat.

"Lower his backrest please Delta." Silently Delta complied. It did not look too good, him strapped in the seat slumped over with a pillowcase on his head. When she pushed the lever, the back of the seat crashed down from the weight of Mark's body and Delta wondered if it was broken.

"Thanks." Madeline gave a weak smile of encouragement to her sister. "Let's go."

As Madeline had suspected, there continued to be little traffic on the bridge. The cars that did pass by were infrequent and they did not slow down or appear to be interested in anything other than getting to their destinations. Just before the area where the temporary railing was, both women pulled their cars over, Delta parked behind Maddy. Madeline could not believe that she made it. Several times her head started to swim and she was worried she would black out, but she willed herself to stay conscious. Whether it was will, or fortune, she did not know. She only knew that it was almost over. Madeline was starting to feel very ill. She knew she needed to get to the hospital soon.

Delta got out of her car and took her jack out. She was going to say she just finished changing a flat tire if someone stopped to question her. Delta was amazed at how Maddy could think of all these details, especially in her condition. She prayed that no one would stop. It would be pretty hard to explain what Madeline was doing with her dead husband in the passengers seat. They had to work quickly and get off the bridge. Delta helped Maddy out of the car and began to shift Mark over to the drivers side and put his seat belt on. It was hard work and she was grunting and straining and trying to avoid looking at the pillowcase. It was a macabre scene but Delta could not bring herself to take the pillowcase off his head, she was afraid to see his face again. Dispassionately, Madeline removed it herself. Madeline could hear

Sins of Samcora

Delta begin to hyperventilate.

"Calm down...Delta...almost done." Madeline watched Delta turn the ignition on and crank the steering wheel to position the car to drive off of the side of the bridge.

"Are you sure about this Maddy," This was so wrong. What were they doing?

"Do it," Maddy instructed. Delta put the car in gear. Both women watched the car slowly creep towards the edge of the road, break through the temporary wooden construction railing and fall off over the edge.

"Hurry...help me down," urged Madeline. Near the front entrance of the bridge was an embankment covered in rocks and large plants with roots stuck into the side. The first section was a steep angle but further down the bank widened out and slightly cleared into an area where Madeline thought she would be able to navigate towards the car. It was fairly dark out, but the smashed Jaguar's lights were still on and provided enough light to orient themselves. Delta tried to help Maddy down as quickly as possible. She did not know how Maddy did it. Delta could barely make it down herself. Delta could hear Maddy's breathing sounding more wet and ragged. When both women finally approached the wreckage Madeline asked Delta to remove the rib binding that Delta had made for her out of the sheet. As she removed it, Madeline slumped down and began to moan. She was at the end of her endurance.

"Help me...into... car," begged Madeline, feeling tortured. Madeline crawled into the wreckage as best as she could. She could see Mark out of her peripheral vision but did not want to look at him. She did not want that memory stuck in her brain.

"Delta...go now. Call... ambulance...Hurry." Madeline could hear Delta huffing and puffing and sobbing as she pulled herself back up to the roadway. She did not know if Delta would be able to climb back up it. She was clearly out of shape but certainly motivated. Madeline felt very cold. The air was cool and damp and she briefly reflected on how sweet the night air smelled before she slipped into unconsciousness.

Delta could see the outline of her sister. She clawed and scrambled up through the dirt and roots as fast as she could, terrified that if there was too much more delay that there would be

Sherry Derksen

two dead people in the car, not just one.

Delta drove away as quickly as possible and called an ambulance from a pay phone. She said she saw a car being forced off the Taylor bridge and go over the edge. When the operator asked her for her name she just hung up, and then began to worry that the operator would think she was a prank call and not take her seriously. Twenty minutes later she was still worried about it so she drove back to the Taylor Bridge. Relief flooded through her as she saw the flashing lights from the ambulance, police and emergency crews. She hoped that Maddy was ok and that she was awake and knew that help had arrived. Everything should be all right now, she hoped.

As daylight began to approach, Delta headed back to her apartment and went over her mental checklist, making sure she did not forget anything. Did she clean the kitchen up good enough? Check. Did she discard the pillowcase and Maddy's bandages? Check. Did she wash off the frying pan and put it back up on the pot holder rack? Double check. Delta was sure that everything was in order. In her distraction and dismay she never noticed that her old Buick was still following her.

Opportunities...

Tom could not believe his eyes.

"What was Delta doing? What was going on?" Tom slouched further down in the seat of the Buick, not wanting to be seen.Trying to peer over the steering wheel, the only thing he could make out was that the car that Maddy was driving had been driven over the edge of the bridge. Did he really see what he thought he did? He knew it was Maddy. It had been years since he saw her but Tom knew her from a mile away. Her face was pretty smashed up but her mannerisms were the same, the way she stood and how she moved. Because of her injuries he could not see the likeness of her face, but he certainly recognized her figure.

Tom thought back to when he had last seen Maddy. She was always a looker. Just gorgeous, but she was a cold mean one. He recalled their last confrontation. He and Delta had a big fight and he went out drinking to get it off his mind. When he got home Maddy was there with Delta, obviously having a woman's sob party and talking about what a bastard he was. He barely got in the door and Delta accused him of being drunk again and stormed out of the living room. He could hear the bedroom door slam shut all the way from upstairs. Maddy started to leave and all Tom wanted to do was talk about it. But all Maddy did was look at him coldly and tell him to go talk to his wife himself.

He really did not remember much after that except somehow they were on the floor and his pants were down around his knees. It was all her fault. She should not have been over at his house interfering with him and Delta. She should not have been

Sherry Derksen

wearing such a tight tee shirt. It's not like he raped her. Hell, he was too drunk to get it up. It was just a little slap and tickle. She did not need to get all bent out of shape about it. Then that was it, she was gone. No more Maddy. Everyone was so up in arms because they did not know why she left. Tom briefly wondered if he had something to do with it, but then he rejected the notion. Maddy was a smart one. She knew that she provoked him and she knew better than to say anything. Nobody had seen or heard from her since, and that was just fine with him. But now, he thought to himself, the bitch was back and what were she and Delta up to?

He shuddered when he thought of how the two of them pushed the car off the edge with that man in there. That was murder right there. Tom being a witness of that would be worth big, big money. This could be the break that he had been looking for. But it was not good to act to quickly. He needed to sit back and survey the situation a little more. He had no idea what was going on and if he was going to capitalize on this he needed to get a bigger picture. Tom continued to follow Delta and now he knew where she lived. He debated going up to her apartment but decided instead to drive and park the Buick back at the mall where he was earlier in the day. He was getting low on gas and would not make it back to his street where the drop in shelter was. He needed time to think things through and he needed another drink.

Parked back at the mall, Tom felt a little exposed because there were hardly any cars in the lot. He decided not to worry about it because the early morning shoppers would be arriving in a couple of hours and he would blend into them. Tom pulled out the bottle that Murray had left and finished drinking it, playing over the events of the day in his mind as he planned his strategy. He felt happily drunk and began to drift off to sleep. Tomorrow he would give Delta a little surprise visit. Tom was fast asleep in the car, curled up on the drivers side and clutching what was now an empty whisky bottle. He was too passed out to notice the police car parked behind him or the officers who were waiting for backup after they ran the plates and discovered that the Buick was reported stolen.

Mission but no control...

It was incredibly sad to him. Dr Brewel hated to lose a patient and he knew he was losing Joan. She was not responding to her treatment. Sinking further into her mental illness, he could not reach her. Once a beautiful and vibrant woman, her fall down the stairs and hitting her head took all of that away. Her violent tendencies were increasing and so was her incoherence yet she kept refusing to take her medications. Dr Brewel did not know what else to do to help her short of certification. He realized her brain injury was overlaying an underlying illness that had not expressed itself before. He was certain she was suffering from schizophrenia and likely had masked it in her younger years. The brain injury damaging her impulse control escalated her symptoms. She had no insight into her hallucinations, unable to see that her imagined persecutors did not exist.

Joan was uncooperative with care and Dr Brewel considered that she might do better with a female doctor. Her general aggression and mistrust towards men was impacting his ability to help her. Dr Brewel had been called in by the Samcora Brain Injury Facility because she was still a patient of his, assigned by court order after she had been released from jail. Joan was transported back to the hospital in Samcora and placed in a locked psychiatric ward for assessment because she had a violent episode at her mothers house in Summerton. Injections of Haldol failed to subdue her as she kicked and swung out at anyone who got near her. The four point restraints during the ambulance ride from Summerton gave her something to rail against until exhaustion

Sherry Derksen

calmed her exertions.

Joan had tried to stab her mothers mail man with a pair of craft scissors. Her mother said Joan was sitting calmly at the kitchen table working on a project when the postman came to the door with a package. Joan leaped from her chair and charged at the poor man and tried to stab him with her scissors. Fortunately the damage was not serious, the postman only had a minor scratch on his forearm. Joan was too small and fragile to do any damage. The postman was more frightened by her behaviour than anything. He helped Joan's mother subdue her until the paramedics arrived because she became incoherent. It was still unclear if any charges were going to be pressed against her.

Because of the incident, Joan's mother became frightened by her daughter. Now she was refusing to have her back in the home. She said she was too old to deal with her violent outbursts. Even though the outbursts seemed to be targeted only at men, she felt too nervous and could not handle it anymore. She said that when her daughter got her brain injury she had stopped being her daughter. Her mind was gone, anyone could see it. She was worried for her own personal safety. This last outburst was proof that Joan should be in an institution being looked after properly. Dr Brewel knew that mental illness frightened people because it was not well understood. Despite that, he was sickened at how quickly some people try to distance themselves from the ill. Joan needed care and now there was no one to help her. Staying at her mothers was her last option before a community home.

She was not able to care for herself independently plus her probation terms required her to be monitored. For now he would form her so she would have to stay at the psychiatric facility. It was his only option to avoid sending her back to the penitentiary. Dr Brewel knew she would not fare well in prison. He also knew that after a month when her hallucinations resolved with the medications she would be forced to take, if there were no further violent outbursts she would be released. She would be set up in a group home, but that was no guarantee she would continue taking her medications. She did not believe she was sick and had no insight into her hallucinations which made it very difficult to get her to comply with taking her meds. It was a tragedy, the revolving door of the mentally ill. As he walked out, Joan did not move. She just

Sins of Samcora

rolled her eyes in his direction as he exited the room.

Joan felt that Dr Brewel was ok, but barely. She needed to get out of the hospital. She had to deal with Mark. His punishment was waiting for him. She decided she was not going to take more pills. She would pretend to take them. The pills made her feel lethargic and she needed to clear her mind and get her energy back so she could fulfil her mission. She heard the nurses talking, she was going to be out of here in a month and then she was going to be assessed to determine if she should be committed for a longer time. She knew she was running out of time to escape the hospital and find Mark.

A new normal...

It was daylight when Delta got home. She felt paranoid and tried not to be seen by anyone as she entered her building and walked up to her apartment. She could barely manage the stairs, she was so exhausted. Once inside, she went to the bathroom and looked at herself in the mirror. Who was she? What had she become? She killed a man. Did it show? Leaning closer, she studied her face more intently, looking for signs of herself. Every second of stress and strain in her life was etched on her face. Lines and crevices everywhere. When did she get all of those? She turned away from her image and jumped into the shower, scrubbing her body with the hottest water she could stand. She could not scrub her sins away. She took a life and in turn it took hers. Crawling under the covers of her bed she fell asleep immediately, sheer exhaustion shutting her down.

Delta slept solid for 22 hours. She had never slept that long or hard in her life. When finally she awoke her eyes opened slowly and she was aware of the softness of her bed and the comfort of her covers. For the briefest moment she forgot what had happened. Then suddenly a tsunami of emotion washed over her and settled into the pit of her stomach radiating pain up to her chest. Did it all really happen?

Delta got out of bed and immediately turned the television on. She had slept through the morning news. The noon local news would be on soon and perhaps there would be something about the crash. Numbly, she sat in front of the television and listened as it droned on. The scratchy fabric from her second hand

Sins of Samcora

sofa suddenly felt fine as Delta regretted ever wanting the cursed leather sofa that she saw at the mall. If she could have been satisfied with what she had, she would have never gone over to Maddy's house and ended up in the mess she was in. But on the other hand, Maddy would have probably been dead instead of Mark. Her train of thought broke as the newscaster announced an update of the accident. Her stomach started to churn as she listened in disbelief.

"As we reported yesterday with our early breaking news, local businessman Mark Jacobson and his wife Madeline were found in a crash off of Taylor Bridge. We still don't have full details yet, but more information is starting to emerge. The police have confirmed that alcohol was not a factor in the crash, in which the Jacobson's vehicle plummeted down a ravine at the Taylor Bridge widening project. Police are speculating that this was a road rage incident and the Jacobson's were forced off the road. They are asking for anyone who might have information or who might have seen anything to call. Mrs Jacobson's condition has been upgraded to serious but stable, and Mr Jacobson has remained in critical condition. We will keep you updated with more details as they come in." The words echoed in Delta's brain, Mark is not dead! How could he possibly survive all that happened? Would he remember that she hit him on the head with a cast iron skillet? How can he be alive after everything? Delta did not know what to think or what to do. She felt relieved that she had not killed him, that she was not a murderer, but this turn of events was almost as bad. He would send the police to arrest her for hitting him. Surely she would be sent to jail for sending him over the bridge. She could have defended her actions in the kitchen but there was no defence for her dropping him off a cliff. That would be considered attempted murder. The knot in her stomach grew tighter.

She did not dare go to the hospital to find out what was happening. Maddy made it clear that she was not to contact her. She had also told her where the lock box key was to the cabinet where some money was hidden. It was a lot of money, more than what Delta would make working at the hospital so she did not feel particularly upset at quitting her job without notice. It was impossible to go back to work anyway. How could she ever fit in with normal people again? Maddy said she was going to hire her

Sherry Derksen

when she got home from the hospital to help with her convalescence. She would figure out from there what was next. But now with Mark alive, what was the plan to be?

Finally Maddy was being discharged. Delta was instructed to meet her at her house. Delta checked herself in the mirror. She looked professional in her nursing outfit but felt anything but. She had put on heavier makeup to hide her bloated face. She was drunk again last night and this morning her face still looked puffy. Delta rarely drank, except for a social glass now and then, when she was with Tom. He did plenty of drinking for both of them. But lately, she had started drinking heavily. She liked the feel of the burning liquid going down her throat. It warmed her and it helped her relax and forget. It helped unknot her stomach and released the pressure from her chest. She liked that place where she felt slightly, but not completely drunk, although she was finding it harder to stop there. In that haze, her mind would let go of the image of Mark and Maddy, and even Tom. At those times, she would get a reprieve from the fear and guilt and regret. Delta found herself drinking regularly, needing the burning liquid to snake through her and take the tension off. No wonder Tom liked to drink, she thought to herself ruefully. She never really understood before when Tom would say he 'needed' a drink but now she did. But, as much as it was her crutch, Delta knew that she was not going to continue drinking indefinitely, she did not want to end up like Tom. She only needed it for the short term, to help dissipate the stress she was feeling until she could figure out her next steps. Delta made sure that she had a new bottle of rye in her overnight bag, grabbed her keys, and headed out the door. She was eager to get more information about Mark's status and what was happening. Maddy would fill her in on everything. Perhaps it was not as bad as it seemed.

"Mrs Jacobson, can you tell us about your husband and how he is doing," the reporters crowded around Madeline and were pushing microphones in front of her face. The nursing assistant was doing his best to push the wheelchair through the throng which was being held back by three overwhelmed looking hospital security guards. It was mayhem. Madeline was surprised to see the number of reporters that were waiting outside the hospital to

Sins of Samcora

interview her, and find out more about the crash. But then, Mark was a big fish in Summerton, so it was news when one of their elite was knocked down. Madeline pretended she could not hear the questions being shouted at her by the reporters and did her best to shield her face from their intrusive cameras. The orderly managed to get Madeline through the crowd and settled into the limousine that was waiting for her. She was glad to be getting home. There were many things that needed her attention.

The leather seats in the limousine felt smooth and cool. Madeline liked the expansive seating and that she was alone in the car. Too many people around her drained her energy. The hospital was small and had no privacy. Anyone could come up to her and see her. It was tiring feeling on public display. She had to be on point all the time, never allowing herself to relax as she had to maintain an uninterrupted impeccable performance as the loving wife. During the limousine ride, Madeline took stock of what she had done so far. She had let her housekeeper, Hazel and two of her gardeners go. She would have loved to see the reaction on Hazel's face, but everything was done through her lawyer, so that small pleasure was not afforded her. As much as she detested Hazel personally, Madeline had to admit that she really excelled at her job. She would be hard to replace, but the combination of her familiarity and Delta's presence in the house was too dangerous. She could not trust Delta to be discreet and keep her mouth shut. It was better to hire different people from a service who knew nothing about Mark or the normal operations of the household. Once she established a new routine she would find someone who was capable so that she could continue with her social obligations. In Mark's circle, which was now her circle, social contact was imperative. With Mark's incapacity, Madeline's lawyer put her power of attorney in place and briefed her while she was in the hospital of Mark's pending obligations, at least the one's he was aware of. It was a lot to deal with and Madeline did not feel that her lawyer was completely competent. She knew that Mark often worked outside the law and that her lawyer was not involved with those kind of dealings. She did not trust any of Mark's lawyers. She would have to find someone to help her run Mark's business and manage her new assets. As Madeline's limo pulled up to her house, she saw Delta standing in the drive along with a few more reporters. It alarmed her at first until she remembered that the reporters had no idea who Delta was.

"Please escort me into the house." Even though he was a short thin man, Madeline felt that the limo driver was better than having no one.

"Yes, Mrs Jacobson," he replied formally as he grabbed his hat and pounded it onto his head while he exited the limo. He took a moment to straighten out his uniform jacket, excited that the reporters might capture him and he would be on television. He would have to watch the local news tonight and if he made it on camera his wife could see just how important his job was. Madeline was annoyed at the media attention. She thought it would have died down by now. Delta rushed up to her as soon as she was helped out of the limo.

"Delta, lets hurry into the house. Don't answer any questions." Delta was on one side of Madeline and the driver on the other. Between the two of them, Madeline was able to get in the house with minimal intrusion from the throng of reporters vying for her attention as they yelled out their questions. It surprised Madeline that there was still media interest. She doubted there would be even one reporter interested in the story if Mark was not so rich.

Ground rules...

"How are you Maddy?" Delta broke the silence first between the two of them. There had been so much commotion coming into the house that they both took a moment and stood in the foyer to get their bearings.

"I'm real sore, Delta," Madeline's ribs hurt and she had a headache. She wanted to sit down. "Let's go to the living room and catch up." Madeline started to walk and Delta silently followed her.

"So, how do you really feel, Maddy? You know, about everything?" Delta searched her sisters face but could read nothing.

Madeline groaned inwardly to herself. She hated these kinds of touchy emotional questions. How did she feel? Apart from irritation that Delta was going to be staying with her she felt fantastic. She was alive, she was in total control of all of Mark's assets, and the plastic surgeon who fixed her broken nose said she would look even better than before.

"I'm ok. Hanging in there, you know." Madeline tried her best to sound weak."How have you been holding up?" Madeline did not really want to know, but it seemed like an appropriate question to ask. Besides, she needed to get a feel for where Delta's head was at.

Delta was glad she finally had a chance to talk about that night. It was a heavy burden to carry alone.

"It's been real hard Maddy," Delta was just starting when Maddy cut her off.

Sherry Derksen

"Madeline."

"Excuse me?" Delta was confused.

"You keep calling me Maddy. You need to call me Madeline, everyone here knows me by that name. If people hear you calling me Maddy they will wonder why you are not using my proper name. It invites questions. Remember, no one can know you are my sister. If they find out they could trace my history through you. That will unravel everything I've built here."

"But, your proper name is Maddy," argued Delta, beginning to feel riled. What was the big deal? Why was she denying her heritage and who was around to hear it anyway?

"I never liked the name. Can we just agree that you will call me Madeline? It's only a name, for heaven's sake. What is the difficulty?" There was no way she was going to allow her to continue calling her Maddy. It was an insipid, stupid name that only reminded her of Samcora. It sounded like a name you would give a stripper. She never wanted to hear it again.

"Fine then," Delta agreed but felt bullied into doing what she did not want to do.

"It must have been so hard on you, Delta. I wanted to tell you more when I was in the hospital, but there was no privacy there. Anyone could have eavesdropped." Madeline changed the topic. Delta would have to get over the name thing. "We have to be careful now, Delta. I have many things to tell you, but first I want to hear all about you and how you have been managing." Madeline spoke tenderly to Delta, trying to sound concerned and interested. She could see the temper flare and it slightly amused her to watch how easily Delta became unglued. She was such an open book. Always too emotional, she wore her inner feelings on her sleeve for all to see and exploit. Madeline decided it was best to change tact and let Delta have a good cry. Delta needed to bond to her, but she also had to learn real quick that it was Madeline who was in charge.

"Can we start over? I'm glad you are here with me and back in my life. I've missed you so much." Madeline sounded sincere even though she was not. Seated on her luxurious sofa she raised her arms towards Delta, beckoning her. Delta embraced her sister and began to cry, softly at first and then in torrents. Madeline held her and stroked her hair while murmuring soothing words to encourage her tears. Delta did not want to be alone anymore, she

Sins of Samcora

craved the love and acceptance of her older sister.

Delta cried and blustered on for over an hour. After she was finished, both women went into the kitchen and made sandwiches and tea. Madeline was ravenous. It took a lot out of her to keep comforting Delta, the woman could certainly go on and on. Madeline was amazed at her tenacity to bawl and could not remember crying that long over anything. Nothing was worth that much anguish. Delta should learn to let things go. After they had eaten, Madeline helped Delta to settle into the guest bedroom.

Delta was shocked by the lavishness. Her room had its own private en-suite with marble countertops and a huge jetted soaker tub surrounded by a floor to ceiling glass block wall. It looked more like a spa than a bathroom. The carpets of the bedroom were plush and soft and the view out the window was stunning. Her private balcony had panoramic views of Ridgeland Lake, which was so expansive that it was difficult to see the opposite bank. The garden below was immaculate with extensive flower beds, the smell of which wafted up to her through the open window in a wall of sweetness. There were beautiful sitting areas with gazebos and pagodas, and a large swimming pool with a hot tub at one end. Delta was dazzled by her room and thought this must be what the interior of a palace would look like. As Delta kept looking around, Madeline began unpacking her small suitcase, and laid out Delta's items on the bed.

"Delta, we should buy you some new clothes. We will go shopping in a few days. You are going to need more things than this." When Madeline came to the large rye bottle, she casually placed it on the bedside table

"I...I don't know why I packed that," Delta never thought much about it when she stuffed the huge bottle of booze into her bag but now it bothered her that Maddy had seen it. Perhaps it was because she had spent so many years lecturing Tom about his drinking and the evils of alcohol. Now she was acting like Tom, not wanting people to see her stash.

"Don't worry about it, Delta," Madeline was non-judgemental. "Life has been too hard for you this past while. A drink now and then to steady the nerves does not harm anyone. Come, I will show you where you can put this." Good grief, thought Madeline to herself. Not only is Delta emotionally fragile, she is

Sherry Derksen

also hitting the sauce. That could be good or bad, it all depends on how she handles her booze. Madeline held the bottle in her hand and led Delta downstairs to the sitting room. In the back corner was an oversized mahogany bar, stocked with almost every kind of hard liquor that there was. Arranged and ready for the next party was an array of beautiful crystal glasses, goblets and flutes which twinkled under the bright display lights that Madeline turned on.

"We will put your bottle right here, Delta. Anytime you want a drink you know where to find it. You just help yourself to anything in this cabinet. My home is your home now, and you can have anything you want." Everything seemed to sparkle and Delta was mesmerized by the shapes and colours dancing off the bottles and glass. Maddy's house was incredible. It was hard to think that people lived like this. All this grandeur and splendour for only two people. Intellectually she knew that rich people lived in luxury, but she never realized how immersive it could be. Delta never met anyone as rich as Mark and Maddy in her life.

"Thanks, Maddy, I appreciate it. I appreciate everything you are doing for me. I am so glad we are together. I am so glad I am not alone anymore." Delta was so engulfed in her surroundings that she temporarily forgot why she was living with Maddy in the first place. She was particularly thrilled with the liquor cabinet and could hardly wait to sample all the offerings. She just wanted to wait until Maddy was in bed so she could drink alone.

"Not a problem, sweetheart," Madeline could see that Delta was salivating for a drink. She decided to leave her alone and let her get tanked. They could talk more tomorrow. "I'm going to turn in. I'm very tired. I hope you don't mind. You know your way back to your room?" Madeline was exhausted. Delta's needs were draining her of her energy.

"Yes, and thank you, Maddy. Thank you for everything."

"Good night Delta. Oh, and by the way..."
"Yes."
"It's Madeline."

Coming home...

Over the next few days, Madeline brought Delta up to speed about what happened during her hospital stay. Madeline explained as much as she could remember. Not surprisingly, she had passed out shortly after crawling into the wreckage on the night of the beating. She had been told that she had come to briefly in the ambulance but Madeline did not remember that. It was the following day, when she felt more lucid and awake, that she began to get her bearings. She had two broken ribs, a crack in her left radius and her nose was broken. The zygomatic arch on the right side of her face was broken but fortunately the bone did not shift and her face symmetry was still good. She suffered multiple soft tissue injuries and had a bruised spleen. Mark was touch and go for a couple of days. She could not believe that he was still alive. She was informed that he never regained consciousness and was in a coma. The doctors were not sure if he would revive or not. It was a wait and see situation. They said that he sustained severe multiple blows to the head, probably from the steering wheel or the flattened roof of the car. The more that they said his injuries were caused by factors in the crash, the safer she began to feel.

Madeline decided not to tell Delta about the police. They had been to the hospital as well and questioned her. Madeline went with the road rage angle. Who could disprove it? She said the crash happened around three in the morning, everyone knew people were driving home drunk at that time and someone forced them off the road. The police said the investigator determined it was a road rage incident and that although the file would remain open that the leads were cold and it was very unlikely they would find the culprit. Unless any new evidence turned up, effectively the case was closed. The police were still canvassing the auto body shops to see if any vehicles without damage stickers were coming in for repair but they did not expect anything to turn up. The most likely scenario was that the car would be found abandoned somewhere. Once the culprit realized his victims were high profile they would likely try to hide the car. Madeline had expressed her understanding and thanked the police for their hard work trying to find the other car. Relieved that the police were satisfied, Madeline did not want Delta to know that they were in the clear. She wanted Delta to still feel nervous, she wanted her to still need her drink. Booze seemed to keep Delta under control. It gave her a mellow, malleable affect that Madeline found easier to tolerate.

"He was on a ventilator because he was having trouble breathing independently and now they have taken it off. He is recovering." Madeline shared the latest news with Delta. It was not even noon yet and Madeline could smell the booze gassing off Delta's breath. She was starting earlier.

"He is still in the coma but the doctors said it is a good sign that his breathing reflexes are back. The inter-cranial damage was minimal on the CT scan but there was a small subdural bleed. They say it is possible that he may recover fully but not certain. Only time will tell. There is not much more they can do for him at the hospital. They want to put a percutaneous tube in through his stomach to feed him and then transfer him to a long term care facility. I said no to that. I told the doctors that I would have the appropriate equipment and staff installed in the house and that he would convalesce at home. They can keep the nasal gastric tube in to feed him for now. You have to help me when he gets home Delta."

"Madeline," Delta still felt odd using Maddy's fake name. "I don't know that I can do that. I don't know that I can look at him." Delta had been trying to put the image of Mark and the bloodied pillowcase out of her head. Her guilt was eating her up inside and the last thing she wanted to do was to see him again.

"Think of it this way, Delta. This will be your chance to set things right. You feel guilty. Well, then help him. I can't think

Sins of Samcora

of any nurse that would be more competent than you." Madeline knew she had Delta even without looking at her. Appealing to her sense of guilt was enough to get her to do anything she wanted. Topping it off with flattery was unnecessary, but Madeline thought it added a nice touch.

Mark had been in the hospital for three more weeks and still had not woken up. Madeline was relieved. She hated the optimism of the doctors. The last thing she wanted was for Mark to rise from his coma. But now he was coming home. The doctors still wanted to ship Mark to a facility, but Madeline would not allow it. Her lawyers secured her rights and she had all of the medical equipment that Mark would need moved into her house. She decided to put Mark down the hall from her bedroom. It was next door to the guest room where Delta was staying and had a sunny window which also overlooked the back yard. Overseers would be coming to the house to check up on him and she wanted to make sure that he looked properly cared for. Madeline was going to make sure he had the best care possible. The longer he stayed alive, the longer she would be in control of his assets. She was so tired of driving to the hospital every day. It was exhausting looking like the loyal loving wife. With him at home, she could relax and begin to enjoy herself again. He had put her through so much already and she deserved a break.

Madeline sent Delta shopping for supplies. She did not want her around when Mark arrived home. There would be too much commotion and she did not want Delta to become unnerved and say something incriminating. He arrived by ambulance and it was a couple of hours before he was set up, and the monitors were in place. Madeline hired a doctor who would come to check on Mark's progress and she confirmed that her nurse would be arriving at the house later that afternoon. The doctor said he would be back later on to make sure everything was in order and left his phone number if Madeline needed him sooner.

Once everyone had left, Madeline just stood in the room and took it all in. It was just her and Mark in the house and it was the first time they were both alone together since the incident. It was so silent except for his monitors. Madeline was glad it was just her and him in the house, it felt right, just the two of them on his

Sherry Derksen

first day back home. This was their house and they should be living in it alone. Although much thinner, he was still so damn good looking. She loved his presence and his power. She loved his intensity. It was not that long ago that she would look at him naked, lusting for his flesh, running her hands along the muscular chisel of his torso and further down feeling the explosion of his desire for her. She loved the smell of his sweat mingled in with his aftershave and the perfumes of their love. She craved him and missed him intensely. She forgave him for what he did to her. When she reflected back on it, she could see where she had made some mistakes in managing him. He was volatile but like any animal, could be handled if you were smart about it. But now, looking at him, he had become helpless and weak. Madeline pulled down his blanket to look at the fullness of him. He had lost too much weight. His once lush muscles softening and shrinking. His strength and body both deflating. He was no longer a match for her. He was damaged and now she rejected him. She pulled the blankets back up to cover what he had become. She closed the door behind her as she walked out of the room. It was too nice a day to be inside. She went out into her back yard and sat in the sun while she waited for Delta to come home.

Mark had been home for a month and everything was going smoothly, or so Madeline thought. Delta was doing a good job as a nurse although Madeline was worried that she was getting too involved. She was spending an inordinate amount of time in his room massaging his muscles, exercising and stretching his arms and legs. Madeline did not know how anyone could be a nurse. The way they had to clean up the shit and wash peoples bodies down revolted her. But Delta did not seem to mind. In fact, she seemed to be calming down a bit lately which gave Madeline more time to get back into a normal routine and enjoy her day. Delta was drinking as heavily as ever, but at least she was occupied. Some days Madeline felt overwhelmed with all she had to manage. Mark's business ventures were complicated and some of the associates she was meeting with were less than savoury. There was a lot of pressure on her to reassure people that Mark would recover. She did not know if he would, and hoped that he would not. Brian Layton and his wife Anne had been coming over to the house to check up on her and Mark. She did not know everything about Brian, but she could read

Sins of Samcora

between the lines of what Anne had told her when they socialized. Brian possessed flexible business morals. He and Mark had been doing business deals for years, and Brian had been involved in Mark's fathers business before that. Madeline decided to approach Brian and see if he would help her handle Mark's financial affairs. She did not want to spend her life worrying about business. She wanted a steady and reliable flow of money, and how that was accomplished she did not care.

Stretched out on her king size bed, Madeline was only half awake. She had another sex dream about Mark and was trying to hold on to the image and feeling of him. She liked those dreams, remembering how Mark could transport her. Her skin felt sensitive as she slowly undulated against her pillows feeling close to orgasm just by the thought of him and the memory of his touch. The memory of how his body moved with hers.

"Maddy, Maddy, wake up," Delta barged into Maddy's room looking disheveled and wild eyed. "What's happening?" Madeline sat upright in bed alarmed and also annoyed that her privacy was invaded without warning. She would have to get a lock for her bedroom.

"It's Mark, come quickly," Delta was hyperventilating.

"What about Mark?" Madeline felt a shock of fear. She did not want him to die. That would ruin everything.

"He's waking up."

Ethics and opportunities...

"What you are asking me to do is unethical. To purposely keep a man in a coma is almost like murder. I don't feel right about it and I could lose my nursing license." Delta felt panicked. Her nursing license was the last thing she was worried about. She was rambling and grabbing at the easiest excuse to refuse. She could not do what Maddy wanted. It was wrong. She looked in panic at the box on the table. She did not want to touch any of it. Where did Madeline get all those supplies?

Madeline looked at Delta with disgust. It was time to play hard ball. This was serious and Delta had to step up to the plate and do her part. Madeline would see to it.

"You are worried about ethical? You are the one who was blackmailing me for money. You were the one who hit him on the head while screaming out your husbands name. You crossed the line when you pushed the car over the embankment with Mark in it. I was half beaten to death. You were the one who should have made the better choices, so don't talk to me about ethics now. We need to keep Mark in the coma." Madeline could see the defensiveness rising in Delta and switched her tact.

"Delta, we are in this together. We had no choice but to do what we did. This is not unethical. This is survival. If Mark starts talking then we will both lose everything and will both go to jail. Probably for the rest of our lives. Mark is extremely connected in this town. There is not a judge or a lawyer who would take our side. Remember how he came at you with that knife. What did you think he was going to do with it?" Madeline tried to reason with her

Sins of Samcora

sister. Why could she not understand what was at stake?

"If he wakes up and recovers what do you think he is going to do? He will destroy us. You know we can't get justice from the justice system, you know that from some of the things we saw back home together. We have no choice." Madeline finished talking and studied Delta to gauge her reaction. She had to play this right. Everything depended on Mark staying in his coma. Delta felt trapped. Maddy was both right and wrong in what she was saying. Mark did come at her with a knife, and she did not forget the terror she had felt at the time. She should have called the police and not staged the accident but it was done. Maddy was right. They would both go to jail. She never did anything to deserve that, she never deserved any of the problems that Mark or Tom gave her. She was always in the wrong place at the wrong time. It was horrible what happened with Mark, but like Maddy said, it was done. Delta promised herself that she would not do it forever. Just a little while until she could figure another way out of this mess. It is not like she would keep him in the coma for the rest of his life.

"Ok Madeline," Delta agreed. It was too complicated to figure out right now. "We will do it your way. But we need to figure something else out soon."

"Of course," Madeline was relieved the debate was over for now. "We will figure it out together. This is a temporary solution." Madeline slid the box of supplies on the table closer to Delta. She knew it was possible that one day Mark would wake up and she had prepared and planned for it.

"Where did you get all this?" Delta was stunned. Inside the box were bottles of Diprivan, IV bags, tubes, and assorted accessories. "Why Diprivan?"

"It's propofol, Delta. A nice clean, easy drug. You know what to do." Madeline reached into the kitchen cabinet and pulled out a large bottle of liquor that she knew Delta had stashed behind the paper towel supplies. Madeline did not understand why Delta hid bottles all over the house. No one was judging her or telling her not to drink. She had full access to the liquor cabinet in the entertaining room. Madeline poured a generous amount of the amber liquid into a large cut crystal glass and handed it to Delta.

"Just a little while," Madeline reassured Delta as she watched her gulp the drink down like it was water.

Sherry Derksen

It had been a few weeks since Mark had woken up. Overall, Madeline was pleased with Delta and her level of compliance. Madeline was concerned in the beginning because Delta was struggling with the idea of maintaining Mark's sedation. But now, a routine was beginning to establish itself and Delta seemed to be falling into the groove. Madeline rarely went into Mark's room anymore. She still had occasional dreams about the Mark she married, and she waited and hungered for those dreams. She felt grief over the loss of her husband, everything that he was to her. She could not accept that the man laying in the bed down the hall was her husband.

Sometimes she would go into his room and watch him. Searching for his essence in that silent damaged body, but she could not see it and rejected him. It was on one of those difficult nights, when she wanted him, and he would not visit her dreams. She got up out of bed and started to walk down the hall. She wanted to watch him again, to see if he might be returning to her. As she got closer to his room she heard a noise. Whispering? There was a noise from Mark's room. Silently, Madeline pressed her ear to the door. It was Delta. She was talking to Mark. Madeline listened harder to try to make out her words. No, she was not talking. She was reading. She was reading the bible. Madeline swung open the door.

"What exactly are you doing?" Madeline looked at Delta who had pulled a chair up near Mark's bed and was reading by the light of a small lamp on his bedside table. It looked like Delta had been crying again. The woman has endless capacity to wallow, thought Madeline.

"I'm reading to him," Delta was startled and felt like she was caught doing something wrong.

"I can see that, Delta. But why?" Madeline looked dispassionately at Delta, waiting for an explanation.

"It helps me to forgive myself for what I have done and for what I'm doing." Delta answered truthfully but not completely. It was true that she was seeking forgiveness from the Lord, and she was going to help Mark attain salvation as well. But she was also trying to stimulate Mark's brain. She knew that coma patients did better when people read to them or talked to them. Even

Sins of Samcora

though Mark's coma was drug induced, Delta thought it would still help him. Of course, Maddy would not understand that, so she kept that part to herself.

"Fine, Delta. Whatever helps you." Madeline did not like what Delta was doing, but was undecided if it had the potential to be a problem. She would need to think it out a bit. "Goodnight, Delta." Madeline decided that she better keep a closer eye on Delta as she softly closed the door behind her.

After watching her for several days, Madeline decided that Delta's new religion was not a problem. For now. After all, she was still drinking heavily and still taking the gifts and money that Madeline had been giving her. If seeking some sort of twisted absolution kept Delta relatively stable, then Madeline thought it would be harmless enough. It was a difficult job, being a nurse to an invalid. Madeline had watched her one day, she needed to understand exactly what Delta was doing almost all day in Mark's room. Delta would clean him and change his adult diapers. She bathed him, brushed his hair, and cleaned his teeth. The worst part was the nasogastric tube. That gave Madeline the creeps. The tube went from Mark's nose down to his stomach so Delta could pump nutritional support into his gut. She spent hours massaging him, stretching his muscles, and exercising his limbs. Madeline had to admire Delta's determination to keep Mark as intact as possible. She was an excellent nurse to be able to do all of that and not feel totally disgusted. Madeline had studied Delta's face when she did her work and marvelled at how she could keep a neutral attitude. Madeline speculated if she herself would be able to do what Delta was doing, and came to the conclusion that she could not. She did not have the stomach for it.

"You don't need to do all that, Delta," Madeline could not see the point of massaging Mark. It must have been awful for Delta to touch him when he was so lifeless looking.

"Yes, I do. If his muscles are not stretched and worked every day, he will continue to atrophy even faster. His muscles will begin to shorten and tighten and his body will end up twisting. The doctor who comes and checks him each week will make a report that Mark is not being properly cared for and will have him shipped to a facility." Delta knew that Maddy did not understand how hard it was to keep fooling the doctor that Mark

Sherry Derksen

was not really in a coma. He was kept asleep through an intravenous drug most of the time but when the doctor came she had to take out the IV and give him an injection. The dosing was challenging and she was always scared she would put Mark into respiratory failure. It was also getting difficult to hide the IV starts and she had resorted to using the veins in his feet so the sites were hidden by Mark's socks. The doctor never removed Mark's socks to check his distal pulses.

"Do you want me to hire you some help?" Madeline could not imagine being stuck in Mark's room all day. Delta was definitely dedicated.

"No, I'm ok with it. Someone might question the IV drugs we are giving him. Its better if we keep it to ourselves." Delta did not want help. She wanted to be the one to look after Mark. It was her responsibility to help him recover. She would not be forgiven if she did not pay her penance. She had to right her wrongs herself. Mark needed her. Delta wished Maddy would just leave. She knew her sister was watching her, seeing if she was keeping Mark sedated.

Both Brian Layton and his wife Anne continued coming over to the house to check up on Mark and Madeline. It was irritating to Madeline, but it was an intrusion that she expected and she was always ready to entertain their questions and accept their sympathies and declarations of ongoing support. Then one day, Brian showed up alone.

"Madeline, you know that Anne and I are concerned for Mark...and of course for you." Brian was not quite sure how to approach Madeline. He needed information about Mark and it would not be to his benefit to start by alienating Madeline. He had suspicions about what was going on in the house.

"Please don't be offended, but I have to say that I am not sure that this is a healthy environment for either Mark or you. Mark is in a vulnerable position. I am not saying that you are doing anything improper, however, there are those who might begin to think that this is...well, unusual." Brian did not want to outright say that he thought Mark would recover better in an independent facility. He did not really know. No one had seen Mark except Madeline since he left the hospital, and she always had excuses why

Sins of Samcora

Mark could not see visitors. It was suspiciously convenient to have full access to the man's money and have him lying upstairs in the house, effectively a prisoner. Brian needed Mark to get better. He was at the end of his resources and desperate for some financial assistance.

Mark owed him more for the Joan Howard cover up. He had gone way out on a limb for him, and as far as Brian was concerned, he was not fairly compensated. It irritated Brian as he remembered how he wanted to explain his position to Mark at the dinner all those months ago. Brian gave up believing that Mark would come through. That dinner was his last chance to try to get Mark to see his point of view. Brian had tried to meet with him after that night but Mark kept putting him off. Finally as Brian decided that he was going to be bold and just barge into Mark's office and demand fair treatment, he again missed his opportunity because Mark and Madeline got into the car accident. Now, with Mark drooling into his pillow it would be impossible to get any money out of him.

Brian needed that money desperately. He was out of time and out of options. Something had to be done. Then it occurred to him that he might try to squeeze Madeline. He should at least feel it out. He was not even sure what to say to her. Brian really did not know Madeline, or what to think of her. Other than his lustful thoughts he never really considered her before. She was just Mark's wife, someone in the background. But now she was fully in charge of all Mark's finances and of his welfare. Arrogant fool, thought Brian to himself. Mark had all manner of plans in place if he was dead, but there were no enforceable instructions if he had extended incapacity. He was just like his father, thinking he was invincible.

Both Mark and Elliot always had to be in charge and never considered that they could be vulnerable. Brian had done a lot of favours for Mark, he thought irritably. Mark should have been in jail ten times over except for Brian bailing him out. Now, here he was, big man, shitting himself in his bed and eating dinner through a tube. Brian could not believe the vanity of Mark, to be so sure of himself that he would leave his business interests so unprotected. The financial legacy of his father and of Mark, built on power and strength, now left in the hands of some woman nobody really knew anything about. Brian tried hard to shift his face into a concerned mask, but all he felt was outrage from being robbed of his entitlement. He had used Anne as a shield of empathy on his other visits. Now he had things to say that he did not want Anne involved in.

Mustering what he hoped sounded like convincing concern, Brian pressed on. "The situation with Mark must be very painful for you, not only because he is so ill, but also you must be feeling overwhelmed with the business aspect of this tragedy."

Madeline was not fooled by Brian's passive face and stroking words. She knew very well what kind of man Brian was. If he was connected to Mark then that told her everything she needed to know about him as a business person. The lunches she had at the club with his wife Anne told her all she needed to know about him as a man. All Madeline had to do was figure out what he wanted from her without revealing herself. She was not so naive to think that this was a simple social call or that he cared about anything other than his own needs.

"Thank you Brian for your concern. You and Anne have both been wonderful. I am not offended by anything you say. It has been hard with Mark being sick. He always took care of everything. It is so difficult without him, especially with his business. I appreciate all your concern because I know you and Mark were close friends and you have his, and my, best interests at heart." Madeline moved from the armchair and sat beside Brian and casually put her hand on his knee.

She knew what she was doing. She knew how close she could get to him. There was an invisible line with a man, where you move close enough that he becomes uncertain if the proximity is still socially acceptable or if you are sending him a message. She could see in him, in his sudden discomfort, that she found that line. Brian could feel the warmth from Madeline's hand. She was a gorgeous woman. Momentarily he thought of her hand moving up his thigh. How she would stimulate him and how she would look with her long hair wild as she groaned and squirmed beneath him as he did things to her that Anne refused to do. Brian suddenly felt flustered and hoped that Madeline could not see that she had affected him.

"Well, Madeline, you know I'm here for you." Brian decided to press on and test the waters, "I know it is a bad time, but

Sins of Samcora

Mark had left some financial business unresolved."

"Financial business with you, Brian?" Madeline interrupted him softly and looked innocently into his eyes. Brian felt mesmerized by her gaze. He could see in her eyes that she was delicate and needed a man to guide her. He suddenly felt sorry for thinking that she could be devious. She was innocent. Mark obviously married her for her vulnerability and for the release that she would provide him in bed. She would be easy to get money from.

"Well, yes Madeline. Mark does have some outstanding business with me," Brian started feeling more confident.

"Thank you for telling me, Brian," Madeline could feel Brian being lulled by her. He was looking at her in that way again. As his passions stirred, his logic faded.

"You just tell me what it is Mark owed you and I will make sure your business is taken care of first priority. I can get the check book now if you want." Brian could not believe his good fortune. Here was Madeline just offering him, without question, what was rightfully his in the first place. All those bloody arguments with Mark to squeeze a few bucks out and here she was just handing it to him.

"Don't you want details Madeline?" Brian hoped she didn't.

"Of course not Brian, I know you are an honest man and all those details were between you and Mark. I don't need to know them, I trust you completely. Most of it would be over my head anyway." Brian could not believe what he was hearing.

"Madeline," Brian tried to disguise the relief in his voice that he was finally going to get some cash. "I appreciate that you are straightforward with me, however, if others ask you for anything, you need to make sure that they are not taking advantage of your circumstances." Brian was not sure if Madeline was trusting him or just too trusting in general. It amused Madeline to see the emotions racing through Brian. She could read them all. She was always able to read men.

"Absolutely Brian, I understand. I am so glad you came here today because I have been thinking about you. I was going to approach you to ask you if you would be my financial adviser." Madeline moved a little closer to Brian, a movement that was almost imperceptible. Her hand was still on his knee, and had been there long enough to confuse Brian. Was she coming on to him? He was not sure but Brian was aware that his breathing had deepened. He was concerned that the swell in his crotch was getting noticeably large.

"Of course, Madeline," Brian said more forcefully than he intended, "I would be happy to represent you and assist you in dealing with anything you need. I will protect you and your interests." Brian got up to leave, relieved to get some distance from Madeline so she could not see how she rattled him. The area on his leg where her hand was felt wet from the heat that came from both of them. She was a beautiful and vulnerable woman and he could see now that there would be scores of men trying to align themselves with her and with Mark's money. Brian suddenly felt fiercely protective of Madeline and yet at the same time he wanted to strip her down on the sofa and dominate her until he felt her full and complete submission to him. He wanted to hear her plead and cry and beg him to come so that he could, and then he would comfort her.

Pay the price, penitent man...

It disgusted her. She could hear Maddy and Brian rutting like dogs in the other room. The affair had been going on for a few weeks now. They should have both been ashamed. Delta tried to talk to Maddy about it. She tried to tell her that it was wrong. What they were doing was wrong. Maddy had promised that they would figure something new out. But every time she tried to talk to her she just kept putting her off. Then there would be some new gift or an envelope with more money in it. After a while the money did not matter. Delta knew there was more to life than money. There was your ethics. There was your humanity. Sure, all the money and gifts that Maddy gave her for her salary was nice, but Delta could not enjoy it with the guilt. Guilt stained everything. No matter what Mark had done, he was still a human being and she was a nurse. It was her calling to help people recover. Not help keep them locked in an unending drug prison.

Delta was not so sure anymore that Mark had been trying to kill them. Maybe he knew what a monster Maddy really was and he was trying to protect himself. He could have also have been disoriented and confused from the initial hit on the head. He might not even have known what he was doing when he was waving around that knife. He had already been hit on the head once, maybe he was not in his right mind? Yes, he was beating Maddy. There was no doubt about that. It was wrong what he had done to her. But did it deserve this? Delta kept questioning herself. She had instinctively hit Mark to get him off Maddy when he was beating her, but when he came to and started to get the knife, they should

Sherry Derksen

have just run.

Now that she looked back, she was sure that there was time to run. She should have grabbed Maddy and ran away and called the police. Then none of this would have happened. Maddy tricked her into thinking that Mark intended to murder them. Maddy was a monster, always twisting things around.

How could Maddy be so cold to Mark and just go on living her life, pretending that nothing was wrong? Oh she was having a great old time screwing around with her married boyfriend while her own husband was lying helpless, thought Delta bitterly. She hoped that Mark could not hear Maddy and Brian. They were so loud and disgusting. It would break his heart if Mark knew what his wife was up to. Looking after Mark for so long made Delta see him in a different light. Maddy only wanted Delta to know the bad that was in Mark, she did not want her to see that he had goodness in him too. Delta knew about Mark's goodness, he had come out of the coma weeks ago.

Delta got to know him even though she still kept him partially drugged. Maddy refused to listen to Delta when she tried to explain that it was getting more and more dangerous to keep Mark continually under the propofol. He needed to wake up for a while so his respiratory system would not fail. But Maddy just said no, keep him under always. So Delta did in the beginning. It was so much easier in the beginning because Delta was afraid of both Mark and Maddy. Now it was not so easy. Each day that she washed his body and massaged his muscles and combed his hair, she saw that he was just a man. He had evil in him, but so did she until she began reading her bible. She paid her penance and walked through the fire of guilt, she was purged of her evil. She could help Mark purge himself of his evil as well. His beating of Maddy was horrific but Delta was sure that in his heart he knew it now. He certainly has repaid the harm he did with an equal measure of his own suffering.

He deserved a chance to redeem himself so Delta decided to stop the propofol. Mark began to regain consciousness. The first time he had come to, he looked her straight in the eyes with such helplessness that it melted Delta's heart. That was the first time that any man had spoken to her without words. Whether he could not, or just did not speak, did not matter to Delta. His intent was clear with his expression "help me," his eyes said. The

Sins of Samcora

effect on Delta was profound. She was so sick of men's words. If that had been Tom waking up, the first thing that he would do would be to get his big mouth flapping away at her and making her feel bad. Tom would be accusing her and condemning her. But Mark was different, he just reached out with his eyes, with no anger or judgements. He just wanted Delta to help him. Delta could feel in her soul that he was a changed man and she felt so tender toward him. He wanted to be saved. He needed her and she had the power to save him.

"Don't worry," whispered delta into Mark's ear as she stroked his head, "I will help you soon." It was getting harder for Delta to restart the intravenous line that kept Mark sedated. She wanted him awake. She had to make a plan. Maddy was crafty and Delta had to be careful. Delta took a long sip from the bottle of whisky that she kept in Mark's room. She did not bother with glasses anymore, she was tired of running downstairs to wash them. Her throat burned as the liquid went down and she relaxed further back into her chair. As Mark slept she began to think of ways to save him.

Cash grab...

It seems that I have two kinds of luck, murmured Tom to himself. Bad luck or no luck at all. But today was the start of a new day and a new chapter in his life. He had just gotten out of prison. He was arrested for theft of his own damn vehicle. That cursed Buick. Murray had the nerve to call the cops and report the Buick as stolen. Then, to add to his misfortune, the damn judge had to be an ugly old fat woman. She was a stubborn bat that refused to listen to him when he tried to explain that he only meant to rent the car to Murray, that he had not really sold it. So what if Murray had a bill of sale. That was nothing. He just signed the bill of sale so that his buddy could register and insure the car more easily. It did not mean that he actually sold it to him. But the judge would not listen. He was sending but she was not receiving. When Tom told her so, and that she was taking out her PMS on him, she got all crazy and gave him a contempt of court charge. He should have been out of jail earlier, most people serve less than a month, but she went out of her way to make sure he served all his time.

Tom was outraged at first, but now looking back, he realized that it was not all bad. At first it was hard because there was no booze. He could not recall when he had felt so sick in his life. They told him in the infirmary he was having delirium tremors, that it was part of withdrawal. He could say it now. He was an alcoholic. Delta always called him that and now he supposed it was true. For the most part, the AA meetings were good. Tom thought they were a waste of time at first but then he began to like the meetings. He felt better, knowing there were others who

Sins of Samcora

experienced the same things he did and suffered the way he did. It was strange to feel sober.

There was something unsettling about feeling sober, yet, it was exciting too. It was like he had another chance to experience life. He had seen what life was like inside the bottle and now he was going to see it outside the bottle. Tom felt like he wanted to be a better person. He had to work through his steps and the only person who he maybe owed an apology to was Delta. Murray, and his old buddies, all the rest of those scavenging bastards could go to hell. Not one of them came to visit him in prison.

It was tough deciding what to do about the camera. Murray did not even notice it was missing from the car. Tom was relieved. If Murray had seen the pictures it would have been difficult to explain, and just added one more complication to his life. In jail, Tom had a chance to catch up on the news. He knew all about Mark Jacobson and his wife Madeline and their supposed car accident.

Accident my ass he thought to himself. But still, he did not want to get involved in that mess. He was glad he had a chance to straighten up in jail, but certainly did not want to serve anymore time for withholding evidence in a crime. Tom did not remember the last time he saw the world sober and he felt too preoccupied with his sobriety to care about anything else. He just wanted to move on with his life. But first, he had to see Delta and let her know that he was sorry for some of the things that he had done. He also wanted to let her know that he forgave her for the things that she had done.

Tom planned to give the camera to Delta so she could decide what to do with it herself. It did not bother him that she was involved in whatever was going on with her and Maddy. It was part of his twelve steps to set some of his life right and he wanted to do that with Delta. He was definitely going to give her the camera, and perhaps she would reciprocate his benevolent generosity by helping him out a little bit. He just needed a little financial support to get on his feet again.

The day was hot and dry and the smell of the flowers intoxicating. The back yard of Maddy's house was the most

Sherry Derksen

beautiful garden that Delta had ever seen. Besides being in Mark's room and looking after him, this was the only place that she felt a sense of serenity and peace. She enjoyed looking for the best blooms in the garden to cut for the flower arrangements that she put by Mark's bedside every day. She wanted him to have the sensory stimulation and the beauty of the smells to wrap him in the same delight she got from the flowers. The sun bit her on her back as she hunched over and selected the lush and heavy blooms. They should have been in the crystal vase by now, drinking in the water through their freshly cut stems, but instead they were lying in the basket on the patio, sweating and wilting and forgotten where she put them down after Tom approached her.

It was a shock seeing Tom standing in the garden, invading her serenity. How did he know where she was? How he could just casually walk into her personal space and begin speaking to her without warning or invite. How did he find her? Why did he find her? Tom and his world were so remote to her now, part of another life and his presence in front of her felt like a clash of two different existences. She had forgotten how much she despised it when he talked. There were no words to describe how she hated his spittle as it sprayed out of his big flapping mouth. She did not have to take it again, did not have to stand passively by and listen to his ramblings. Delta did not care what Tom had to say. Yes, he was in jail, she got that. Yes, he considers himself a recovered alcoholic, whatever. Yes, he is sorry he was such an asshole. Delta did not want to hear it. Why couldn't he see that she was just numb to him, numb to everything? She did not care anymore. All she wanted from Tom was for him to shut his big ugly mouth and go away.

As he continued to speak she realized he would not go away. He was going to continue to attach himself to her like the parasitic leech she realized he was. He explained that he was at her apartment and then when he discovered that she had moved out, he figured she would be here with Maddy. He cheerfully said what good timing it was that he found her out here, in the garden. Cold shivers crawled up Delta's spine as Tom recounted how he was peeking in the window. How he had seen what happened in the kitchen and the accident. How he had pictures of it on his camera.

"So I have decided to forgive you for everything that you have done to me in the past Delta," Tom rambled on feeling

Sins of Samcora

like a big man, "and I know that if there was stuff I did to you that you understand it was because I was sick. I have this disease called alcoholism. So you see, none of it was ever really my fault." He must be insane Delta thought to herself. How could I have put up with this rambling idiot for as long as I did? Why could he just not shut up and be quiet? Quiet and gentle like Mark.

"So, I was thinking," Tom continued, "that I would give you this camera and maybe you could help me out a little, you know, to help me get back on my feet from after my illness. It looks like you and Maddy have it made here." There it was. Delta knew the moment he approached her in the garden that he wanted something from her. At least he had finally gotten to it and hopefully would shut up soon.

"So, how much do you want," drilled Delta, not really caring how much it was. She was tired of the game. She just wanted to be rid of Tom so she could get back to Mark. "How much damn money do you want now?"

"Well," said Tom defensively, feeling disrespected, "You make it sound like I am blackmailing you. I am helping you out here and you are acting like a bitch. I don't need to take crap from you, I can take this camera straight to the police. That would fix you," Tom was beginning to wind up and feel more belligerent, forgetting that if he took the camera to the police, then he himself would also be charged for withholding evidence.

"How much?" intoned Delta without flinching. She looked him straight in the eye, unimpressed and unmoved by his threats. She was desensitized to him and his bullying antics.

"Ten thousand then," spat out Tom, not really sure why he picked that number. Not really sure if she could afford that or if she could afford much more.

"Fine then. I will get the money. You come back and meet me in the garage around two in the morning. I will leave the side door unlocked so you can get in. Don't let anyone see you. If you don't have the camera with you the deal is off." Delta turned away from Tom and started walking back to the house, not bothering to give him another glance.

Tom continued standing there for a few moments in shock. He had never seen this side of her. She felt and sounded foreign to him. He realized that he no longer knew the woman who had been his wife for so many years. He began to feel uncertain and thought that a drink would feel good about now. Tom shook his head and began to walk away. No, he was not going to let Delta take away his sobriety.

Both Tom and Delta's back had been turned to Madeline when she first walked out into the yard. Madeline also had not seen them right away, only realizing they were there by the gazebo when she heard their voices. She quickly turned from the direction she was heading and crouched down, silently crawling to the backside of the structure so she would not be seen. She was less than four feet behind them and could hear everything. Madeline tried to keep her breath under control so they would not detect her presence. She stayed behind the gazebo for several minutes after they left, trying to work the cramps out of her legs and thinking about how to handle this newest problem.

The vengeance...

Eyes feeling scratchy and dry, Delta struggled to focus on the blurry green readout of the digital clock. It was already a quarter past two in the morning. "Where did the time go?" She felt so groggy. How the hell could she have fallen asleep? Massaging her temples she tried to clear her head. Her tongue felt dry and fuzzy and too big for her mouth as she tried to work up some moisture.

"I didn't drink that much, how can I be this hung over?" Seeing Tom took a bigger toll on her than she wanted to admit. Maddy had seen the strain in her earlier, commenting on the deepened lines and paleness of Delta's face. It was a rare gesture when her sister had brought her a cup of hot tea with an embarrassingly generous but appreciated splash of bourbon in it. The warm aromatic liquid spread it's warmth like tentacles and induced a soft relaxed state which released the twisted knots in her shoulders. The last thing Delta remembered was the feeling of weightlessness as her body melted further into the soft chair beside Mark's bed. She was not even aware when the tea cup and saucer bounced on the carpeting beside her after rolling out of her limp hand.

Delta had moved one of the plush velvet wingtip chairs to Marks bedside where she liked to sit while she had her nightcap. She liked the quiet and in the stillness of the room she could unwind as she whispered her secrets and confessions to Mark. Delta believed that he could hear and forgive her for what she was doing. Maddy rarely entered the sanctuary of Mark's room

Sherry Derksen

anymore. The last day she came was the day she watched how Delta cared for Mark, observing the healing intimacy of her touch on Mark's body while she rubbed in lotions and massaged his atrophied muscles. It seemed to affect Maddy but Delta was unsure why. Was she jealous? Repulsed? Maddy was so hard to read with her practiced and perfect face. Her fake smiles. Always so in control. Her aloofness was unsettling. She would be more likeable if she showed some damn emotion once in a while.

Delta was not afraid to show strong emotion. It was a testimony of basic humanity to show and share what you really felt. Tom often accused her of being too emotional and an ugly crier. Mocking her while she emoted to his cruelty with loud gasping sobs and snot bubbling out of her nostrils. Sure, she was an ugly crier and he made her that way. Asshole. Tom. Damn, she was groggy. It was still hard to see.

Trying to clear her eyes she rubbed them vigorously. It felt like there was oil on her eyeballs. She needed to pull herself together and get to her meeting with Tom in the garage. Delta hated being late. That was always Tom's trick and had been the source of many of their fights. But for $10,000 Tom would make sure he was on time, hell he was probably early. That would be a first. $10,000 was a lot of money to give that bastard. Being blackmailed by her husband that she had devoted years of care, time, and anguish to felt like an emotional rape. She did not really care about the money itself. It was his continual unrelenting sucking of her resources that upset her. He never considered how hard it was for her to accumulate that amount of money. What she had to do. How she had to sacrifice.

Maddy had seduced her with more money than she ever thought she would have and instead of joy it brought her pain and confusion. Blood money. Complicated money. But even so it was her money and he had no right to just demand it of her. She had sold her soul for her money and he just waltzes in to take it. With wobbly knees, Delta pulled herself up in the chair. Her head swimming she quickly sat back down trying to breathe through the nausea. She knew what she had to do about Tom. She just needed a minute to get her nerves together. Delta could not let Maddy know what she was planning. She needed to handle this herself, in her way. Tom was in for a big surprise.

Sins of Samcora

He never wore a watch but Tom could feel in his body that it was 2 o'clock in the morning. He was certain of it. The air at that time always seemed to feel weighted with an oppressive scent that he was never quite able to describe. Two o'clock was when they called for last rounds and as was his habit, he would order a couple more drinks and then go outside for a piss. He hated pissing in the bar toilet, so nasty in there. He rather enjoyed watching his stream wash down the side of the building in the alleyway. Shake and zip and then a quick smoke before heading back in to finish up his drinks with the handful of regulars who were still around. He used to look up to see if the stars were out but he stopped doing that some time ago. The vastness and depth of the night sky would grab him and draw him in. It was eerie shit. Empty and cold.

Standing in the cool garage waiting for Delta was upsetting him. More eerie shit. She should have been here already. Maybe she changed her mind? Maybe she was lying to him about the money? Maybe she did something stupid and called the police? The side door of the garage was open as she said it would be, and that gave him some small measure of comfort. Even so, the whole situation was unnerving. Could he be charged with break and enter? He did not want to go back to jail. After all this was not Delta's house. Clearly it belonged to the sucker they clocked in the kitchen. Delta had acted strange. He felt like he did not even know her anymore. What would he do if she did not show up? Maybe she was setting him up? She used to be so predictable. Did she want to get back at him? She always blamed him for everything, nothing was ever good enough.

"Do you have the camera?" A woman's voice cut through the shadows of the garage. He never heard her come in and her voice cut through his thoughts sending his pulse into overdrive. It took him a second to come back to the present, to why he was standing in this stinking garage freezing his nuts off. How long had she been there? Had she been watching him, amused at how jumpy he was standing in the dark garage?

"Of course I have the camera you stupid cow. Do you have the money?" Tom felt his hostility bubbling up. She always had a way of making him feel unbalanced. He did not trust her and he did not like this cloak and dagger business one bit. "I can't see a

Sherry Derksen

bloody thing, turn some lights on," Tom demanded, hating being off guard, hating her. Wordlessly she moved forward and he felt her beside him. He could now see the shape of her. She had her head down and was hunching over. She seemed smaller than she used to be and her defeated body posture made him feel less vulnerable. Made her feel more familiar. Tom felt a large envelope being pressed into his hands and his excitement rose at the size of the package. He did not expect ten thousand dollars to feel so thick in his hands.

"Shit, that is a lot of money," Tom said under his breath. Flashes of what he was going to buy ran through his head. He could make a fresh start with this money. Should he have asked for more? If it was this easy to get ten grand, maybe he should have asked for more? Was this really happening? She could easily cheat him. Tom wanted to count it.

"Are you cheating me? Is it all here? There will he hell to pay if you are screwing with me." With an ugly glare, Tom looked up from the payday in his hands into her face. His eyes, now adjusted to the darkness locked on her and widened with surprise. Her arm moved up toward him so fast he did not immediately register what was she holding in her hand. What the fuck?

Tom only saw the syringe as she withdrew it from his neck. It had felt like a bee sting. He had gotten stung once as a kid, hot burning pain mixed with pressure and fear. FUCK! Speechless, his breath clamped off at his throat. Tom felt a rush through his body before he lost total motor control. A cold shockwave starting in his feet and exiting the top of his head. The last thing he heard was his own body slamming into the concrete floor.

The woman dragged his limp body into the car and fired up the engine. She was glad he did not split his head open on the concrete when he fell. She forgot about that part, forgot to plan that he might have bled when he fell. Relieved that she did not have to clean up his blood she drove with him crumpled in the passenger seat until she found an alley that seemed dark enough and deserted enough for her purpose.

After parking and shutting off the lights, she took a new feeding tube out of it's sterile package and fed it through his nose until it entered his stomach. She knew her rough estimate length should be about 63 cm. With her syringe she aspirated some

Sins of Samcora

stomach contents to make sure the tube was placed properly. Can't be too hasty, can't be too careful. It was too easy to get the nasogastric tube in the lungs when the patient was unresponsive and the gag reflex gone. There could be no mistakes with this. She fished another larger syringe out of her equipment bag and began pushing alcohol from another container into the tube.

She had taken the strongest proof alcohol that she could find from the liquor cabinet. She knew that alcohol was one of the few substances that transferred directly into the bloodstream through the stomach lining. She also knew that the drug she injected him with would keep him unconscious and suppress his body's reaction to expel the toxins as his blood alcohol levels got higher and higher. Once all the alcohol was pumped into his stomach she removed the feeding tube. With the volume of alcohol in his stomach she estimated that it would take about two hours until his blood alcohol toxicity would begin to shut down his respiratory centre. Then he would simply suffocate.

Checking his pockets she found the camera. Good. It was all coming together now. Double checking that no one was around and watching she opened the passenger door and dragged him out of the car. It was easier to do than she thought it would be. Driving away, leaving him there to die in the filth of the alley seemed like justice to her. He had hurt her badly and she still bore the trauma of that. Now he wanted to hurt her again. He had never been accountable for all the pain he caused. She would have let it go if he had stayed away but he did not. His bullying and extortions had finally crossed the line. She knew he would have never stopped at $10,000 dollars. Once he cycled through that he would be back for more and more.

He had lived by the bottle so he could die by the bottle. He was a mean drunk. No one would even care. Just another drunk found dead in an alley. If they even bothered with an autopsy it would be death from blood alcohol poisoning. She had made sure that she brought some high quality booze. For some reason, she wanted to make sure that his last party was a good one.

Predators and their prey...

"I love you." Brian's breath was wet against Madeline's cheek, the sudden confession grunted out as he completed his final ejaculatory thrusts mounted on top of her. Madeline despised his words. Tangled with him in bed, sweaty and sticky from another afternoon session of sex she wanted to wash his declarations of love off as badly as she wanted to wash his smell off of her. Eyes closed, getting into her groove, she had been fantasizing that it was Mark who was thrusting into her. She had been so close to an orgasm.

Mark was magnificent in bed. She liked the rawness of his rutting, the unabashed fury of sensations he could bring out in her. There were no declarations about feelings during sex with Mark. Love talk was reserved for conversation, not copulation. Brian's intrusive comment turned her off. Now she had to pretend to come to get this finished. She never had to fake orgasms with Mark. Mark's power and intensity overwhelmed her inhibitions, overwhelmed her innate sense of shame allowing her to do and behave the way she wanted to, needed to, so that she could release. She could easily express both her innocence and her depravity to him with no judgement.

Sex was so different with Brian. Everything was a negotiation and she had to be aware of his sensitivities so she would not shock him with the truth of her desires. He rarely commanded in bed, he was more of a human dildo responding to her orchestration.

"I love you too," Madeline purred back, breathless silky lies stroking his delicate ego as she faked her rapture and

Sins of Samcora

pressed another kiss into him. She wrapped her legs tighter around him, grinding into him to coax out his last shudders and pretend that she had responded. She knew men and knew her gestures would be interpreted as acceptance of him and proof of her love. She did not love him, but it would serve her no benefit to let him know that.

She was not exactly sure what she felt for Brian but it was somewhere between indifference and convenience. He was an average lover, but Madeline liked the arrangement. Brian was easy to lead around and she enjoyed steering his mood by steering his cock. It made him more controllable as she aligned her business goals. She liked the way things were and did not want their relationship to advance.

The affair started, predictably, with Brian's attempt to get some of Mark's money. Yet, his greed was not offensive to her. Greed was an honest emotion. Madeline understood survival and respected the courage that drove Brian to make claim to what he felt Mark owed him. Whether Mark legitimately owed money to Brian was irrelevant to her. Although the amount of money was significant, she was not bothered by it. There was plenty to go around.

Much of Mark's enterprise was over her head and if she was being honest she did not really want to deal with the fine details of Mark's businesses. With Brian as her advisor and protector, she was receiving valuable return for the cash outlay. He had proved himself adept at navigating the myriad of vultures that oozed out of the woodwork after Mark became non functioning. Madeline was surprised at how highly skilled a negotiator Brian was and now understood why Mark had kept him around. She had always thought of him as a backward cowboy, a slow stubborn type who craved a bygone era because he could not cope in the one he was in. She saw that she had been wrong in her assessment. She had a new appreciation for his talents as she witnessed him easily navigating the nuances of complex business, particularly with some of Mark's less savoury associates.

All in all, Madeline felt satisfied with the arrangement. Before, she would have never considered a fling with a married man, but now she could see that she had the best of both worlds. She, as his mistress would be getting his best behaviour and because he was married, he still had to go home to his wife which

Sherry Derksen

gave her the space she craved. She could tolerate Brian, but having him around her all the time would be suffocating. The beatings she took from Mark had taught her the importance of maintaining freedom and the upper hand. Men treated you much better when they didn't feel like they owned you. She would never allow another man to encroach on her independence again. Madeline began to think about the pool of men that were possible candidates for her next affair. Fidelity had no place in the modern world. You were a fool if you did not recognize that the balance of desire and satisfaction were powerful currencies.

"I'm going to tell Anne I want a divorce." Brian's announcement was like a hammer shattering her serenity. Involuntarily, her body clenched. Madeline forced herself to relax, to slow down, and to not let Brian see the frustration in her eyes.

"Why?" Madeline spoke steadily, careful not to show her emotions, her utter rejection of his statement, her utter rejection of him. She felt like screaming. What was wrong with him?

"I would have thought you would be happy about it." Brian was feeling uncertain, and a little foolish. Madeline was not responding the way he thought she would. She should have been happy with the news. When he played it out in his mind, he saw her celebrating. Not just freezing up and asking him why. He sat up in the bed, wondering if he should leave, yet not really wanting to leave just yet.

"It's a big step. You don't need to leave her for me, you know." Madeline sat up in bed as well and pulled the sheets around her naked body.

"I love you even if you stay married to her." Madeline hoped to calm his emotions. She could sense him beginning to pout. She hated that weakness, that ridiculous grasping at the unattainable. It always amazed Madeline how people were ruled by their emotions, letting how they felt direct their lives instead of intellectually determining what was best, regardless of their inner conflicts.

"I thought you wanted to be with me." Brian looked directly in Madeline's eyes, hoping his expression could tell her what he was feeling so that he did not have to say it. He was feeling rejected and hurt. When did she get so much power over him?

"I am with you. I've never asked you to leave Anne.

Sins of Samcora

I've never asked you to choose." He was being amazingly indulgent. Why did he want to change things? He was ruining what they had.

"Have you thought about your career? Your social network that is tied to you and Anne as a couple? Your kids? I have never asked you to jeopardize all you have built for yourself." Madeline's anger was growing but she was careful not to show it. She felt like she was his mother, having to point out how simple minded he was being. Nothing was a bigger turn off to her, except perhaps his arrogance in thinking that she was waiting for him, for his leftovers. His lack of humility in assuming that she would be willing to build a life with him enraged her. Did he forget that she herself was still married? What did his fantasy include about Mark? Just because he was a judge did not reduce any complications she would have in divorcing a comatose man. Besides, she had no intentions of ever divorcing Mark. He was her husband and she was never going to let him or his bank account go.

Madeline had to calm down and maintain her rationality. As petulant and annoying as Brian was right now, she did not want to jeopardize her relationship with him. It had too many advantages. If he turned on her he could do her some real damage. She had to try to salvage what she could. Madeline moved her body directly in front of Brian and gently cupped his face in her hands. The sheet that was wrapped around her fell away, revealing her nakedness. His eyes cast to her body.

"Do you doubt my love for you?"

"No." She was incredibly beautiful and Brian loved when she touched him the way she was. Her caress was innocent, a feeling that he lost many years ago, but rediscovered through her. She was so open with herself, with her body. He had never noticed how much life had hardened him until he fell in love with Madeline and reawakened to her tenderness and passion. How could she remain so pure married to a prick like Mark? In his heart he knew that she loved him. She had to. It was inconceivable that the love he felt for her was one sided. But, she was right. He would lose respect, family, and contacts if he divorced Anne. He understood all that, and the implications of those losses. He also understood that true love is rare. What he and Madeline share is uncommon and precious. A life without her would be no life. But then, a life without money would also be no life. He would come out financially intact in a divorce to Anne, but Mark had an ironclad prenup with Madeline. He knew because he adjudicated it. She would get nothing, which would mean that he would get nothing. Both of them were used to a certain standard of living that would be difficult to turn back from. Even the strongest love spoils in financial hardship.

"I know you are right but I don't like it." Brian's percolating emotions finally started to level out as Madeline leaned forward and began to kiss his neck and whisper endearments to him. She smelled so good and her lips were like little butterflies tickling him. Her hand reached between his legs and she stroked him. His feelings of rejection faded as his erection bloomed with the skill of her hand. It was remarkable that she was not jealous of Anne. They never talked about it but Madeline must know that he still slept with his wife. If Anne was aware of Madeline, she would have gone ballistic. He flipped Madeline onto her back, he needed more of her. Even if he did not leave Anne, he had to find a way to be with Madeline more often. Brian pulled Madeline closer and in unison they rolled into each other, writhing, and grasping and gripping each other tighter as they began to indulge their desires.

After he was gone, Madeline reclined in her jetted tub, letting the hot water relax her knotted muscles. The perfume of the hot soapy water and her satsuma candles soothed her. Brian had been exhausting. She felt relieved that he was redirected away from the idea of divorce, but Madeline sensed that her problems with Brian were just beginning. His attachment was growing. Deflecting his divorce talk was easy enough, the disturbing element was that he entertained the fantasy to the point where he told her about it. That he would even consider such a thing showed an incredible lack of judgement on his part. She was not flattered that he wanted to be with her. That was nothing new. She had lost count of the number of men who had told her throughout her life that they wanted to be with her, that they love her. Verbal declarations were nothing but empty words. True nature is revealed by what is done, not by what is said.

The only man who showed her his love with actions was Mark. He did not proclaim his love in secret whispers in the bedroom, he declared it at the altar for all to hear. Mark was so

Sins of Samcora

different from Brian. He was perfect in every way except for his brutality, and even that, she would have been willing to live with. She had just needed more time to figure him out, and how to circumvent his explosions. She knew she would have figured out a way to manage the action.

Her life was perfect until Delta came on the scene and started demanding money. That ruined everything. Mark would have never noticed how much money she siphoned off if she did not have to take so much to satisfy Delta's greed. That final fight in the kitchen should never have happened. All of her problems started when her sister came back into her life.

Madeline ached to be with Mark again the way they were in the beginning. Before it all started to unravel. Thinking about Mark intensified her deep longing for him. Did she love him? Was this what love felt like? She missed the man he was, her glorious, strong husband. He was the only person she ever met who was stronger than herself and that absolutely intoxicated her. His sex transported her. No other man could make her feel what she felt with him.

It grieved Madeline that they had no time to work out their problems, their relationship had been cut off. She had tried one final time, on a night not long ago when her desire for Mark was overwhelming. She went into his room and stood over him and studied him to see if there was anything left of who he used to be. But there was not. That body laying in the bed was not her husband. He was a thin weak shell with no fight left in him. Nothing but a veneer of a man she used to want. Her husband was dead to her.

On that day of the final confrontation, that devastating beating, he could have killed her. But now here he was like a vulnerable infant, no spark, no power. He did not survive her. No one had ever survived her and now he was no exception. Madeline utterly conquered him. He burned himself in the fire of his own violence and she wanted and waited for him to rise like a phoenix but he could not rise. He would never be able to rise because she was too strong for him now. She would keep him down, controlled, and under her will. She would press him down hard.

Madeline recognized her feelings for Mark as lust and excitement for the man he used to be. These feelings were easy to confuse for love but were not love. Compassion and mercy

Sherry Derksen

accompany love and she experienced none of those. What she had loved was the match. She had always known that she was just as powerful and violent as Mark and it was a turn on to be paired with an equal. Someone who she could not so easily manipulate. His failure to recognize her power was his misstep. His misstep had been his complete undoing. He lost and now he was lost to her.

The predator had her prey.

Back to life...

The room was brighter with the curtains pulled back. Delta opened the window inviting the warm morning air to carry in the soft sweet smell of gardenia from the garden. The fragrance of the heady blooms masked the lingering smell of antiseptics and body odour that permeated Mark's room. Morning had always been her favourite time of day and today Delta felt happier, knowing that she was going to spend it alone with Mark.

Maddy had been refusing to see Mark but even so, whenever she was in the house Delta felt on edge like she was being watched. It was always a worry that she would burst through the door at any moment and interrupt her privacy with Mark. Today she felt more relaxed knowing that Maddy would be out for the day with Brian and her time with Mark would be uninterrupted and more importantly, unmonitored.

She felt disgusted with the way Maddy was behaving, carrying on with that man, Brian. No self respecting woman would have an affair like that, especially when your own husband was convalescing in your home. Well, at least the harlot would be away for the day. With her gone Delta did not need to stress as much that Maddy would find out about the changes she had been making to Mark's care. Changes that would have infuriated her if she was aware of them.

Like the fact that Delta was waking Mark up every day now. The propofol was a nice clean drug but it was not intended for continual use. The risk of Mark getting respiratory issues from the depression of his nervous system was a major concern to Delta.

Sherry Derksen

It would be irresponsible of her to keep him drugged around the clock like Maddy wanted. It was inhumane. Besides, Maddy was not coming through on her promise that they would figure out another solution to their problem with Mark.

Delta had tried to broach the subject several times but Maddy always refused to talk about it. Except to make clear that she was in charge and it was her decision to keep Mark drugged. She was so stubborn and bossy. Delta was afraid to bring it up anymore because the last time Maddy threatened to start monitoring her activities more closely to ensure she was doing what she was told. Delta could not bear to have her private time with Mark invaded. It was easier to lie so she just told Maddy whatever she thought she wanted to hear.

Her strategy was working, Maddy rarely asked about Mark or came to see him anymore. She was too busy screwing around with her new boyfriend to care. Delta realized that Maddy was not interested in rehabilitating Mark. Her intentions were obvious, keep Mark in a coma indefinitely. Maddy had warned her that Mark was dangerous and that the both of them would only be safe from him if he was incapacitated, but she did not agree. He was in her charge, a vulnerable soul who needed her care, who needed her support. Yes, he had done some very bad things, but he has paid for that now. Doing bad things does not make you a bad person. He just had a devil in him and the situation got out of control. Maddy was living in a fantasy world. Mark needed rehabilitation. You can't do this to a person. He needed to get back to life. They all did. Whatever the cost.

Delta took another large swig from the second glass of orange juice that she had brought upstairs from the kitchen. The sparkling cut crystal glass felt satisfying and heavy in her hand, both from the quality of the glass and the liberal portion of vodka that laced her orange drink. The cool liquid had a nice bite which helped pick her up. She had felt tired and hung over again this morning from the wine she drank the prior night. She had to stop drinking the wine. It gave her a lazy, stupor kind of drunk, not the nice happy glowing drunk that hard liquor gave her. But once she had started on the bottle it was hard to put down.

She walked over to Mark's bed to stop the IV drip. She liked watching him regain consciousness, it gave her a feeling

Sins of Samcora

of hope seeing him come back to life every morning. Each time it erased some of her guilt for hurting him and maybe one morning she could come back to life too. It was her favourite thing to do, to wake him up. Keeping him drugged was against her grain. She was a nurse. A healer. It was always a risk though. She knew it. The drugs were very disorienting and Mark had been hallucinating.

When that happened in the hospital with critical care patients, they called it ICU psychosis. Delta knew it was because the drugs were interrupting his circadian rhythm. He was losing his sense of night and day and his brain was beginning to misfire. The risk of him yelling out or making noises that would alert Maddy were high, but Delta was always prepared with a tranquilizer needle ready to take him down instantly if he made too much of a ruckus. But he never did. Mark was a wonderful patient. Cooperative and compliant. He seemed to instinctively understand what was needed from him and always woke up calmly. Even though Maddy was gone for the morning Delta had her tranquilizer injection ready. If things got out of hand she had to be ready. That was just good nursing practice.

"Good morning," Delta watched Mark trying to adjust his eyes, to focus on her and his surroundings. Unsteadily, he reached his hand up to his face and felt that the nasal gastric tube that had been snaked into his body was missing.

"I took out the feeding tube already. I bet that feels better. I was thinking today you might try swallowing the normal way." Delta informed. The nasal gastric tube was usually in Mark so that Delta could feed him and give him water while he was under. Medically there was no reason why he could not swallow with it in, but it seemed so unnatural and foreign and in the way. She wanted Mark to feel normal when he was awake. It was risky each time she pulled it out. If Maddy ever noticed it was out she would know that Delta had been waking up Mark and feeding him normally. There would be no way to explain why it was out.

The tube was also part of the staging she had to do when the attending doctor arrived to check up on Mark. It was critical that there was no evidence that Mark was not really comatose. Delta always worried about Mark during those monthly visits because she had to remove the IV and propofol and instead tranquilize him with a stronger injectable drug. The potential side effects were scary and the mixture of drugs at the dosage she needed to take him down were risky, but there was no other choice. Mark had come a long way, but he was not ready yet to be trusted in the care of anyone else but her. Only she could know that he was awake again. As much as Delta feared the visits from the doctor, she was also proud when they ended as the doctor would invariably give her a compliment about the quality of care that she provided Mark. The doctor was pleased that the atrophy in Mark's muscle was minimal and that he had no bed sores from his immobility. It was unending hard work exercising him and massaging him to keep him supple, but Delta was grateful to do it. She liked the physical contact, the intimate connection of touch. Plus, the work purged her guilt. Everyone had to pay for their sins and this was the way she was paying for hers.

Delta took a basin of warm water and began to wash Mark, getting him comfortable and ready for the day with her. He said nothing all the time, just followed her with his eyes. Delta liked the silence, a welcome reprieve from a life time of irritating words and whining from Tom. Tom could not shut his mouth if his life depended on it. Mark was a very different kind of man, so refreshingly quiet. Yet, he spoke to her all the time with his eyes and his movements. When he did use words, he chose few and shared them softly and gently. Sometimes Delta felt a little foolish, like a school girl who had a crush.

Sometimes she thought she might be falling in love with Mark. Not the nasty base kind of love that dogs like Maddy and Brian were playing at, but a pure spiritual love. Her spirit brother. She did not imagine that they would ever be lovers, she did not want that for herself. But she did think that once he realized and came to appreciate all that she did for him, sacrificed for him, that they would have a lasting deep bond of love and respect. It was fully her intention to not only heal his body, but to heal his soul, purging him of the evil that was in him which had driven him to beat Maddy so viciously in the first place. Once he was purified, he would be grateful and would forgive her for her role in his injuries. Once healed, he would look back on this period and recognized that it opened him to the light.

That was how it happened for Delta. She had been purified by her experiences of fear and pain at the hands of Tom,

Sins of Samcora

Maddy, and Mark. It brought her closer to God. Now she was a more complete person, one who was not deluded by frivolity and distraction. She knew her salvation was her mission, which was to rehabilitate Mark. Mark was luckier than she had been, he at least has her to be his mentor, leading him out of his dark places into that glorious salvation. This is the true calling of people who say they love each other. They help each other purge sin and replace it with joy. Replace the devil with God and you can become whole again. Mark would rise from his sick bed a stronger and better person.

Fooled again...

      Mark was fully conscious now. His body felt heavy, stiff, and sore. He was disoriented and confused but he had enough of his wits to know he was in trouble. Big trouble. Each time that woman woke him up he was able to put more and more together. Delta. That was her name. He was not sure if he was still dreaming. His life had become an unending dream state. She had told him what happened but he could not quite remember everything. The only thing that he knew for sure was that his current circumstances had to do with Madeline. He was going to kill her and relish every moment of it. This Delta, she was crazy but she was his only link to getting out of this mess. He knew her type, she had no will, no backbone. She was merely Madeline's puppet. She was also stupid and stupid people are dangerous.

      He had to play his cards right. He tried to prop himself up on his elbows but was too weak and fell back. He felt so thin and hollowed out. The room was spinning and he had to close his eyes. He was remembering more now. Delta was drugging him. She must have been lowering his dosage because sometimes, even though he could not open his eyes or move, he could hear her. He could hear her confessing her guilt to him. He could hear the house. He could hear Madeline and Brian. His revenge would be complete after he bathed in a lake of their blood. His plans to pay back his suffering were fierce and deeply violent. He could not even sit up, how was he going to walk out of here? Mark willed life and strength to come back into his legs, into his arms, but it would not. His body was wracked in pain. Inactivity had made his muscles unimaginably

Sins of Samcora

stiff.

"Here sweetheart, let me roll the bed up for you so that you can sit up awhile. I have some food for you here to eat," Delta was in front of him again, with some soupy oatmeal sweetened with blueberry puree. She rolled up the head of the bed and propped Mark up with pillows behind his shoulders. He looked a little pale but was opening his eyes more. She could see that his dizziness was fading. She fed him and all the while Mark studied her face, trying to see the enemy and figure out his strategy.

"So weak," Mark whispered hoarsely to Delta. His throat felt parched and sore. The level of exhaustion that he felt at simply sitting up and eating was shocking. He was unused to his body failing him. All the strength he honed in his gym was gone, his cut and chiseled muscles gone, his body broken and useless to him. He could not indulge in his anger. He had to focus all his energy on clearing his head and planning a strategy to escape. Delta obviously was his ticket out. As much as he hated her, he needed to let her think that he was compliant. She had her hand on the trigger that fed him the drugs, she was the last person he intended on pissing off until he was back on his feet. It was so difficult to piece everything together. She wanted his forgiveness. She wanted to help him get better. The getting better part sounded good to him. Yes, he would forgive her, but only after his hands were around her throat and he squeezed the life out of her miserable body.

Delta poured herself another drink and sat down in the entertaining room, close to the liquor cabinet. She needed a couple drinks to take the edge off her anger. She had another fight with Maddy and she was beyond sick of it. Everyone has their limits and Delta reached hers. Maddy was just going too far. She obstinately refused to make any attempts to improve her personal moral code. She was far too interested in prostituting herself with that filthy Brian Layton. Delta told her what she was doing was wrong, told her she should break it off with Brian and act like a proper wife, but she refused. How dare she laugh at her and call her a drunken bible thumper. She was not a drunk. She could stop anytime she wanted. It was just a difficult time for her. She knew exactly what a drunk was. Her life was marred by her alcoholic husband for years and she was nothing like Tom.

Sherry Derksen

This business with Mark was far from normal. Who could have survived that kind of continual stress? It was horribly insensitive of Maddy to comment on it, knowing all she had been through. As far as being a bible thumper, well, that was a compliment. At least her soul was saved, something Maddy should be more concerned about for herself. More time thumping a bible and less time thumping Brian Layton was what that Jezebel needed!

The amber liquid burned down Delta's throat as her old comfort, that hazy numbness began to grow and relax her. She turned it over and over in her head but finally accepted that there was no hope in persuading Maddy to yield to reason. Maddy was so entrenched in her sins that she could not see the madness of what she was doing. How could a human being be so disconnected to the suffering of others? To the suffering of her own husband? Yes, Mark had done vile things, but he was a changed man now. If Maddy could only hear him speak, hear the sincerity in his voice when he prayed with her. Why could she not open her mind and heart to the possibility that God can transform lives? It was time to heal, time to repair the damage. They had been at odds too long now. They argued about everything, particularly about Mark. She was hostile and shut down any attempt to discuss the possibility of waking up Mark. There was no way out with Maddy, you cannot negotiate with bullies. Delta realized that she would have to make all the decisions about Mark by herself. All the suffering had to end. The situation had grown untenable.

Her sister was intimidating. There was no way that Delta could tell Maddy that Mark was doing so well with his rehabilitation. He was very diligent with his daily exercises, both physical and spiritual. He was working very hard on getting the strength back in his body and he was working just as hard at getting the strength back into his soul. Every time she restarted his sedation he asked her to hold off a little longer and read a few more passages from the bible. At first she thought he was just trying to avoid the sedation but now she felt ashamed of herself that she had ever thought that. Clearly he was just hungry for the word. He was renewed spiritually and he was almost ready to wake up permanently. Delta had no idea how to let Maddy know that it was time for the nightmare to end.

Sins of Samcora

Delta tugged down her tight blue jersey dress. Her pantyhose felt hot but she liked the snug feel thinking it helped flatten the look of her belly. It had been a long time since she cared about what she wore, since she felt feminine. Today was a special day. Mark was going to get up out of bed and sit in a chair to eat his breakfast. She had been standing him by the bedside for the past week and today it was time to practice walking. She set the table up only five steps away from the bed. It should be manageable. This would be a day for celebration. The first time walking since the incident. Stopping the propofol drip she knew he would rise out of his sedation soon and while waiting she adjusted the place settings on the small table that she had set up. The food was pretty simple. He was starting to have some difficulties with swallowing so she made a simple cream of wheat with maple and milk. The warm thickened cereal should feel good on his raw and irritated throat. The continual re-insertion of the feeding tube was starting to take its toll. She knew she should be leaving it in all the time but he disliked it so much. It was a small concession to help him feel more human. His voice had been so hoarse the prior day. She had to start thinking about how to inform Maddy that she was rehabilitating Mark. Maddy would not receive the news well and she did not even know where to start the conversation but Delta was determined that the drugging had to end. It was getting harder and harder to hide what she was doing. Once Maddy could see Mark's rehabilitation she would understand. Even so, the thought of Maddy's reaction filled her with dread. Best to avoid it a little longer, at least until Mark was able to walk on his own.

She felt girlish and giddy thinking about sitting down with Mark at the table and eating together like normal people do. She yearned to be normal again, have a normal life. Mark's sudden groaning drew her attention. He was coming to but having more trouble than usual. She felt bad about it, but the dosing accident had been an honest mistake. She did not remember drinking more than usual or how she had gotten confused and set the infusion rate wrong on a new bag of propofol. She was so tired lately. She realized the error a few hours later and lowered the infusion rate but his respirations had fallen to four per minute and she was not sure how long it had been that way. There were no oxygen tanks in the room to give him support so there was nothing she could do for him

Sherry Derksen

but wait it out and see what would happen. She could not call anyone for help. She would have to handle it herself. She definitely was not going to tell Maddy about it. His sedation went way too deep and Delta was not sure how long his breathing had been affected by it. She felt afraid that the hypoxia to his brain damaged him and she vowed to herself to be more careful. It had been almost a week since her mistake with the medications and Mark was still having problems fully waking up. He was so sluggish and his motor skills had deteriorated. It scared her that her drinking had interfered with her ability to do her job safely. She knew that at some point she would need to start thinking about the role that alcohol had in her life. For sure, once she and Mark were out of this house then she would quit drinking. She was determined not to end up like Tom.

"Wake up honey, wake up," Delta softened her voice and brought her mouth closer to Mark's ear. She had bathed and shaved him and he smelled so good in the cologne that she doused him with. He was getting way too thin, but he was still a gorgeous man. There were still traces of the shape of his hard muscle, the wasting of his body was not complete. She felt sinful when her mind travelled to his flat belly and lower body. She had never made love to an athletic man. She could only imagine how Mark would have been, powerful, wild, a stallion. She had never been taken and overwhelmed by a man, she only knew Tom with his fat beer belly and stinking breath. Delta retrieved her bible. She had to stop sinning and reading scriptures helped her. She decided to read aloud to him, to give him strength and hope as his mind rose out of the haze.

He felt so disoriented. Was it day, was it night? No, it had to be day, it was bright and he was only released him from his prison in the day. It was so hard to see, his eyes were sore but slowly Mark's vision came back. He was still in a twilight zone, like he was awake but dreaming. Wake up Mark! Clear your mind, he willed himself. It seemed harder to sort himself out this time. He could hear Delta sermonizing to him and in a way, it was helping him. He would pay attention to her voice and work at sorting out the words. Once he was able to make sense of what she was saying, he knew he was awake and that the dream was over.

Mark trained himself to keep his mouth shut as much as possible. It had been hard because he was outraged at his

Sins of Samcora

predicament, and also because he had been hallucinating again. He could not trust himself, nor what he heard and what he saw. His vision was beginning to sharpen and he watched Delta as huge spiders descended from the ceiling and began to drop on her head. Slowly they crawled through her hair and down onto her face. When Delta was speaking one of them scooted into her mouth while another one was hanging on to her bottom lip. What was she saying? Mark closed his eyes and told himself that there could not be any spiders, he was hallucinating again. He had to clear the fog out of his mind. After he squeezed his eyes shut, he opened them slowly but the spiders were still there. But at least he could hear better now. He recognized that he was waking up.

This time felt like he had been out much longer, but he was not sure. He felt like his entire life was a dream and he missed what it felt like to be alive. Mark knew that he could not keep on this way much longer. The drugs were going to kill him if he did not get off them soon. Mark knew that he had to be very careful with his words, his only hope was to befriend Delta and persuade her to let him go. He would say anything to her to stop the drugs. His life was a nightmare. At least she was still helping him get his strength back. Each day he had felt like he was getting stronger, but today he felt set back and was not sure why. He had to act soon, he had to escape her.

"Let me massage your legs first to get some blood flowing," Delta began. She had finished reading to him and wanted to get going. She was feeling hungry and was craving the refreshing taste of her orange juice. She cranked the bed up so that Mark was sitting upright. He was finally starting to look a little more lucid.

"We are going to have breakfast by the window today," she announced. Delta swung Mark's's legs around so that they were dangling off the bed and then she gave him instructions.

"Hold on to me," she began, her speech slipping into the rhythm of a seasoned nurse.

"I will help you lift off the bed and then we will swing around and you can take a few steps to the table. It's only a few steps away, I know you can do it. We will count then together."

"Moron," thought Mark silently to himself. Mark kept his anger reigned in, and despite his rage against Delta, he was thrilled that he was going to rise off the bed. It almost seemed to

Sherry Derksen

good to be true. His voice revealed his joy at being on his own two feet.

"Thank you Delta. OK, I am ready, one, two..." Mark hefted himself up and although he was very wobbly, he noted that he was stronger than he thought he would be. He felt ecstatic. It was pretty easy to walk over to the table as far as his legs were concerned, however, he became very lightheaded and sat down with a thud once he arrived at the chair. It was shocking how much energy it took to walk only five steps.

"Ok, breakfast time!" Delta sat beside Mark and put a napkin in his lap. Mark began to feel very weak and he leaned back in the chair and took some deep breaths. It felt so incredible to have the sunlight stream through the window onto his body that Mark groaned.

"You will be fine, Mark," Delta reassured. "Just eat your breakfast and you will start to feel better." Delta assessed Mark. He was very pale, his body was unused to his activity, but as he continued sitting his colour began to improve.

"Thank you Delta, this is just wonderful." Mark gushed unashamedly to Delta. He felt like he had hope again. He was sitting at a table, drug free, about to eat his breakfast. He had his independence back. He may have leaned on her, but he walked to this table on his own feet. He was off his death bed and he had no intention of ever going back into it. After breakfast, Mark felt even stronger. This was the first day that he felt like he had a chance of escaping and it was intoxicating. Was he strong enough to overpower Delta? Mark did not want to go back into the bed. He wanted to take his shot to escape but it was risky. Should he wait? He felt so elated he could have started laughing.

"Read to me from the bible Delta," he requested. Breakfast was over, the dishes were empty and the glasses of juice almost finished. Mark needed an excuse to keep sitting at the table, and he thought if he could get Delta reading her bible, he could buy some time. He needed time, to think and to plan. Delta looked at Mark with admiration and pleasure.

"Of course, I would love to read to you." Delta got up from her chair and retrieved the bible from the bedside table. She was so proud of him. She gave him some freedom today and he was asking her to read to him. Briefly she wondered if he was going to

Sins of Samcora

try something and now she felt ashamed that she questioned it. This morning was going better than she hoped for. He truly was rehabilitated. Delta sat back down and prepared to read.

"Could you sit a little closer beside me Delta," asked Mark. "I'm feeling weak and honestly, I feel a little more secure with you closer. I don't want to go back to the bed just yet because I'm enjoying the sunlight from the window. I was hoping you could read to me for a short while if that is all right with you?" His request seemed innocent enough and he was looking a little green around the gills. She pulled her chair in closer beside Mark, secretly thrilled that he needed her this way. She felt important and purposeful.

"Is this better? Do you feel more secure now?"

"Yes, thank you Delta, it's much better. What are you going to read to me?" Mark tried to sound as casual as he could. He had to fight down his rising excitement that the plan he devised was coming together. Delta lowered her head and began reading. After a few minutes she felt more relaxed and became absorbed in the text. So absorbed that when Mark reached forward, in her peripheral vision, she thought he was just reaching for his juice glass. She never noticed that he had grabbed the flower vase that she lovingly filled with the fresh flowers that she picked just for him. Only a split second passed before she noticed that the heavy flower vase was propelling towards her head.

In that brief moment, she managed to lift up her head and turn it away from the point of impact. The vase hit her on her lower chin. The impact was surprisingly hard and she fell back in the chair to the floor. Delta felt disoriented but did not pass out. Mark rose up from his chair and threw himself on her body. The force of his body on her took all the breath out of Delta. Mark began punching her in her face, his own face twisted into an evil expression. He had one hand on her throat and was squeezing while and the other hand was punching her. She could taste the blood from her nose draining into the back of her throat. Breathing became difficult with his fingers digging into her neck.

Her shock gave way to rage. Bastard! Delta twisted and turned her body. Mark was much larger than her but he was still weak and uncoordinated. He was trying to hold on to her but his attack was weakening and she managed to kick herself free.

She rose to her feet and ran over to the bedside table

Sherry Derksen

and began thrashing around for her needle that she preloaded with tranquilizer. Evil bastard! He tricked her and now he needs another nap, she thought coldly to herself. She was such a fool. He was just like Tom, a liar and an abuser who just wanted to take advantage of her. All she did was show him goodness and this was her reward? It was plain to see that he was exactly like Tom, incapable of change. They both were incapable of anything but cruelty. Maddy had been right about him all along.

Mark was on the floor desperately trying to get himself to his feet but he was beginning to feel lightheaded again. He seriously miscalculated how strong both he was and how resilient she was. He planned it and saw it so clear in his mind, that she would be knocked out by the vase and he would strangle her and walk or crawl out of the house. But she just did not go down. Now she was going for her damn needle. Damn it. Mark needed another plan. He would stay on his hands and knees and try to recover a bit of strength. When she came for him, he would leap forward and tackle her. He could not believe how incredibly tired he felt. He did not anticipate how quickly his strength would deplete. He had made a serious tactical error and he knew this was the only chance he would ever have to escape. He could have just laid down and passed out but he knew that would be the end of him. He would pull every ounce of his being into fighting her and surviving.

Once Delta had her needle in her hand she began to come towards Mark. She could see his plan, it was so obvious. He must not realize that he was too uncoordinated to be subtle, Delta thought to herself angrily. She came close enough to Mark so that he would spring at her and when he did, she side stepped his tackle easy enough. He landed on his face and rolled onto his side staring at her while trying to sit up. She began to advance around him. Her strategy was to keep circling around him so that he would have to keep moving himself to avoid her and he would wear himself out. He seriously overestimated his endurance she thought to herself.

She did not care where she injected him. Anywhere would be fine. She just had to tranquillize the beast. The worst part would be getting the asshole back into bed without Maddy finding out what had happened. Delta felt her blood run down her neck. She would have to assess the extent of her own injuries after she put Mark down. She did not think that her nose was broken, and she

Sins of Samcora

likely had a cut on her chin or jaw. The patch job should be easy enough and she would just tell Maddy she fell if she was questioned about it.

Maddy had been right. Mark was a dangerous man and always would be. It was his nature. He attacked her for no reason at all. Mark was fatigued from turning his body around to fend her off and it was obvious that he had no more strength to kick at her. He just laid down flat on the floor and began panting heavily. Mark was looking white and Delta could see the sweat and the tremors on him, a result from his overexertion. He had no more fight left in him. She came up beside him and bent down from the waist so she could reach his body with the needle. He was so spent he made no effort even to look at her.

He could feel the needle puncture his skin and enter his body but just before she was able to depress the plunger down on the syringe he suddenly rolled over towards her. Mark grabbed her ankle with one hand and with the other he pushed against her knee cap as hard as he could. The strength of his push was not that hard, but Delta had been off balance. The abrupt shift in her weight was too sudden and before Delta could put her other leg behind her, she found herself free falling backwards. Her hands flew up to break her fall, leaving the full hypodermic needle still sticking out of Mark's thigh. Even before Delta hit the floor, Mark grabbed the hypodermic out of his leg and plunged it into Delta's calf, depressing the plunger and driving the tranquilizer into Delta's body. Mark could feel the moment when Delta went unconscious, and panting heavily he let go of her ankle. As Mark tried to sit up his head began to swim and he knew he was going to pass out. He laid back down quickly and rolled over on his side trying to stay alert. The room was spinning around and just before he passed out he saw his salvation. Delta's cell phone on the floor.

Help for the helpless...

"Did you see the look on their faces?" laughed Brian as he pulled his sleek blue Ferrari up to Madeline's house. Madeline was sitting beside him, luxuriating in the supple black leather seat. They had just come from the winners circle at the track where his horse Fastblast won his first major race.

"No one believed in me, or in Fastblast, but I knew it. I just knew it!" Brian pounded the steering wheel, punctuating his statements. It felt good to be successful again. All the money he had spent had been worth it for the top trainers and vets to get Fastblast into condition. Brian knew in his gut that his horse was something special. The gossip saying that he had made a bad decision when he first bought the horse would end, replaced by tales of his victory and shrewdness. It had bad health, but its lineage was extraordinary. Brian had a feeling in his gut about that horse, and it paid off. Now everyone was celebrating with him, telling him that his instincts were right about Fastblast.

"I'm really pleased for you Brian," Madeline responded. "You certainly know your horses, and you certainly know how to make a winner." Madeline could not care less about horses but it did amuse her to see Brian so happy. There had been too much tension in the house with Delta moping around and she was so sick of her sister's drunken reformation lectures. Life had begun to feel heavy. Madeline yearned to feel happy and carefree again even if it required a few sacrifices.

If she had to have this arrangement with Brian, she decided that she was going to make the best of it. It was nice to

Sins of Samcora

have a little bit of fun for a change. She found she enjoyed the track, the excitement of the races and the interesting mix of people. There was a lot of old money and old men who were looking for new money and young partners to inflate their bank accounts and egos. A fertile field for her to network and find another man when the inevitable happened and she had to break it off with Brian.

Brian still entertained occasional thoughts about divorcing Anne so he could spend more time with her but he did seem to be backing off that idea so perhaps she could extend her affair with him longer. Perhaps he was finally beginning to accept the practicality of remaining married. They still had more than enough time together. Too much time as far as Madeline was concerned.

"Yes, I do know my horses," agreed Brian. " I also know my women,"Brian gazed at Madeline appreciatively. She was gorgeous and he loved the way she kept herself fit. He leaned over and pulled Madeline toward himself and kissed her.

"I think we should go in the house and have a little celebration over my victory," Madeline was not in the mood for sex but she knew it was an important component in keeping Brian on the hook and under control. It was not that she hated sex, in fact she liked it. But it had no emotional connection for her. It was little more than an activity, albeit a pleasurable one, and she was feeling tired and drained from the racetrack. Madeline was shrewd enough, however, to not let Brian see that she was viewing his attentions as an inconvenience.

"I think a celebration is in order," Madeline returned his kiss slower, deeper. Brian's breathing quickened and he leaned back in the seat, revelling in Madeline's attentions. His need was immediate, but he wanted to prolong his pleasure. Abruptly, Brian pulled away and opened his door. He wanted to continue in bed. Madeline followed him as they made their way into the house.

Brian held the door open for Madeline as they entered the foyer. He wanted to grab her right there on the landing, but he was forced to behave. He knew the drill. Madeline refused to make love anywhere except her bedroom. She was too afraid that Nurse Delta or any of the household staff would accidentally walk in on them. It would look improper. Madeline also did not want any gossip about their affair to start circulating. Brian could appreciate

Sherry Derksen

the reasoning, and he actually began to like her little rule. Knowing he was not allowed to touch her in any way until they were upstairs added to his excitement and anticipation. At the top of the stairs, Madeline looked backwards at Brian and motioned for him to stop. She made him watch as her eyes travelled down his body and lingered. Teasingly, she began walking backwards and signalled him to slowly follow as she unbuttoned her shirt and opened the garment up, keeping her eyes steady on him. Reaching behind herself, she grabbed the door knob to her room and as she opened the door she let her shirt slip off her shoulders and fall to the ground, fully exposing herself to his view. She reached her arms above her head and arched her back, stretching herself and posing for him, enticing his attentions. Brian could no longer stand the restraint, the seduction inflaming his desire anew, he wanted her now. He was so intent on Madeline that he almost missed the groan.

"What was that?" Brian stopped in his tracks thinking that he heard a man groaning. "I heard something." Madeline felt instantly cold. She heard it too, the sound was loud and came from Mark's room.

"I didn't hear anything, except you, lover." Madeline tried to get the moment back, tried to divert Brian's attention. It was obvious she had heard the groaning too but she did not know what else to say. There was nothing to say. She had to let Brian have a moment to process and hope that he would dismiss it in his mind and come to her. "Please, shut up Mark." Madeline silently willed as she wondered where Delta was and why Mark was making so much noise. It was difficult to contain spread of panic in her body as she watched for cues from Brian. Brian walked down the hall and stood outside of Mark's door, listening for more sound, unsure of what he thought he heard. Madeline stood and watched Brian, waiting for him to move. Brian was about to dismiss the sound and then Mark groaned again, this time louder. There was no denying the sound cutting through the silence.

"What the hell, Madeline, is that Mark?" Without waiting for a reply, Brian grabbed the handle and barged into Mark's room. He was not prepared for the sight he saw. Nurse Delta was lying on the floor flat on her back, her face bloodied. Mark was laying on the floor beside her on his side trying to crawl towards her. Mark looked up into Brian's eyes.

Sins of Samcora

"Help," Mark croaked out weakly.

Monster in the making...

It had been two painful hours but at least Brian did not call the police. He lifted Mark onto the bed and adjusted him. Madeline put a pillow under Delta's head and covered her with a blanket. She was still out cold. After removing the syringe from her calf, Madeline had taken a cloth and cleaned up Delta's face. She had a split lip and a cut in her cheek. Delta looked like she was breathing fine, in fact, she just looked like she was sleeping. What had she been up to? Madeline saw Delta's cell phone on the floor and discretely picked it up and put it in her pocket. Brian did not see her do it but she was sure Mark did.

It took Mark a long time to get his story out. He was weak and disoriented. His confusion was deep and Madeline was not sure how much Mark actually realized about what was happening to him. Mark's accusations were directed exclusively at Delta. Did he remember what had happened that night in the kitchen? What did he believe Madeline knew and what her involvement was? He was clever and dangerous but he had been drugged for so long. What did that do to his memory? To his brain?

Secretly Madeline had wanted Mark to rise from his drugged prison and she was excited that he found a way to do so. She also knew that she could not let it happen. It was impossible to move on from where they had both been. She wanted to be challenged by him again, but disappointingly, she knew he was not up to the match. Already she was thinking about solutions to her new situation. He was saying nothing that was implicating her. She realized that she had to deal with both Mark and Delta. Clearly her

Sins of Samcora

foolish sister had been up to no good and Madeline would need to press her down along with Mark.

Brian was in disbelief as Mark detailed his struggle with Delta and how she ended up being tranquilized with the needle that was intended for him. Mark looked with steely eyes at Madeline but was very careful not to accuse her. He had seriously misjudged her capacity for treachery. He wanted her to think that he thought she was innocent. It was far too dangerous for him to let her realize that he knew she plotted with Delta to keep Mark drugged and pretend that he was still in a coma. If he let her believe that he considered her innocent, then he might have a chance out of this mess. He needed to make sure the gold digger felt safe. Mark was also uncertain of the relationship between Brian and Madeline. He thought he heard them together, heard their sex, however, with all the drugs that had been pumped into him, he could not be sure. His head felt thick. Mark and Brian went way back. Brian was not stupid enough to throw their business relationships and interests away for a lay. Brian would help him. He owed him. He still owed his father. Brian would be nothing without Elliot and Mark.

"Unbelievable, Mark," Brian shook his head. This was quite a tale. "Why would Nurse Delta want to keep you drugged?" Brian could not figure it out. What was in it for her? He had met Nurse Delta in passing but never really spoke to her. His impression was that she was unremarkable. Brian had to admit, the first thought that ran through his mind was that Madeline was somehow involved. It would be convenient for her to keep Mark out of the way, but Mark did not accuse her. Plus, she seemed just as shocked as he was to see Mark awake. If Madeline knew what was going on here, that Mark was being sedated against his will, she would have never risked bringing Brian up to her room so many times. Any time, he could have heard something like he did now. It just did not make any sense. Madeline was not devious enough to do such a thing, he would have seen it in her somehow, Brian reasoned. Madeline was too naive, too innocent.

"No, Madeline is not smart enough to fool me," Brian decided. "Madeline's talents are in the bedroom." Brian dismissed her potential involvement and turned his thoughts back to the motive of Nurse Delta.

"Mark, is it possible that Nurse Delta did this to you

to keep her job here? She gets paid a very high salary to look after you."

"I don't know, I don't care. That can be dealt with later. Just call me an ambulance, Brian!" although Mark's voice was thin and shaky Brian could still detect the authoritarian tone in him.

"Hang on there Mark," Brian instructed. "I'm going to help you and get you out of here." It must have been a nightmare. Being incapacitated and drugged. Feeling helpless and not being able to ask for help. Brian shivered at the horror he thought that Mark had endured. "I'm going to call an ambulance, I'll be right back," Brian reassured. Brian left the room and motioned for Madeline to follow him.

Outside the room Brian turned to Madeline, looking intently into her face, searching for truth. "I'm going to ask you only once Madeline, did you know anything about this," Brian felt he already knew the answer but he just had to ask. He had to see her expression. As a judge, he prided himself on being able to read people, on knowing when they were telling the truth or not. Madeline felt trapped. It was beginning to unravel, but she had no choice but to play it out to the bitter end. There was no point in showing your cards until you absolutely had to.

"No, Brian how could you even ask that?" Madeline was upset at the current events and began to cry. Her rare tears were honest, but the intent behind them was not. Madeline knew she had to put on a believable performance which would require tears. Her fear of being found out gave her enough emotion to create her display. She tilted her head up defiantly and gazed directly at Brian, knowing that he would not see the guilt in her because she did not feel guilty. She missed Mark, but she had never felt guilty about him. He had hurt her. Her actions were for survival. She had entered the marriage intending to be a dutiful wife and only carve off a little of his wealth for herself for when it was her time to go. It was an honest transaction that his brutality interrupted. He deserved what he got.

"I'm sorry baby," Brian moved forward and scooped Madeline in his arms. "I know this is shocking for you. But now I need you to trust me. You don't cry anymore, sweetheart. I will take care of everything for you like I always do. Listen to me carefully now, I want you to go to your room and wait for me. Do you think

Sins of Samcora

you can do that," Brian spoke gently to Madeline. It irritated her that he was talking to her in a tone that made her feel like she was some backward child, but she could sense a shift in him. He had some kind of plan and she was not sure what it was.

Madeline did not know what would happen next. Her only play at the moment was to listen to Brian and make it look like she was cooperative. He was holding all the cards now and she had to wait and see how he played his hand. At least he was not accusing her. At least he was not calling the police. After all, he had an interest in how this situation turned out as well.

"Yes, Brian, I'll do what you say." Madeline tilted her face up to Brian and tried to look reverent. She wanted him to believe that she had utter trust in him. Brian's heart melted. He lifted Madeline up and carried her into her bedroom and laid her down on the bed. He felt fiercely protective and was not going to let anything happen to her.

"You stay here until I get you, no matter how long it takes, ok?" Brian spoke in a deep and serious manner, a tone she had not heard in him before. He was definitely up to something new. Madeline knew better than to defy him.

"O.k.," Madeline agreed. Brian kissed Madeline on her eyes, "Don't cry anymore honey, I will take care of all of this for us. I love you."

"I love you too." Easy words thought Madeline.

Brian backed out of Madeline's room and quietly closed the door. Madeline sat up in the bed. She had no choice. She decided to do as he said. She would wait it out and see how he was going to handle it. At least now she could stop trying to cry.

"Unbelievable." Brian was trying to process all he had heard. He could not even imagine what it must have felt like, what Mark had been through. It was akin to living murder. He agreed with Mark, however, that it was not good to call the police. There was too much complexity involved and the police might get too interested in some of their other activities. The situation was better handled in house. When you handled things directly it gave more flexibility in your arrangements.

Brian went downstairs and poured himself a drink, standing in the back entertainment room and staring out past the Ridgeland Lake. It was a peaceful view and he needed a mental

Sherry Derksen

break to calm down and think everything through very carefully. He had to weigh the options and come to a decision. What was he going to do? Mark had to get to the hospital or at least have some kind of medical intervention. That would be the right thing to do. That was exactly what he would have done a few months ago before becoming addicted to Madeline and the money.

What would Mark do once he recovered and saw how much money Brian had taken? Even though Mark disagreed, Mark did owe him some support for all the legal favours he had done, especially the Joan Howard favour. Even so, Brian could admit that he took way more than what he could actually justify. Plus, he was not in a position to pay it back anytime soon. It felt so good to have access to cash flow to be able to look after his horses properly. His stable was not full of old farm nags, his animals were top bred. Fastblast was an outstanding beast and worth every penny that he invested in him. His horses gave him tremendous pleasure and happiness.

Madeline gave him happiness too, she made him feel young. His passion for life was renewed. How could he just give that all up? Mark was territorial and their relationship would never survive his infidelity with Madeline. If he saved Mark he would be condemning himself. He knew that after Mark recovered he would be relentless in finding out every last detail of what happened to him. It was only a matter of time until Mark found out about the money and that he was bedding his wife. Mark being awake was a problem.

The incredible deception of Nurse Delta was hard to believe, but Brian appreciated the ingenuity of her plan, it was a damn good idea. Undoubtedly she could be hired to continue on drugging Mark, however, if she was capable of doing that on her own accord, then what else was she capable of? If she so easily turned against her employer, Mark and Madeline, then she could not be trusted to turn against him. Plus she was clearly incompetent proved by her laying unconscious on the floor. Suddenly Brian knew what he had to do.

Madeline did not understand why people spent so much time entrenched in their feelings of guilt. She could not honestly say she felt guilty about anything. Decisions she made,

Sins of Samcora

both good and bad were the response to events in her life. Logical decisions that supported her survival in what sometimes felt like a harsh world. It seemed obvious what Brian's response to the situation should be yet he needed time. "Time for what," thought Madeline? To decide Mark's fate, his fate, her fate? What presumption to think the decision was his alone. There was no point in doing anything until he revealed his position. Madeline was not too worried he would call the police. After he worked through his shock he would see the obvious. He would see for himself that he was in too deep to let Mark walk away. Madeline simply rested and waited for Brian to return.

"Madeline, you may not understand why I needed to do what I did, but my arrangements are for your protection." Brian's tone was serious, his voice lowered conspiratorially.

"Ok," Madeline spoke cautiously. Where was he was leading? Brian was not sure how to tell her what he had done. He had no idea what her reaction would be, so he decided to push ahead and tell it plainly.

"I've taken care of the nurse, she will not be a problem any more." Madeline sat up straighter. Brian had no clue that Delta was her sister. Even though they were not close she was still her sister, her blood.

"What have you done Brian?" Madeline waited for it.

"I have friends in low places," Brian explained. "When you are a judge, you have friends from all walks of life. I happen to have a few friends who owe me favours."

"Is she dead?" Delta was her sister. Madeline felt her spirit of vengeance stirring. It was a beast that was best left sleeping.

"No, no, nothing like that," reassured Brian. Did she really think him capable of that? Was he capable of that? Madeline slowly let her breath out.

Brian continued explaining himself. "I like to think of it as poetic justice. She drugged Mark for all these months and now it's her turn. She's being shot up with heroin. It won't take long to addict her and I will be keeping track of her. If she tries to make problems then I'll get her picked up for drug trafficking and drug use. A bit of jail time will straighten out her attitude. Trust me, no

Sherry Derksen

one believes junkies or anything they have to say. I can arrange to have her case put onto my docket and will send her away for a long, long time. She won't bother us again. I suspect that after she is a junkie, that she will just drift away on her own and we will never hear from her again. After all, who is she going to tell? What can she say? That she was drugging her employer?" Brian seemed satisfied with himself, he had it all figured out.

"What about Mark?" Madeline could pretty much guess what happened.

"Come and see," Brian was beginning to sound more upbeat than Madeline thought he should. Did he not see her as delicate, vulnerable? Was he not worried about her sensitivities? Their relationship just made a big evolution and Madeline wondered if he even realized it. He took her by the hand and walked her out of her room and into Mark's room. Everything was as it was before. The furniture was straightened up. Delta's blood was wiped off of the floor and Mark was laying on the bed with an IV in his arm and a bag of propofol slowly dripping into his vein.

"Mark is back to sleep and that's the way he must stay. But this time, instead of outsiders, we need to do this ourselves. The less people involved the better. Mark is dangerous to you. To us." Brian felt vulnerable. Would she understand? Does she want him or Mark? Would she call the police?

That was it. He laid it all out. If she truly loved him, then she must understand that this was for the best. Mark would make an example out of both of them. There would be no divorce. What Mark did to Joan Howard would pale in comparison to what he would do to Madeline. There was no other way to keep both Madeline safe and the money flowing. There was no money without Madeline. That damn iron clad prenup took care of that. He was boxed into a corner. Brian studied her face carefully, searching for reassurance. Did she think he was a monster?

Madeline could not believe what was happening. Brian fixed everything. It was back to where it should be. Madeline was not thrilled with what was happening to Delta but she could appreciate that it was a good and clever solution. After all, Delta was not dead. That was all that really mattered. Madeline would figure out a way to help Delta later on when it was safer to act.

"It was the only choice, Brian," Madeline put her

Sins of Samcora

hands on Brian's shoulders. "When I was waiting here for you, all I could think about was how afraid I was of Mark. I've never told you but he was a brutal husband. You are the one I love." Madeline stood up on her tiptoes and kissed Brian roughly on his lips, daring him to reciprocate. He grabbed her hair at the back of the head and held the kiss deeper and harder than even he intended. He felt bold, and intoxicated, standing in the room kissing Madeline while Mark was laid out ten feet away, oblivious to what was happening. Now it was all his, Madeline and the money.

Things were different and he liked it. They were married by their complicity. Now, she was more his than if she were his wife. Brian began stripping off her clothes, tearing the delicate garments away from her body until she stood before him, naked. He knew he was being too aggressive, too domineering but he could not stop himself. His emotions were running too high. He spun her around, wordlessly forcing her on the floor and claiming her with no tenderness or preparation. The only sounds were their gasping and grunting, and the clashing of their bodies. After a few moments Brian realized that Madeline was meeting him in his animalistic frenzy, that she too was seeking release in their violent consummation which ended shortly in an overwhelming release which they would both remember as the best of their relationship.

Evolution of an affair...

It had been a month since Brian had discovered Mark. Madeline did not enjoy giving Mark his medicine, but it no longer bothered her. She was feeling insulated to the reality of what was happening to her husband and to herself. It was difficult to believe that it was possible to keep a person drugged that long. Brian enlisted the help of a doctor that he acquitted two years ago in a particularly nasty malpractice suit. She never knew his real name, Brian only referred to him as the Doctor but she thought she heard Brian call him Doug once. All she knew about him was that he was a prior heroin addict and if it were not for Brian, he would have lost his license to practice and would have been in jail. The Doctor was now in charge of Mark's health, which was a relief to Madeline because she did not have to worry about the hospital's assigned Doctor showing up for his monthly inspections. She had asked about the new drugs that Mark was now on and he had told her that Mark could be on them for years.

When Madeline inquired if the drugs would affect his brain permanently, the doctor simply replied "Does it matter?" She decided it did not. Madeline had noticed that Mark's body was beginning to curl up as the atrophy accelerated in his muscles. The contracture would continue to twist him up if his muscles were not stretched, massaged, and exercised regularly. Delta had done a wonderful job of keeping Mark supple, but with her gone, Madeline could not be bothered. She did not care if his muscles shortened and deformed him. The thought of touching him was revolting to her. Brian arranged for a rotating casual group of care workers to come

Sins of Samcora

in to clean up and look after Mark, thinking that this arrangement would raise less suspicions and eliminate the risk of another opportunist like Delta. Brian had been right, there were no comments or issues raised from any of the workers, but the drawback was that the care Mark received was inferior.

One evening when Madeline had gone into the room to change Mark's medicine bag, she noticed that the day worker had laid Mark onto his side. He was propped up by pillows and his blanket and hospital gown were pulled away, exposing his buttocks. Madeline's initial reaction was anger, the workers should have more respect than to lay her husband out naked. Her fury quickly abated when she looked down and saw the raw ulcerations from Mark's bed sores. Madeline averted her eyes and tried to calm her gag response. She changed out his medicine bag as quickly as she could and exited the room.

Under Brian's guidance, she secured a declaration of Mark as her legal dependent. She now had full unrestricted control over all decisions and assets. Brian structured her finances so that it no longer mattered if Mark was alive or dead, she would still be financially autonomous. She should have felt relieved that any reliance she had on Mark to stay alive was no longer needed. Yet, as much as she despised looking at what Mark had become, she wanted him to remain alive. She loved the memory of what he used to be and it frustrated her that Mark had been unable to survive her. As long as he lived, she could continue to fantasize that he would rise from the ashes and become the man he once was. She missed his intensity, his sheer male force. She liked that she was able to utterly subdue and control his power. It was exciting to think she had almost met her match. The challenge was over, he was withering away.

The more time Madeline spent with Brian, the more she missed Mark. Brian was so inferior. He believed that Madeline was innocent in everything, firmly attaching the blame of Mark's situation on Delta. Foolish man, she thought to herself. She could never respect a man like Brian. Men like him only felt strong when they thought everyone else around them were weak. Madeline tried a few times to find out where Delta was, but Brian staunchly refused to tell her. The final time she quizzed him about it he had gotten angry and told her never to ask again. She could have respected him more if he would not tell her because he was determined to keep the secret to himself. But his excuse was not self protection, it was that he wanted to protect Madeline. It annoyed her, him thinking that she was unable to bear the details of his treachery with Delta while he could blind himself to what he was doing to Mark.

Delta was feeling less important to Madeline now anyway. After all, it was she who began the entire cascade of events ending with both their current situations. Delta initiated her fate by inserting herself into Madeline's life and blackmailing her for money. Delta would just have to figure out how to deal with her own circumstances, just as Madeline always had to deal with her own life. Right from the beginning Delta had her own agenda, even if she did not recognize it in herself. Now Delta was experiencing the consequences of her decision to cross Madeline when she tried to rehabilitate Mark in secret.

Madeline was very aware that Brian also had an agenda. He wanted what had belonged to Mark. But he was not Mark, he was not clever enough to handle all that Mark had created. Like Delta, he would come to enjoy the consequences of his decisions as well. It seemed like everyone in Madeline's life, except Mark, had an agenda which included bleeding her. She could accept a certain level of extortion from people, whether it be for money, sex, or relationships. She considered life to be symbiotic, a certain amount of interdependence was healthy and interesting. But Brian and Delta had both gone too far. They moved from symbiotic to parasitic. She was tired of the presence of the both of them in her relationship with Mark. She was beginning to feel like she used to when she was younger and living in Samcora, just before she ran away. The encroachment on her life and spirit was too much. She was going to figure out a way to reclaim her autonomy.

Payback...

"I have to go, I will see you there in two hours". Brian hated having to break off his conversation with Madeline, but his other line was ringing and he could see on his call display that it was a client that he had been trying to connect with since the prior day. After dealing with his business, he hung up the phone and leaned back in his chair. He was at his office and it was still only ten in the morning, but it felt like it should have been closer to five. It felt increasingly harder to focus at work. The familiarity of his old routines were becoming stifling. He wanted to be with Madeline, or at the stable with his horses. Brian could not remember when life had felt so good, when everything was finally going his way. He had reached a level of relative contentment, a place where he never imagined he could be. When he thought about it, Madeline had been right. It was not a good idea to dissolve his marriage to Anne. Brian was pretty sure that Anne did not know about his affair but she had been changing. Whether she could feel the distance that had been growing between them, or she had just decided to reinvigorate their relationship, he was not certain. Whatever was driving her was definitely getting his attention. She had not lost that much weight, but he could see that at least she was trying to improve her health. She was fixing herself up much better and had started to dress noticeably sexier. They had a long way to go, but he was starting to think about her, almost care about her. She was his wife and would always be his wife and she was beginning to excite him. Brian felt conflicted at first, feeling somehow loyal to Madeline. But Anne is the mother of his children and would always be present in his life.

Sherry Derksen

Besides, Brian admitted to himself, it was exciting to go from one woman to another. Not so long ago, he wanted nothing other than to be with Madeline only, but now he found he could not choose. He wanted them both. Both of them together made the perfect woman for him. Anne was loyal and dependable. Madeline, pure adrenaline and lust and came with a large bank account. Brian looked at his watch. He had a long time to wait before his rendezvous with Madeline, he might as well try to focus and get some work done.

Noon time had finally arrived and Brian navigated his car to the address that Madeline had given him. He liked role playing games with Madeline and sometimes they would meet in hotel rooms or bars. But this time, Madeline had given an apartment address to meet at for their tryst. Brian replayed their earlier phone conversation in his mind, allowing his imagination to wander and his arousal to build.

"I wanted something new, lover," Madeline's smooth voice gave no clues as he questioned her on her unusual choice of venue. "I have something different planned for you, something you're going to love, something we have talked about." Madeline teased, sounding sexy and mysterious. Brian could hear the lust in her voice and his interest was piqued. What did she plan for him, he wondered? Madeline was fantastic at sex play. She was willing to do anything he wanted and together, they had played out many of his fantasies. Fantasies that he was afraid to tell Anne about, lest she think of him as deviant or perverted.

"What did you have in mind?" Brian did not really want to know. Half of the excitement was the surprise.

"Come and see," Madeline was teasing him.

He had a surprise for her too, a leather rope and a neck belt that he was going to bind her with. Madeline was a strong woman and he immensely enjoyed subduing her. She seemed to like rough play. That was something he knew he would never get Anne to do. He was really going to enjoy the afternoon. Brian found the apartment and it was only when he was almost at the door that he realized there was something very familiar about the address. This was the same apartment block that Mark had assaulted Joan Howard at. It was a different apartment though. The strange coincidence mildly bothered Brian, but it did not dampen his enthusiasm to see what Madeline had waiting for him inside. He would ask her later

Sins of Samcora

why she chose this apartment, but for now, it did not matter. What mattered right now was what was going to happen inside the room and the heat in his pants. He knocked on the door, feeling the familiar surge of anticipation. The door had not been properly shut and it slowly swung open from his knocking. He stepped into the apartment and quickly surveyed it. The interior was unfurnished and standing in the middle of the living room was Madeline, stark naked with her hands behind her back. She looked primal, wild. Brian shut the door behind him and locked it. He could feel his erection rising looking at his naked lover. He still did not know the theme of her game, but it was starting pretty good. She did not speak to him, only looked at him, wide eyed and innocent. She reminded him of that night he took her forcefully on the floor, the night that he discovered what was happening to Mark. As Brian began slowly walking over to Madeline, he used one hand to loosen his belt and unzip his pants while the other hand was holding his leather rope. Excitedly he was trying to decide which game he wanted to play, if he would tie her up with the rope, or if he would whip her with it. When he was a foot away from her he stopped and leaned forward to give her a greeting kiss, but before he reached her lips he stopped abruptly. "What was going on?" He felt suddenly confused by a sharp pain and a horrible pressure in his abdomen. He looked down and there was the hilt of a knife sticking out of his stomach. What the hell? He looked into Madeline's face but he could read nothing there. Her face was expressionless and stone cold. Brian felt his legs buckle beneath him. He felt so strange and knew that Madeline had cut into his abdominal aorta and he was bleeding to death. He was too stunned to process what was happening and at the last second before he blacked out he felt a rush of horror that he did not have enough time to ask God to forgive him for all he had done. Brian lay crumpled on the floor dead, and Madeline looked at him dispassionately. Now that it was done, she just wanted to get in the shower and wash any traces of him off. After Brian fell the blood began to bypass the hilt of the knife and pulsate out in tandem with his final heart beats, slowing down as his blood volume began to lower. She did not think it would spurt out of his abdomen so far. Murder was so unpredictable. No matter how well you plan there always seems to be some surprise. She was glad she had the foresight to worry about blood splatter on herself and had taken off

Sherry Derksen

all her clothes. But first she had to take care of some other business. "It's ok to come out now, sweetheart." Madeline called her friend who was waiting in the bedroom.

"I've taken care of the bad man for you". Slowly the door to the bedroom opened and Joan Howard had stuck her head out. She knew that evil man. He was responsible for hurting her along with Mark. He had sent her to jail when she did nothing wrong and where horrible things had happened to her.

"Come and see, Joan," encouraged Madeline softly, tenderly. Joan tentatively came out of the room and Madeline pulled the knife out of Brian's stomach and passed it to her. Joan took the knife in her hand and knelt down beside the dead body of Brian and began talking to him. Madeline walked to the bathroom and washed the blood off of herself in the shower and put her clothes back on. When she emerged she saw that Joan was still sitting beside Brian and she was rocking herself back and forth, but now she was covered in his blood like she had been rolling around in it. Madeline noted that the knife was now sticking out of Brian's chest where Joan must have put it. Madeline thought that it was sort of funny in a gruesome way, that Joan was sticking him like he was a piece of meat she was checking for tenderness. Madeline thought briefly that perhaps she should dispose of Joan as well, but it was clear that Joan was deranged. She was deep into her psychosis and with her history, even if she was able to figure out what had really happened, who would believe her? There was no logic in connecting Madeline to Joan and Joan's apparent murder of Brian. No one had seen Joan come to Madeline and Mark's house three months earlier. Madeline recalled how grateful she felt that Delta had not seen Joan, that she was upstairs in the room with Mark, spinning in her obsession over him and drinking herself into a stupor. Joan was clearly psychotic and she was looking for Mark. She wanted to kill Mark, but there was no way that Madeline was going to allow that. Mark was hers and she would decide his fate, not some psychotic from his past. At the time when she first encountered Joan, Madeline still needed Mark to be alive and Brian had not finished getting her financial affairs in order. No, Joan would not be killing anyone just yet.

Madeline had always been aware of Joan. She was not about to lose track of that wild card. Always know the competition

Sins of Samcora

and your enemies. It was important to understand the type of women that Mark had been attracted to before she targeted him and Madeline knew Joan was the last regular girlfriend before herself. Overall Madeline was unimpressed. Joan had little to offer Mark besides her physical beauty. She clearly had limited intellect if she thought that getting pregnant would ensnare Mark. Capturing a man like him required significant more subtlety and nuance. She always believed that it was Mark who assaulted Joan, even before she experienced Mark's violence herself. Once she found out that it was Brian who was the judge at Joans trial she was convinced of the truth of it. Madeline had no sympathy for Joan. She had made her play for Mark and failed because she did not understand him. There was no risk of Mark and Joan ever becoming a couple again. Even so, Joan continued to be a threat because she was crazy. Madeline knew about her brain injury, her hospitalization, and incarceration. Her desire to avenge.

Joan had come to the house and it was lucky that Brian was not there at the time. She was deranged and standing in the foyer she threatened and cried and flailed around with her thin arms. It took little effort during the scuffle to subdue Joan. Her neck was so thin that Madeline's hands easily wrapped around it to squeeze off the air until Joan passed out. Madeline stopped herself and left Joan crumpled on the floor until she revived. When she did revive, Joan continued sitting on the floor, defeated and mumbling about getting justice. It was at that moment that Madeline formulated her plan. She would give Joan the justice she was looking for.

Madeline thought it would be more difficult to contain Joan in the apartment that she rented for her than it was. She was surprisingly malleable and easy to direct. Joan never left the apartment, always sitting in the same corner of the bedroom, rocking back and forth faithfully waiting for Madeline's daily visits when she brought food and encouraged her plan to punish Brian and Mark. The routine seemed to bring a sense of stability to Joan. Plus, Joan did not seem to notice how much more she was sleeping, oblivious to the sedatives that Madeline put in her food. Joan remained controlled and complacent. Although she was firmly fixated on both Mark and Brian she agreed that Brian would be the first to pay.

Sherry Derksen

Sedatives. There were not that many left. Madeline had used the same pills when she sedated Delta that night Tom came to the garage. What did Delta think she was going to accomplish by paying off Tom? That would have only whetted his appetite for more. He would have dug his hooks in and never let go. That night that Madeline killed him by pumping all that booze into his stomach through the nasal gastric tube was a night of justice and Madeline could not bring herself to feel sorry about it in any way.

She did not feel bad about Brian. He was a parasite. Madeline had gone over to Joan's a couple of hours before Brian had arrived, and had made her phone call to him on her cell, allowing Joan to hear her. She explained to Joan that she would entice Brian in, and then when he was in she would call her out of the bedroom to do what she wanted with him. Madeline had no intention of letting Joan attack Brian. She was far to weak and unpredictable. Brian would have easily overpowered her. Madeline wanted quick and clean. Joan was only necessary to take the fall for disposing of Brian. She was so unstable that she probably would think she did it anyway.

"Good-by Joan, honey," Madeline whispered in her direction as she left the apartment and locked it behind herself. Stepping out into the hall she briefly wondered if she should call the police herself. But no, the incident will be discovered soon enough, Madeline decided. Joan will make a fuss or try to leave, or the stink of Brian will alert the neighbours in a few days. Either way, it did not matter to her. Joan's fingerprints were all over the knife, and she had all kinds of motive. It was the best thing for Joan anyway, reasoned Madeline to herself. She would be convicted and sent to a locked psychiatric facility. There she would receive the help that she needed, the help that until now, society had been unwilling to give her.

Sins of Samcora...

Back at the mansion, Madeline took another long hot shower. It felt good to be in her house and to feel clean. Now with Brian, Delta, and Tom all out of the way she could begin to relax and enjoy her home. It was just her and Mark, the way it should have been all along. Although it would never be the way it was before at least they were alone again. Bound in their marriage to each other until death do they part.

Everything bad that happened to Madeline had its roots in Samcora. Roots like Delta and Tom who slithered up ruining her perfect life with Mark and setting the stage for her oppression by Brian. She would bear no guilt for her decision to cut those roots down and survive the toxicity. Brian, Tom and Delta all chose to encroach on her and any sins against them were not hers to bear, they were the sins of Samcora.

There were only two loose ends to deal with. She had to eventually find Delta but there was no urgency. Delta was effectively silenced and could say nothing without implicating herself. Delta's word against the word of an upstanding citizen like Madeline, a loving wife who selflessly cares for her comatose husband would hold no weight.

Madeline considered her second loose end, Tom's camera. It was evidence. She walked downstairs and took the camera out of the wall safe and erased all the pictures he took. She had almost cleared the pictures as soon as she had taken the camera from Tom but something inside of her said to wait. It was never good to move too fast. She had to think about the implications of every move she made. But now, it was clear that there was no purpose for any of the pictures so Madeline wiped out all the memory and was about the throw the camera away. Before depositing it into the trash she changed her mind and decided that she would keep it. It would make a good memento. Besides, it took great pictures.

Epilogue

The pain was excruciating. She would have given anything for another hit. She needed to shoot up so bad, but he would not let her. Stopping her, he was causing her pain. Who was he? Why was he hurting her? He said he wanted to help her but she did not want his help. He had tricked her into coming to his shack. He said they would get high together and now she was trapped by him. He refused to give her what she needed. She wanted that magic that erased her mind, that took her to sweet oblivion. But he would not listen to her, or be moved by her need.

"You are stronger than this," he said. She hated him and his preaching. Just let her be. She did not want to be strong, she did not want to be saved. Just let her die in peace. In the fog of her drug dependence she lost her will and she did not care. All she wanted was the glow of her poison. Her horse. Her meth. Either would do. It hurt so bad, Delta felt herself drowning.

He watched Delta's raging and exhaustion as she slipped into sleep. Or was it unconsciousness? He was never sure. She was so hard to rouse and he was afraid that she may not rouse again and die here on his bed. He hoped she would stay unconscious for a while to make it easier to let the drugs pass through her as he starved her need. It was time that she needed, rest to regain any strength she possessed.

He had taken her to his cabin. Well, if you could call it a cabin. It was really just a shack where he stayed when he went fishing. But it was far away from the city and from people and he could be alone with Delta to help her. She could scream as loud and

Sherry Derksen

as long as she needed and no one would bother them. It broke his heart to see her. He had her chained to his bed, it hurt him to do so. It hurt him to have to be the one to break her, to break her addiction.

She was covered in filth. Her arms and legs were black and blue from the needle tracks. She was injecting herself in her feet because her arm veins had collapsed. It hurt him to watch her acting like an animal, but she was an animal now. She was turned into an animal by the drugs. He knew all about that. He himself was enslaved not so many years ago but he got himself clean and vowed to help others get clean as well. He knew not to listen to anything that she said, that the drugs had her mind and she would not be able to reclaim her identity until those poisons had left her body.

He was sure that she did not remember him, but he remembered her. Tom's wife. She had looked friendly enough, he never understood why Tom was always so annoyed with her. He had difficulty finding her at first but then she began to show up at the usual drug houses. Those places that he used to go to himself before, when he was like her.

He had seen the pictures that Tom emailed him and saw her in them. Of course she was much thinner now but it's still her. He saw the picture where she and that other woman pushed that hot shot over the ravine in the car. That was no car accident. Unconsciously he fingered the jump drive that was on the chain around his neck, reassuring himself of what he had seen. Tom said he needed his help and that there was big money in it. Then he had seen Tom's obituary.

Book Club Questions

Both daughters (Madeline and Delta) grew up in an alcoholic household. Do you think their core personalities would be different if they grew up in a sober household.

Do you think Madeline's lack of empathy was caused by her environment or is a genetic trait? Would she still have psychopathic behaviors if she grew up in a healthier environment.

How did the book make you feel about addictions?

Why do you think Delta turned to alcohol to help her cope even though she watched it's devastating effects on her mother and her marriage to Tom?

What feelings did this book evoke for you?

If you were making a movie of this book who would you cast for the characters?

What did you like the best about this book?

Do you think people have a right to a relationship just because they are related by blood?

Madeline and Delta both isolated themselves from the larger community. Do you think that Delta's co-workers had any idea she was in so much emotional pain? Do you think that superficial friends like Anne Layton would be able to recognize dangerous psychopathic behaviors like Madeline's?

How do we, as the larger community, recognize the walking wounded?

Made in the USA
San Bernardino, CA
02 November 2018